OFFICE OF THE LOST

CHAOS AND ORDER BOOK ONE

J. SCOTT COATSWORTH
KIM FIELDING

OWL

Tin Box
PRESS

Published by
Other Worlds Ink
PO Box 19341, Sacramento, CA 95819
in conjunction with
Tin Box Press
Portland, OR

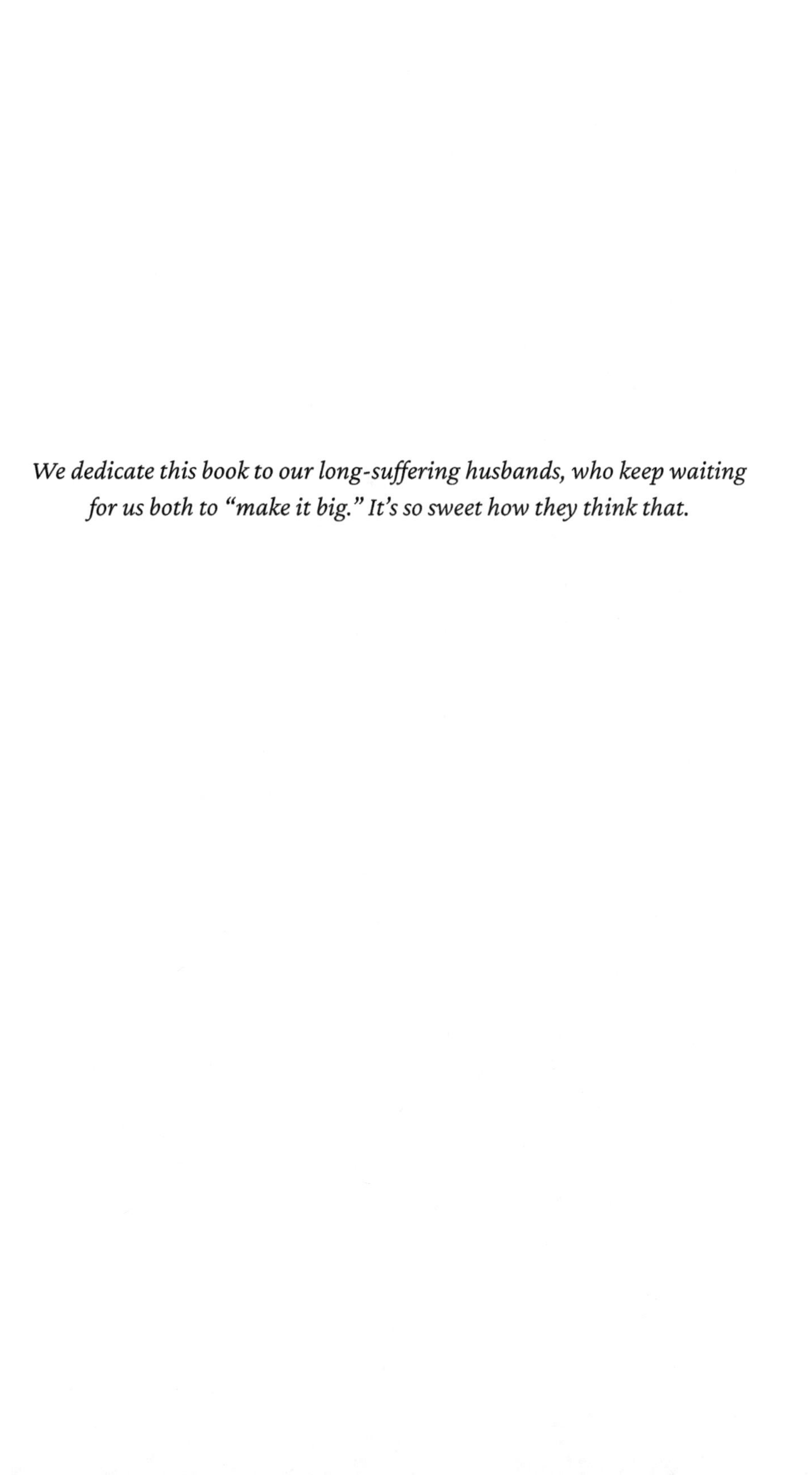

We dedicate this book to our long-suffering husbands, who keep waiting for us both to "make it big." It's so sweet how they think that.

CONTENTS

FOREWORD

Scott

I first met Kim almost a decade ago, when I launched the Queer Sacramento Authors Collective with two local author friends. Kim soon joined—and even though it was a little bit of a stretch to include her then-hometown of Turlock, about 90 miles south of Sacramento, in a Sac area writer's group, we were thrilled to have her.

We've since become fast friends, with her attending many of our local QSAC events, and sharing with each other the trials and tribulations of being an author.

We'd discussed writing something together for a couple years when the idea for The Office of the Lost came up. Writing with another author is fraught with danger—if the authors are not compatible and respectful of one another, it can rapidly degenerate into a very unpleasant experience.

Luckily for us, we worked seamlessly together. We fleshed out the main plot of the book, and the we alternated chapters. I wrote from Crispin's point of view—a finicky everything-always-has-to-be-perfect fae whose job it is to put everything back in order. Kim wrote Leopold, a wild-bundle-of-chaos human going absolutely nowhere in life.

And something magical was born.

I hope you enjoy this frothy, romantic, fantastical combination of our talents. If you do, we'll be back for more with book two.

Kim

When two compatible authors work together on a story, something magical happens. It's like word alchemy, and the result is something far different than either author would have written alone. It's also a whole lot of fun.

So when the opportunity arose to write a book with my friend Scott, I leapt at the chance. I've long been a fan of his work, and I knew he had the type of whimsical imagination that would help lead us to wonderful places. The process was great, with each of us embracing one of the protagonists but also providing plenty of input on the project as a whole. I wouldn't claim that we plotted every-thing out with precision—my muse much prefers if we write by the seat of our pants—but I think our combination of improvisation and planning suits our characters perfectly.

I'm sort of in love with Leopold and Crispin, and I hope that soon you will love them too.

1

CRISPIN

Crispin Eladrin Moss'caladin was a by-the-numbers, check-all-the-boxes kind of fae, the only desk fae in the Office of the Lost with a ten-point-two perfecality score. This made his chest swell with pride whenever he thought of it, since it technically wasn't possible to rise above a ten-point-oh.

He hummed happily as he worked his way down the Recovered Assets form, filling out every line with careful precision, dipping his quill in the ink pot with exactly the right angle and timing to collect the perfect amount of ink with nary a drop spilt on desk or parchment.

He was barely aware of the sounds of the other desk fae around him, sitting at the hundred or so identical white marble desks extending out from his like blocky petals of some strange stone flower.

Item Recovered? Check.

Item in Good Shape? Check.

Description of Item: Slightly used spelled red oak wand, possibly from the Third Dynasty.

World of Origin? Therrin.

And on and on, cataloging all the minute details of how he'd acquired the formerly lost object.

He glanced up at the hands of the enormous clock on the near wall. Five minutes to five. Perfect timing. He'd be home to his tree bole in the Greatwoods on Torevor—and his pet squirrel Minkis—right on time. *Punctuality is Perfecality.*

As he was slipping the form and the small box with its recovered contents into his outbox, a shadow darkened his sparkling clean desk, dimming its reflected glow.

Crispin swallowed hard and looked up into the beady eyes of his supervisor, Bidulla Krönk.

She was an ogre of a woman. Literally. Her sallow skin was the color of a rotten lemon, two pointed yellow teeth protruded a good three inches past her lips, and paint nearly melted off the walls when she smiled.

Like she was doing now.

"Hello, Curator Moscow." Her voice was like a rake over gravel.

"That's Moss'caladin." He tried not to sweat, rather unsuccessfully.

She nodded. "Yes, Moscow, just like I said." She sank down on the corner of his desk, and the far side lifted an inch off the ground. "I'm told you are doing excellent work."

He wanted to cover his ears to block out the avalanche of sound, but decided that wouldn't be at all proper. He should have been thrilled that his perfecality score was at last being noticed, but instead he wanted to shrink under his desk and hide until she left. He'd spent his entire career—well, if you could call five years a career—under the desk, figuratively, and he couldn't imagine for the life of him how his cover had been blown. "Thank you, ma... Supervisor Krönk. I was just heading out—"

"I'm afraid that won't be possible." And when she said *afraid*, it felt more like *rumbly angry.* But that might have been just her voice. Which, to be fair, was comparatively lovely for an ogre. Still, ogres weren't known for a subtle expression of emotion.

"Why is that?" He found himself blinking and instead tried to stare at her politely, which somehow felt worse. She also had a strong... personal aroma, which was making his eyes water.

"Something urgent has come up, a task that we feel is more wisely left to one of our best curators."

We? There was now a we who were aware of him? His heart dropped. "The best would be Curator Deepmountain, ma'am." Theodor ur Deepmountain was a dwarf, and one of the most experienced members on the team. And by experienced, Crispin meant ancient; his long, wispy white beard was probably older than Crispin. Surely she'd see the wisdom in his suggestion.

She growled—or was it a purr?—and his entire desk shook. "We think this particular task needs more... finesse than Curator Deepmountain possesses. The Oracle specifically asked for you."

Me? He suppressed a squeak, but there was the damnable blinking again. Crispin forced himself to stop.

Then he blinked again. She was complimenting him, in a heavy-handed, very ogre sort of way. The proper thing to do with compliments was to acknowledge them. Right? "Um, thank you?"

She nodded as if finally he'd done something right. "Here are the details. If you need anything, staff will provide it." She handed over a dark blue folder with the Office of the Lost "OotL" logo embossed in gold. Some people called Crispin and his co-workers "oodles" as a result of the rather unfortunate acronym, but he stuck steadfastly to "curators."

He peered over her shoulder. Three sylvan fae hovered behind her with clipboards and magical quills that never needed dipping.

Crispin sighed heavily. It was clear that there was no way out of this one, so he might as well acquiesce gracefully. "I see. Well then, I'll go home and get a good night's rest so I'm fresh for this *most important task* in the morning, and...."

Bidulla shook her head. "This matter is top priority." She pointed at the proffered paperwork, and sure enough, it was stamped "Top Priority." The red ink seemed to sizzle as he stared at it.

"You'll leave tonight. With your... skills"—she said it as if there was still some doubt as to whether he possessed any—"you should be able to convince the subject to return with you forthwith."

If the Oracle wanted him *and* the job was stamped top priority, it must really be important. *I should feel honored.* "All right. I'll go forthwith and... wait, what?" The final word ascended into an upper pitch that only canines could usually hear.

She stared at him as if he'd gone daft.

His mind raced. She wanted him to leave tonight, without a proper bath, without saying goodbye to Minkis, and to collect a *someone*? Not a something? *This is all going too quickly.* "May I ask what is so urgent about this particular recovery?"

She sighed, which would have blown his carefully completed paperwork out of his outbox if it hadn't already sparked and vanished into the archival vaults. "I'm not at liberty to tell you that. Suffice it to say that this mission is of the utmost importance. Make this happen and you have a very bright career ahead of you, Curator Moss'caladin." She said it right that time, leading him to believe she'd known it all along. Ogres did love their games.

Left unsaid was what would likely happen to him if he failed. It would be back to the forest for him, hunting deer and learning sword-craft with his know-it-all older brother. He shuddered. "I'll do my best, ma'am." There, that was better. He'd managed to get an entire sentence out without his voice cracking.

He signed the paperwork, and with a *ding*, a copy appeared inside Thea, his portable transport device that had somehow survived the ogre assault on his desk.

"See that you do." She got up, and the far end of his desk settled back to the ground with a small *crash*. "I expect great things from you, Moscow." With that, she turned and made her way, with far more agility than he would have expected, across the crowded room, her staff trailing behind her like a cloud of gypsy moths.

"But you said if I needed anything...." But she and her attendants were gone.

"Very well then." He'd never heard of a recovery mission for a *being*. Once he brought them back to OotL, would they be stuffed into the vault next to the collected diamonds and wands and other important bric-a-brac? Or would Her Ogreness come to collect them personally, leading them off somewhere without an explanation?

Not my responsibility. Crispin frowned. He liked things neat and tidy, and this case was shaping up to be anything but.

He opened the folder. Inside was a brief description of the subject —a Leopold Lane, who looked more like a Leo than a Leopold. Good enough looking, if a bit unkempt for Crispin's tastes, dark hair in contrast to Crispin's blond.

Thea whistled. "Handsome, though he's a bit scruffy for you."

"He's a recovery asset. Not interested." Then he saw the destination world.

Earth.

His heart sank.

No one liked to go there. It was loud and dirty and filled with inefficiency and redundancy. Very little magic remained, largely because it had been mostly stamped out by the horde of smelly humans who seemed dead set on ruining their world before anyone else could get around to it.

He'd been there a few times to collect lost things, and every time afterward he'd needed a three-hour soak in his blue ceramic bathtub to clean off the grit and the anxiety that clung to him.

In and out, quick. That's how it would be. Then he'd be home to Minkis in time for a midnight meal.

He headed for the Necessary Room to collect whatever he would need. In half an hour, he was packed and in the Hall of Mirrors, ready to effectuate the mission and keep his perfecality score above ten-point-oh.

2

LEOPOLD

The dime rolled off the counter, bounced on the tile floor, and rolled under the bakery case.

Ignoring the glares and aggrieved sighs of the people in line behind him, Leopold fished around in his jacket pockets in search of more coins.

"You can just tap your phone right here to pay." The short blonde barista pointed perkily. She was the type who did everything perkily. Leopold was willing to bet she even managed to be perky when she was asleep, which for some reason annoyed him to no end.

"I'd rather not." He didn't find another dime, but eventually he unearthed a nickel and five pennies, along with an expired light-rail ticket, a crumpled but probably unused Kleenex, and a metal screw-looking thing that looked as if it was probably an important part of something but he didn't know what. He set down the coins and shoved the rest back into his pockets.

"We have an app," chirped the barista. "You can download it for free and use it to pay for your orders. And you earn points! Which you can use to get free coffees and stuff."

"I don't have a phone."

She blinked at him as if he'd suddenly sprouted a few extra heads.

And although it wasn't really any of her business, Leopold shrugged. "It broke."

"Oh!" She looked relieved, her world suddenly tilted back onto its proper axis. "Well, when you get a new one then."

He nodded curtly before shuffling aside to wait for his order. He shouldn't have splurged on the fancy coffee; he could have caffeinated himself more cheaply at a fast-food joint. But what the hell—broke was broke, and he might as well enjoy a lot of sugar and whipped cream with his last bit of pocket change.

The coffee shop was busy. People typed at laptops, chatted with friends, or scrolled on their phones. In one corner, a young woman with dark braids swayed to the music from her headphones while she drew in a sketchbook. A couple of tables over, two men in suits and ties were having a lively discussion about autonomous vehicles.

The espresso machine and blenders whirred, the sound system played a woman singing in what he thought might be Portuguese, a toddler burbled an incomprehensible monologue to his father. It was a comfortable place. If Leopold chose, he could no doubt park himself in an empty chair and nurse his overpriced frothy concoction as long as he wanted.

He wouldn't, though.

"Leonard!" called another of the baristas, this one a tall young man with a nicely shaped beard and one large silver hoop earring. He set a plastic cup down in the pickup portion of the counter. "Leonard! Order's up!"

Nobody came forward. Three more names were called in quick succession, these with prompt responses, and then Leopold realized that all three of those people had been behind him in line. He approached the counter and peered at the remaining cup.

"Leonard?" asked the barista.

"Leopold."

The barista shrugged. "'S probably yours."

It probably was. And Leonard was somewhat of an improvement over the last time he'd treated himself to coffee, when he'd been called *Leopard* instead. *Honestly. Who would call themselves Leopard?* At other times he's been Leslie, Leeann, Leland, Leon, Leofric, and once —memorably—Legolas. Which was, well, yeah, kind of awesome, but clearly a mistake of epic proportions.

He was fairly certain he'd never once been Leopold. Maybe he'd get there if he could afford fancy coffee more often.

Clutching the drink that might or might not have been his, Leopold exited the shop.

Early February in Sacramento wasn't really winter, at least not as most people would measure it. In fact, from what he'd heard, the area had been in drought for several years, with the Februaries dry and unseasonably warm. But that was before he'd moved here, and this winter had broken records for the amount of rainfall. By now, people had shifted from *thank goodness* all the way through *well, we really need it* and were now settled into *I'm so sick of this miserable weather.* Leopold didn't blame them. Gray skies. Flooded homes. High heating bills. And, as he stepped off the curb, a deceptively deep puddle that swallowed his entire left foot.

He yelped and lost his balance, and although he managed not to fall on his face, the cup went flying. It landed on the hood of a parked BMW, spattering sweet expensive coffee onto the windshield—and onto the nicely dressed woman who had just emerged from the driver's seat.

"I am *so* sorry!" Leopold said. Or started to say, anyway, because before he could get the phrase out, the woman was screeching at him as if he'd attempted to murder her. Yeah, coffee stains were not going to do her cream-colored wool coat any favors, but at least it had been iced coffee, so she wasn't burned or otherwise injured.

She was wearing Leopold's pick-me-up and he couldn't afford another, and his left foot and lower leg were soaked and thoroughly chilled, and now a guy in a lifted pickup was honking at him, and it had suddenly started to rain again, and dammit, Leopold was just *done*.

"I'm sorry!" he yelled at the woman, who didn't pause her tirade. Then he glanced at the pickup driver, who was now flipping him off, and Leopold hobbled across the street.

His apartment was only a few blocks away, on the upper floor of a house that had been pretty nice a hundred or so years ago but had long since sagged into despair. His place—a cramped bedroom, a living room with a closet-sized kitchen, and a Lilliputian bathroom—was in a converted attic reachable by two flights of rickety outdoor stairs. The climb had been miserably hot in summer and was now cold and damp, making the ascent both dangerous and uncomfortable. Today he walked up the stairs more slowly than usual because his ankle was sore from the puddle incident, and he somehow managed not to fall to an untimely death on the cracked and weed-infested pavement of the parking lot far below.

In addition to the rickety exterior stairs, two of the windows were cracked, the floors were uneven, and the electricity went out whenever the people downstairs used their microwave. The house was a firetrap and couldn't possibly be up to code. God help them all if there was an earthquake.

But still, Leopold liked it. He found it charming that none of the walls were plumb and none of the corners formed perfect right angles. His landlord had seemingly used the dregs of several paint cans, resulting in walls that had large patches of varied whites and beiges. Leopold liked that too. He loved it when the floors and rafters creaked and when the pipes made noises like dying ancient sea monsters.

Also, it was cheap.

As soon as he was inside, he stripped off his jacket and let it fall on the floor, then kicked off his sodden shoes. Next came the socks and wet jeans, and he rummaged around in his pile of clean but unfolded laundry until he found a pair of gray sweatpants and two socks—one white and one navy. He didn't care that they didn't match.

What he *should* do, he knew, was sit down and calculate his finances. Rent was coming due and he didn't think he had enough to cover it. He *should* pick up some extra hours at work. He had been holding two jobs to make ends meet, but after the forklift incident at the warehouse he was down to one employer, a bus company. And if his record held, something dumb would happen there while he was on duty and then he wouldn't be detailing buses anymore either. So he *should also* be looking for a new job right now.

But thinking about numbers made his head swim, and the idea of filling out employment applications and going to interviews made him shudder. The weight of all those *shoulds* made him just want to fall into bed and sleep for a week, at which point he might awaken to find he'd won the lottery and all those *shoulds* could go to hell. Except that he didn't have the money for a lottery ticket, and even if he had, the effort to go out and actually buy one was beyond him at the moment.

So instead, he curled up on his lumpy couch—of indeterminate original color but now a rather dull and uninspiring chocolate-milk brown—and started channel-surfing.

He didn't watch anything in particular; he rarely did. What he enjoyed was viewing a few minutes of a show, trying to guess what was going on, and then flipping to the next and the one after that. Sometimes he made up storylines that tied the fragments together, so that the people bickering in the old sitcom diner became pals with the mechanics fixing up the sports car, and the cartoon girl with the pet monkey taught Spanish to the elderly congressman.

Today he watched a few minutes of a reality dating show followed by a snippet of a sport he thought might be rugby and then a bit of an old cop show. Then a nature show involving squirrels— apparently there were squirrels on every continent except Australia, where there were pseudo squirrels, and Antarctica, which in the summer was almost as cold as Sacramento on a rainy winter day.

Shivering, he cranked up the thermostat, which responded with a very convincing death-rattle but nevertheless spat out a bit of warmer air. Perhaps its final exhale.

He'd just clicked over to a sci-fi space battle when the television sizzled loudly and the screen went blank. He thought at first that it was simply Todd and Krys zapping a frozen burrito downstairs, but then he realized the power wasn't out completely, which meant the problem likely lay in his television. *Great. Just what I needed.*

He was still slumped on the couch, trying to decide whether to get up and... do something, when someone knocked on the door.

Leopold slumped even more and waited for whoever it was to go away. But they knocked again, harder, and he sort of had to give them credit for trudging up two flights of stairs in this cruddy weather. With an aggrieved sigh, he hauled himself upright and plodded to the door.

A very pretty young man stood on the little landing, looking less than thrilled. He was slender, with straw-colored hair, eyes somewhere between gray and blue, model-esque cheekbones, and a deep frown. People often frowned around Leopold; he tended to have that effect. What was unusual about this guy, however, was that he wore a tweedy three-piece suit like that of a 1950s British schoolmaster. Or so Leopold imagined, anyway.

"I'm not interested in your God," Leopold announced.

The man blinked and cocked his head sideways, a bit like a bird. "I beg your pardon?"

"If you try to convert me, it won't go well. Really, dude. Last guy who tried ended up quitting his church." Leopold tilted his head. "Or maybe that's not your gig. But if you're trying to sell me something or get a donation, I'm flat broke. And if you want my vote for something, I'm not registered."

He'd actually attempted to register a few times but was never successful. "Irregularities" in his records, he was told. Whatever that meant.

But now his visitor was shaking his head. He dug into his suit pocket for a moment and, when he pulled out a phone, seemed mildly surprised. "Oh," he muttered to himself. "Well, yes, I do suppose it will work."

It was one of the big phones that had always seemed rather impractical to Leopold. The prim and proper stranger fixed him again with that bright blue-gray stare. "Are you Leo Lane?"

"Leopold." Shit. Now he'd admitted who he was. Maybe instead of correcting the guy, Leopold should have simply denied it.

The visitor nodded firmly. "Yes, excellent. Mr. Lane, we need to—"

The rain started to fall so suddenly and so heavily that for a moment Leopold thought someone had aimed a firehose at them.

The man in the suit made a funny little yelp and ducked his head. Water had already plastered his hair to his skull, and... he had really weird-looking ears. Sort of pointy, like Mr. Spock.

"Mr. Lane, may I come in and speak with you? Please?"

Well, he seemed a bit odd but not dangerous, and leaving him outside in the downpour would be heartless. So even though Leopold had a thousand and seventeen reasons to say no, he stepped back and gestured for the man to enter, and then closed the door behind him.

The guy stood just inside the small apartment, dripping onto the floor, surveying the room with an expression of minor horror. "Was there a battle fought here?"

"Ha ha. Hilarious. Look, I know the place is a mess, but I don't know you from Adam and you don't have any right to criticize my housekeeping skills."

If anything, the man looked even more appalled. "You mean you allowed your home to get... into this condition?"

C'mon. It wasn't that bad. Sure, clothing—both clean and dirty —lay strewn on the floor and furniture. Dishes, glasses, and packages of food covered the kitchen counter. And there were unstable stacks of books and magazines and newspapers, and little collections of rocks and pinecones and dried flowers, and the table held three partially completed jigsaw puzzles, and one of his three kitchen chairs had a busted leg he'd been meaning to fix, and the houseplants on the windowsill had died from neglect but the pots were sprouting mystery weeds, and he had no idea what was in the sagging cardboard box in the corner and couldn't remember how it got there, and…. Okay. But still.

"Look, dude. I'm busy. I don't think you came here to tell me I'm a slob. Spit it out and then you can be on your way."

He wasn't busy. And this guy was very easy on the eyes, even sopping wet. But Leopold wasn't patient, and also, something about the man made him uneasy although Leopold couldn't quite put his finger on what.

The man made a visible effort to pull himself together, taking a deep breath and straightening his back. Before Leopold could demand to know what the hell he wanted, he cleared his throat. "My name is Crispin Eladrin Moss'caladin. I am a Curator."

"Like… from a museum?" The curators at the Crocker Museum always chased him away from the art, as if afraid he might touch and contaminate it.

"No. Well, in a way…" Crispin tugged at the bottom of his jacket, looking extremely uncomfortable. "I collect certain specific items for the Office of the Lost."

Leopold blinked. "Um… so you want a donation? Like I said, I'm literally broke. But I think I have a couple cans of corn somewhere. Or an extra blanket. Or…. What *are* you collecting, dude?"

Crispin sighed and held up the phone. It held a perfectly clear picture of Leo's face, and not in one of his rare photogenic moments.

His hair in the image was lanky and unkempt—was *kempt* even a thing?—and his squinting brown eyes were pinholes in a washed-out white face. *Too bright a flash.*

Crispin cleared his throat, tugged at his collar, and swallowed hard. "I'm afraid, Leo, that I'm here to collect… you."

3
CRISPIN

None of this was going as planned.

Crispin was a huge fan of *as planned*.

First off, the damnable Hall of Mirrors had dumped him a good half-mile away from his destination, in the midst of the rainstorm from hell, in a park next to a frightening display of men with round hats that all had numbers, every one of them glaring at him in the intermittent flashes of lightning. He'd run off in startled fear, his world-appropriate clothing feeling itchy and growing soggy —and looking stunningly drab, a far cry from his usual flair for color. None of the squirrels in the park seemed friendly, tucked away under the dry canopies of the trees as he ran past, noting his passage with apparent disinterest.

He had eventually found his way out of the park to the questionable shelter of an awning of an abandoned... he wanted to say restaurant, but it had zero charm and, due to the whole abandoned part, zero food. His stomach had rumbled at that. Before his workday had taken a turn for the worse, he'd planned to have a perfectly respectable meal of nut mush and elven mead with Minkis, if his rather unreliable pet squirrel had decided to come in for the night.

14

And now here he was half-soaked, on the simultaneously bland and crazy planet Earth, a world he'd managed to avoid for years. At least this part of it didn't stink. Much. Though there was an uncollected can of refuse in one corner of the little courtyard that emitted a rather foul odor. No matter. He'd be off-world soon enough and then safely back home once he dropped off his collection at the office.

The stairs he'd just climbed would have put the rickety ones on the haunted world of Thauria to shame for their sheer ability to seem both insubstantial and very creakingly real, and now he stood in a place that could charitably be called the seventeenth pit of hell, talking to a man who clearly wanted nothing to do with him.

His target, Leopold Lane, was... rumpled. That was the best and most generous word he could come up with to describe the person before him. He was shirtless and thankfully not too out of shape, not that Crispin would have said anything. That would be rude. He wore baggy gray pants and mismatched socks—maybe that was a thing on Earth these days?—and his chestnut-colored hair was messy, but not in a way that looked adorable. More like the dead cat he'd seen on the side of the road on the way over from the park.

Still, the man didn't seem unkind, only confused.

"Excuse me?" Leopold's eyebrows shot up. "What, are you with the army or something?"

Something flickered in the corner of the room. Or, in an angle of the room? None of the corners of this place seemed straight. It was like stepping into one of those weird paintings where everything curved up and around to meet itself in impossibly complex ways. Or like a bathroom on Herschel IV. "No, no army." Crispin tried a different tack. "Leo, have you ever felt... lost?"

"Oh geezus, you're one of those. And it's Leopold, not Leo. Or Leopard, or Legolas...." He shuffled over to a big white metal box that looked like it had seen better days fifty years before and was now surprised to be still standing. He cracked it open and pulled out a single clear bottle with a blue label that said Zima. "If we're gonna talk batshit, may as well have a little of this. I've been saving it for a special occasion, and you seem"—he looked over his shoulder and gave Crispin a once-over—"special."

There was another flicker at the corner of his eye, this time behind the sagging cold box that had clearly seen better days. Crispin wondered if he was having a stroke. "Sorry, Leo–pold." He was proud to have caught his own mistake this time. He rarely used nicknames, but somehow it had initially seemed appropriate. Oh well. He could admit when he was wrong.

Leopold opened a cabinet and pulled out two glasses—as mismatched as his socks—and after pushing aside a number of strange colored pieces of cardboard or wood, set them on the table. One was a thick glass beer stein that wouldn't have been out of place in Theodor the dwarf's kitchen, while the other was a plastic glass in the shape of a thin pink bird. Its long neck acted as the handle, the webbed feet splayed on either side provided support.

Plastic. Crispin shuddered. *Vile stuff. Another Earth specialty.*

"Guest's choice."

Crispin blinked, confused, until he realized that Leopold meant the glasses. "That one, please."

"Fair enough." The man half-filled the stein with the fizzy liquid and handed it over, pouring the rest into the second glass. "Oh, where are my manners?" He chucked the bottle into an overflowing bin and rummaged through a rag pile, emerging victoriously with a black piece of cloth. "Knew I'd washed this one."

"That's... clothing?" His charge was one of the slovenliest people Crispin had ever run across, and Leopold's charm, bare bones as it was, was dangerously close to expired.

"Yup. Grabbed this at a con a couple years ago."

There was something printed on it: a picture of an old man in a brown robe with a long shiny blue sword. The words had all but faded beyond recognition, except for the first two. "Help me...." It seemed... appropriate. Maybe it was a sign.

"He kind of looks like you," Leopold continued, "all prim and proper. Are you a Star Wars fan, Crispy?" He grabbed his drink and sank down on the tattered scum-brown sofa that was crouched against one wall like a feral cat.

Crispin frowned. There was so much wrong in that question. In this room. In this... person. Maybe he'd be better off returning to the office and telling his boss he'd been unable to complete the recovery. Let her send someone else to do it.

He discarded the idea as soon as he thought it. She'd been very clear on the importance of this particular collection, and if he failed, he'd lose his stellar perfecality rating. "No. Not a fan of any wars, star or otherwise." He sipped the concoction. It sizzled unpleasantly in his mouth.

The lights flickered again.

"Is there something wrong with your... domicile?" He couldn't quite bring himself to call it a home.

"Oh, that." Leopold rolled his eyes. "It's an old house. Neighbors are using the microwave. That's all."

Crispin had no idea what *little waves* had to do with anything, and he didn't want to know. "We should get going...."

Leopold's eyes widened. "You were serious?" He looked up at the sagging ceiling. "What, is the ship here to collect us?" He downed his drink and set the strange bird-glass on a cardboard box next to the sad-looking couch.

Then everything happened at once.

The shadows lining the walls moved.

The room shook.

Crispin dove for Leopold out of instinct, holding out Thea, his portable transport device and friendly companion—who had decided to be a phone in this gods-forsaken world—and landed in a sprawl across the surprised man.

Leopold sputtered, scrambling away from him. "What, are you crazy? Get off of me." Then a look of horror crossed his face.

Crispin looked over his shoulder at the ceiling. Something dark and foul was growing there, as the shadows bubbled up from behind the cold box that had housed the Zima. He caught a hint of a gaping jaw full of dark sharp teeth and a whiff of something that smelled like the grave, at which point the lights flickered out for good. *What in the fells of Hargsmarsh?* "We have to go!"

Leopold made a strangled sound in the dark.

"Thea, take us back to OotL. Now."

The phone's screen lit up, and for a second Crispin wished it hadn't. Tentacles with sharp claws on the tips were reaching for them from the small kitchen in the horrid little flat Leopold called home.

Then the phone's light expanded, and he and his charge were sucked into it.

One of the tentacles had wrapped around his leg—and it was oh, so cold—but then the creature was gone.

Crispin blinked, looking around anxiously. Something wasn't right.

They should be in the Hall of Mirrors, his mission accomplished. Instead he was all alone, still surrounded by the sparkly blackness of the Un-Place, relieved only by a slight glow from the device in his hand.

He pried a severed tentacle off of his leg and tossed it aside. It sizzled into nothing.

"Leo?" Remembering his manners, he tried again. "Leopold?"
Nothing.

He lifted his mirror. Thea was still shaped like a phone, but her screen was cracked. "Thea?"

In response, she played a line from *The Lost Snork's Lament*. "No one knows where the blind man goes...."

"Come on, Thea, talk to me... where are we?"

The screen flashed, sending a kaleidoscope of lights and a drunk-sounding hiccup.

"Did the dark cloud do something to you?" He looked around. "Did *Leo* do something? Where has he—?"

The rest of his words were cut off as he landed face-first in a mound of grass.

He pushed himself up and scrambled backward spitting out a few purple blades and managing to sit up and look around. He was in a forest, a very purple forest, and something was howling in the distance. *Damnable grass will probably stain my....* But his tweedy jacket was gone, replaced by downy fur, and he seemed to have... antlers?

He was distracted from that revelation by a voice. "What the hell did you do to me, Crispy? And where the hell are we?"

Crispin turned to find his charge, at least he assumed it was still Leopold, staring at him and looking really annoyed. The human also had brown fur—except for a rather fetching white patch on his chest—a pair of short antlers, humanlike hands, and an elongated snout.

He looked just like a....

"Oh crap."

4
LEOPOLD

Purple. That was Leopold's first impression, and it didn't make any sense. But then again, neither did the sudden attack of vertigo and accompanying nausea, or the weird heavy feeling in his head, or his general sense of... *wrong*.

In fact, he was fairly used to disasters springing up around him, so much so that he became suspicious when life seemed to be going too smoothly. But he'd never felt so disoriented, so certain that his existence had just taken the wrong exit off the freeway. *Wrong. That word again.*

He staggered around for a few moments, trying desperately not to puke, and wasn't sure whether to be relieved when he heard a familiar voice. It was that bizarre man, the one who claimed to be collecting him, although Leopold still didn't understand why. Crispin Something. And when Leopold lurched around a large tree— a large *violet* tree—there Crispin was, his back to Leopold and his smartphone held high.

"What the hell, Crispy?"

Only, when Crispin turned around, he was.... *Oh God.* "What did you put in my Zima?" Leopold knew his voice was shrill, but being unwittingly drugged was bad. And it was especially bad for him, because he'd long since learned that if he ingested anything more intoxicating than half a bottle of beer, *very bad things* happened. The sorts of things that involved flashing red-and-blue lights, hyperventilating insurance adjustors, and the need for Leopold to pick up quickly and move far way.

Maybe he ought to be relieved that the only effects this time—so far, at least—were hallucinations of a purple forest and of Crispin turning into a deer. A deer in tweed trousers.

"Oh, crap." Crispin slapped a hand over his mouth.

Leopold stalked closer. "*Oh crap* is right. What the *hell*, dude? You don't just go around slipping drugs to strangers. What did you give me and when is it gonna wear off?"

"I did *not* drug you." Crispin managed to look simultaneously offended, distressed, and confused. He somehow also managed to still look like Crispin, even with brown fur, a long muzzle, and short velvety antlers. His ears were even longer and pointier than before.

"Nobody gets this wasted on half a Zima. Not even...." Leopold's thought trailed away when he realized how odd his mouth felt. His tongue and teeth were all... wrong. *Damn that word.*

And then there was the strange tickly feeling on his skin. He glanced down; his t-shirt was gone. His chest, like Crispin's, was now covered in short fur. Maybe he should be relieved he hadn't hallucinated away his sweatpants and socks.

His scalp didn't feel right either, however. When he put his hand to his forehead, he felt antlers. "This is bad," he moaned. "I don't want to be a deer." Deer in the woods usually got shot. Would the hunters have purple guns?

"You are not a deer. You have—well, we both have—temporarily taken the form of piwati, an endemic sentient species in Vlotho. Which is, I assume, where we have landed, although I don't understand why. I visited here once before to collect a rather interesting flower. It had the most delicate teeth...."

Leopold decided there was no point in continuing this conversation. He sat down on the grass, which was the precise shade of grape Kool-Aid, and waited to sober up. The grass was pleasantly soft, at any rate, and it smelled really nice. Like a bakery or a pan of sizzling bacon, only not. While Crispin returned to talking into his phone, Leopold plucked a blade of grass and stuck it on his tongue.

Yum! He took another piece, and another, and was considering getting on all fours and grazing properly—until it occurred to him to wonder what he was *actually* putting in his mouth, back in his non-delusional apartment. None of the options seemed good, so he sighed and stopped eating.

It wasn't a horrible trip, as these things went. The weather was pleasant and the foliage interesting. Some of the trees had leaves that reminded him of the amethyst ring one of his foster mothers had worn. Maybe when he got a second job and saved a bit of money, he should paint his bedroom walls that color. The landlord probably wouldn't mind, and anyway, Leopold's damage deposit was a lost cause after the Great Spaghetti Sauce Eruption of last month.

Crispin trudged over and folded elegantly to the ground in front of Leopold. "I'm having a bit of difficulty," Crispin admitted.

"Did you take the drugs too?"

"I don't know what— There are no drugs. We are both quite sober. But I'm afraid we're in a bit of a pickle."

Leopold chuckled. "Then everything would be green instead of purple, wouldn't it? Unless it's a purple pickle. Which sounds like a tongue-twister. Or bad porn." He laughed again.

"Please be serious. This is not a good occasion for joking." Hands on furry hips signaled Crispin's disapproval.

"Right. 'Cause everyone ought to take delirium seriously."

Crispin sighed. "This is reality. I attempted to collect you, as I was sent to do. But there was some kind of... of accident." Crispin shuddered. "So instead of returning to the Hall of Mirrors at OotL, we've ended up in Vlotho. And the portal isn't working properly." He tapped the phone, which he still held in one hand. The glass was cracked.

"I have no idea what you're talking about." Leopold was starting to wonder if this Crispin character was a bit *woo-woo* in the head.

"It's quite simple. I am a curator. As I mentioned before, I collect items—or, um, sometimes people—for the Office of the Lost. I have been instructed to collect you."

Leopold decided to humor him. Why not? He had nothing better to do right now, and that grass was looking mighty tasty. "Collect me for what? And what's this office thing? A government agency? 'Cause if Sacramento has some kind of bizarre tax or something, I'm sorry I didn't pay, but I didn't know anything about it. And now I can't pay on account of being broke."

While Crispin paused, apparently deciding how to answer—or as Leopold's hallucination struggled to keep up with real-time events—birds twittered prettily. There was just enough breeze to make the grass ripple and leaves sway, and the temperature was nearly perfect. Off in the distance a dog howled, but here everything was peaceful. This was better than getting rained on or flipping channels in his apartment. No wonder people took drugs.

"The Office of the Lost," Crispin began in an instructional tone, "is in a place outside of worlds, yet simultaneously inside them. The Hall of Mirrors is the nexus that joins realities together."

"A hub. Sure. Like O'Hare."

Crispin blinked at him for a moment as if confused and then shrugged. "I don't know this O'Hare world, but yes. A hub. That makes us quite important, you see." He puffed up his chest slightly. "And the hub contains the Office of the Lost, which is where I'm employed. Our function is to collect and protect items that, while they may seem insignificant, are in fact crucial to the successful conclusion of certain events. The Oracle sends us out to find them. For example, last month I traveled to Hbrthnot and acquired the last remaining copy of the autobiography of Queen Thragell the Fourteenth. Our oracle has foretold that the volume will one day be indispensable to—"

Leopold frowned, which felt weird with his extended jaw. "I'm not an *item*. I'm a person."

"Yes. Well." Crispin reached as if he intended to straighten his tie, but all he had on his chest was fur and he let his hand fall. "Occasionally we're sent to collect living... specimens. From your world we have a pair of passenger pigeons, which are quite simple to care for, and also a pair of woolly mammoths, which require a very big room and regular manure removal. And I'm afraid that if I don't bring you in promptly, my next assignment will be cleaning up after them."

He looked upset and Leopold was tempted to console him, but he didn't because none of this was real.

Anyway, woolly mammoth shit wasn't the issue here. "Fine. You collect stuff. But why me?" Because Leopold suddenly remembered that when Crispin had first showed up at the door, he'd asked for Leopold by name, which meant he hadn't just wandered there randomly. Plus he'd had that sucky photo of Leopold on his phone. And that was weird, because the only ones who knew where Leopold lived were his bosses, his landlord, and his neighbors. In fact, the entire rest of the world was pretty much blissfully unaware of his existence.

"Why *me*?" he repeated, this time a little plaintively.

Crispin, looking forlorn, sat down on a purple-tinged log and sighed. "I don't know. Bidulla Krönk—she's my supervisor—didn't say. She rarely explains my assignments."

"Well, your boss made a mistake, 'cause I'm nobody special. I have no particular skills and no money at all, and although I'd love to be related to royalty or a billionaire or a celebrity or something, I'm not. My dad was a truck driver and my mom worked in an elementary school cafeteria." And they'd both died before Leopold was ten, but that wasn't relevant right now.

"The oracle is *never* wrong," Crispin announced huffily.

"Whatever." Leopold was getting tired of this trip. He wanted to make himself a peanut-butter-and-onion sandwich, catch twenty minutes or so of some ridiculous reality show, and doze off to the sound of rain pounding onto the roof. He stood. "I'm just gonna walk around until I sober up."

He started to do just that, but Crispin leapt up and ran to block him. "Leopold! You must remain with me. We're late already and...." He took a few deep breaths before making a visible effort to get himself under control. "My perfecality rating is at risk of dropping below a perfect score."

"Perfecality isn't a word, dude." But Crispin looked so upset, with his big purple eyes—wait, purple eyes? Whatever—and his distressed furry face, that Leopold didn't have the heart to abandon him. Even if the guy had spiked his Zima.

Leopold flapped one hand. "Fine. I'm ready to go to your office place. Beam me up."

"But that's the problem. Thea should be bringing us to the Hall of Mirrors, but instead she's... doing this." He held up his phone.

A slightly tinny female voice was warbling about Tommy working on the docks. She was off-key and getting the lyrics wrong.

"That's Bon Jovi," Leopold pointed out. "Well, sort of."

"This is Thea. Well, no. This *object* is my portable transport device, which often takes the form of a mirror but may incorporate any shiny surface. Thea is the intelligence behind the device. She is supposed to take me and my, er, acquisitions back to OotL, but she isn't. There seems to be something wrong with her."

"Oodle? Oh yeah. Gotcha." Leopold scratched his head. The antlers were a little itchy. "Screen's cracked. I feel your pain. I've never owned a phone that's survived more than a week without me breaking it. Except one, an old... Nokia? That one I lost. At least yours is sort of working."

The song ended abruptly, which was a relief. Crispin held up the phone and spoke loudly. "Thea. Please send us to the Hall of Mirrors this instant."

"No can do," sang the phone with a giggle. She repeated it on a loop. Then a loud exploding noise came from the phone, and Crispin dropped it in alarm as he let out a terrified yelp. It landed on a soft tuft of grass, and when he picked it up, the phone didn't seem in any worse shape than it had been before.

Now it was singing about heaven and sex. Bruno Mars, Leopold thought.

Crispin returned to pleading and arguing with the phone. Leopold, growing bored, yanked up some foliage and began chewing. He was hungry and the stuff tasted pretty good. But even as he munched, worry started to gather somewhere beneath his skin. There was something wrong. This hallucination had been going on for a while, with no sign of disappearing. Even more troubling, though, was its consistency. Sure, the contents were damned weird—turning into an alien deer thing, being collected based on the orders of an oracle—but the details weren't shifting. He and Crispin were having coherent if unlikely conversations. The greenery continued to be, more accurately, purplery. That howling noise was still going on in the distance.

Only... about that last part. The howling sounded as if it were growing closer, didn't it?

"Uh, Crispin?"

"If I could get Thea to concentrate, perhaps she could suggest—"

"Are there, um, predators in this place?" Which shouldn't matter since none of this was real, but the hair—the *fur*—on Leopold's nape was standing up, and his heart was racing, and his few bites of grass were feeling heavy and cold in his gut.

"Predators? I don't know what—" Crispin stopped himself and tilted his head, as if hearing the howls for the first time. His eyes widened; his nostrils flared. Leopold was sniffing the air too, and there was a definite whiff of something. It was coppery and musky, and it made him shudder.

Crispin swallowed loudly. "Oh, crap."

5
CRISPIN

I should run. I really should.

Crispin willed his limbs to move, yelled at them in his head, in fact, but they stayed rooted to the ground as the danger approached, the manic howls growing in intensity.

Thea flashed at him, the light like a kaleidoscope through the fractured screen. "Danger, Will Robinson!"

Leo was already halfway across the clearing, but his head snapped back at that. "I think your loopy little travel device drank some of that spiked Zima, too."

"The Zima wasn't spiked." Or maybe it had been. His head felt weird. Instead of running from the howling, he felt a strange compulsion to run *toward* it.

Something hopped into the clearing. It was about the size and shape of an Earth rabbit, or maybe a westcat from Therrin (which as everyone knew were far nicer than the eastcats). Crispin knelt to look at the little thing. "Are you running too?" It stared at him with eyes almost as big as its head, trembling and shifting from foot to foot. It had five of them, so it took a moment to complete the exercise.

Poor thing looks frightened.

He felt Leo staring over his shoulder. "Bad juju."

"What?" He wasn't sure what bad juju was, but whatever it might be, this thing didn't seem to have any. "He's adorable." The rabbit-cat trilled, a sweet sound that put Crispin in mind of a choir of angels. Really tiny angels with teensy-weensy harps.

Then he noticed that the forest had gone absolutely quiet. No more howls. No birdsong. No rustling purple foliage. "Maybe whatever that was... decided to go away?"

"Bad juju, dude. We should go. You don't mess with bad juju."

Despite being sketchy on the details of bad juju, Crispin was inclined to agree. He reached down to grab the little critter. *At least we can get you to safety.*

It opened its mouth, and he jerked his hands back. If its eyes were almost as big as its fuzzy head, its jaws were three times as big and lined with razor-sharp teeth.

Then it howled.

Crispin stumbled back as the rab-cat leapt at him, missing him by a hair's breadth. "What in the holy oerk of Greebals?" He scrambled backwards, knocking Leo to the ground.

The thing howled again, and suddenly Leo was in front of him holding a big stick. He swung it as the thing leapt again, and sent it flying through the purple trees with a yip and howl.

"Score!" Leo thrust his hand into the air and did a little dance. "Out of the park. I always wanted to do that." He seemed to have recovered from his earlier round of grousing about the Zima.

"We should go." Crispin's body shook, and he felt ill. He was lucky he still had his hand. *I was about to pick it up.*

Leo grinned. "Why? I just sent that little toothy fur ball to hell." He looked longingly at a patch of purple blades. "The grass here is really good. You should try it."

"He wasn't alone." Crispin scrambled up as five more, no, ten, no, seventeen—he'd always been really good at counting things—

hopped out of the under-foliage. Leo swung around just in time to see the grand entrance.

For half a second, the two parties—the desk fae and his *collected* vs. the rab-cats from hell—stared each other down. The forest was again absolutely quiet.

Then someone screamed like a baby—if Crispin was honest with himself, it was him—and he and his charge turned tail and ran on hooved feet into the purply-violet wood.

They stumbled over lavender shrubs that had little yellow flowers that rang like bells when disturbed, adding to the cacophony, and past plum fernlike things that reminded him of the fairy ferns back home, only these didn't glow and were ten times larger. They rustled ominously as he and Leo passed, and Crispin wondered briefly if they wanted to eat him too. *Consumed by a fern* was not the legacy he wanted to be remembered by when he one day slipped into the Black Woods.

All the while, the howls and growls followed them, now coming from all sides, and even from the canopy above. "Thea, what are those things?" The question came out in gaspy breaths as he stumbled over a mauve log that was half as high as he was. Thank god his hooves gave him good purchase on the rough surface. He prayed to the holy oerk that the rab-cats couldn't fly.

"Doing an analysis now."

That sounded like the old Thea he knew. He felt a sudden ray of hope. *Thank the gods.*

Then his little companion erupted in a stream of manic laughter.

Leopold grabbed his hand. "Come on! I think I see light ahead!"

They hadn't known each other all that long, but the statement sounded uncharacteristically chipper for the morose human Crispin had collected—or tried to collect—in that dank apartment back on Earth.

One of the little rab-cats nipped at his ankle, and he gave a howl of his own, kicking it away and into the forest. Ignoring the ache, he hobbled after Leo toward the alleged light, looking up just in time to see Leopold's legs fly up into the air—fortunately still attached to the rest of him—as his antlers caught on a low-hanging vine. He came down hard on his back, the air forced out of him with an audible *whoosh*.

Crispin rushed to his side. "Leo! Are you all right?"

The howling once again drew closer. They were being surrounded, hunted. His human struggled to say something.

My human. He had no time to reflect on that thought. They had to get moving or they'd be rab-cat food. "It can wait. Breathe. We have to go!"

Leo scowled at him. He closed his eyes, as if he could concentrate his way through the whole mess, and at last air filled his lungs again. "It's Leopold, you daft bastard. Not Leo."

Crispin grinned, not even minding the insult. "Glad to have you back." He put a furry arm under Leo's and helped him get up. "Just a little further, I think." They stumbled together through the thinning undergrowth, toward the light.

The howling suddenly stopped, cut off as if someone had just flicked a switch, or maybe waved an enchanted wand. The forest was again as quiet as a graveyard, an association Crispin wished he hadn't just made. A mounting dread seized his heart. *What's scary enough to shut up a pack of rab-cats?*

He said a prayer to the Mother of Fae, who also happened to be his own mother. Which always made things a bit awkward, her being a semi-deity and all, when he asked for a blessing in her name.

Cerillia Ailedrin Moss'caladin had not been happy when he'd chosen a desk job over being a hunter. But that was drama for another day. Right now he had more pressing issues.

They tumbled into a moonlit clearing. When had the sun set? Not that he'd have been able to see it through all of the godsforsaken layers of forest canopy on this depressingly wild world. Wild had always been more of his brother's thing. Give Aspin a bow and arrow and set him loose in a dark forest and he was in fae heaven. Crispin much preferred a cozy armchair under a woolly blanket in front of a fireplace hearth, a mug of hot chocolate in hand.

"Why... did... they... stop?" Leo was laying on Crispin's stomach, somehow managing to make his brown fur look pale and wan. Or maybe it was the blue moonlight.

"I don't know." Crispin pushed away from Leo, disentangling his arms and legs. He looked back over his shoulder, expecting the toothy little rab-cats to burst out of the shadows at any moment. "Thea, a little help here? Are you... working yet?"

His little assistant responded with a sputtering of sparks and a column of smoke.

"That can't be good," observed Leopold.

He shook his head. "I've never seen her smoke before...." His gaze fell upon a large foot. Two of them, actually, covered in shaggy brown fur. They seemed to be connected to a pair of legs as thick as tree boles.

"So is there a repair shop for... for whatever that device is called?" Leo continued.

Crispin didn't reply. His eyes were too busy traveling up the thick expanse of those legs, past the heavy belly that overhung them like a mushroom cap, and up to the giant head that even now was tilting down to look at them.

"Crispy?" Leo sounded annoyed.

"It's... there's a...." He stared at the... huge thing that stood before him. Its mouth spread in a toothy grin, and he felt faint. *It's going to eat me.*

He had never been eaten before and was sure he would find the whole thing quite disagreeable. All those years of work, and it was to end in the pit of a giant's stomach. It didn't seem fair.

Leo must finally have noticed it too, because he responded with a particularly Earthian stream of words. "Well, fuck me sideways. What the holy hell is that?"

The shaggy beast opened its mouth, and Crispin closed his eyes, not wanting to see his own end.

"Could I interest you gents in a spot of ripple bark tea?"

Crispin started to hyperventilate. "Could you... some tea?" was all he could manage, followed by a series of hiccups.

"Yes, of course. Follow me back to the hedging and I'll get you right and refreshed." He turned and lifted one of his huge feet, and when he set it back onto the ground, the whole clearing shook.

"I think he's invited us back to his place." Of course Leo seemed much less frightened than Crispin was.

Crispin nodded. "Back to his flat. A giant invited us for a cup of tea." It was all way too much.

His eyes rolled back in his head and he collapsed, managing to just miss the soft patch of velvety purple moss he'd been aiming for.

6

LEOPOLD

Leopold was beginning to suspect that spiked Zima wasn't really his problem.

For one thing, this hallucination had gone on for a really long time and with way more sensory information than he'd normally attribute to drugs. His head was still sore from when his antlers collided with a tree branch, for instance, and he could still taste that delicious purple grass. While it was entirely plausible that a bad trip might include those nasty little rabbit things—and even a guy who looked like the love child of a bear and a redwood tree— Leopold doubted that his brain could manufacture an unconscious desk fae who was currently sort of a deer.

Also, Crispin was *heavy*.

"Is it much farther?" Worrying about sore arms was preferable to worrying about having ingested a doctored malt beverage. And a tainted Zima was preferable to the other alternative: that all of this was real.

Leopold shuddered, almost dropping Crispin in the process.

"I can carry him, you know," said the giant cheerfully. "Wouldn't bother me a bit. Last week I found a thermox lost in the forest, the

33

poor thing. Tucked her into my pocket, she went to sleep, and I didn't remember she was there until I went to change to pajamas. And a thermox weighs a lot more than your friend."

Being forgotten in a giant's pocket didn't seem like a good fate, not even if Crispin could be annoying as hell. Also, if something bad happened to him, Leopold had no idea how to get home. "I've got him."

The giant shrugged and plodded through the foliage, booming cheerfully about repairs he'd been doing to his cottage roof and about his upcoming vacation to a place Leopold had never heard of and couldn't pronounce. As best as he could tell, the main attraction of this holiday spot was a waterfall that did erotic dancing after nightfall.

He didn't even try to picture that.

Just as Leopold's arms were threatening to give out, the giant led them into a large clearing with boysenberry-hued ground cover and thistle-colored thistles. In the center of the clearing loomed a stone structure roughly the size of the Cathedral of the Blessed Sacrament in downtown Sacramento, but with all the charm of a mud hut.

"I know what you're thinking," said the giant. "*Oh, this guy's just hopping on the tiny house bandwagon because he thinks it's trendy.* But that's not true. I owned my teensy-tiny house long before it was cool."

"Uh, sure." Everything was relative. Apparently.

"Well, it's sort of a mess inside right now, and besides, I don't think my furniture would be very comfortable for you. How about we take our tea out here in the garden? It's a beautiful evening."

"That's fine. Um, as long as there aren't any more of those killer rabbit things around." Leopold gave their surroundings a nervous scan. Then he wondered about giant teacups. Would they be drinking the tea, or swimming in it?

The giant laughed, a sound like cannons firing. "No, of course not. In fact, they should all be hibernating this time of year. It's weird that you encountered any at all."

"Yeah. Weird." He did spy a little motion in one of the trees, and a bushy tail vanished as soon as he looked in its direction.

The giant lumbered into his cottage and Crispin began to stir, twitching his limbs and mumbling something about his perfecality score. Leopold set him gently on the ground and, when Crispin managed to focus his eyes, Leopold offered him a hand up.

"Wh-where...?" Still a little wobbly on his legs, Crispin peered at their surroundings.

"The giant's cozy little cottage." As if it was the most usual thing in the world. He was proud of himself for keeping his head, drugged or not.

"Giant." For a moment Crispin looked as if he might faint again, but then he steadied and narrowed his eyes at Leopold. "It's all very well for *you* to be so blasé about it—you think you're hallucinating. I, however, am aware that this is really real."

"I'm sorta coming to that conclusion too."

Crispin raised a refined eyebrow. "And you're not panicked about encountering a giant?"

Leopold sighed. "Dude. An elf whisked me away to... I dunno. Another planet? And turned me into a deer thing. And we were attacked by bloodthirsty bunnies. Giants just seem kinda par for the course at this point."

"Only *one* giant, I hope." Crispin cast another uneasy glance around as if he expected several more behemoths to come bursting out of the foliage. "And I did not *turn you into a deer thing*, and I am a desk fae, not an elf."

"Whatever." His new elf—friend?—was one of those types, nitpicking over every little thing. "Look, I've had enough adventure for one day. Take me home." Then they could be done with one another.

Crispin stamped a foot. Well, a hoof. Which was actually sort of cute in a Disneyesque sort of way. "I *can't*. I've told you. I must bring you to the Office of the Lost, but I can't even do that because Thea...."

His voice trailed off and he frantically patted his pants pockets. "Thea! Where is my—"

"I've got it." Leopold pulled the device out of his own jeans pocket and was grateful that he'd at least been able to keep that portion of his outfit. He had no idea how other magical deer creatures carried their stuff if they didn't have pockets.

Crispin momentarily cradled the phone to his chest but then scowled at the screen, which wasn't any less cracked than before. A bit of purple moss had worked its way into the phone's crannies, which probably also wasn't helping. "Thea?" he said nervously.

Thea whistled, one of those *leering* whistles construction workers gave to passersby they found attractive. But it was a very off-key, slurry kind of whistle.

Crispin frowned. He was kind of cute with his face all scrunched up. "Can you please take us back to OotL? Now?"

She made a sound like someone stepping on fractured glass, followed by an obnoxious honking.

"The glass. It's broken." Crispin swallowed audibly. "I don't think I can replace the screen in... this place. Is there perhaps—"

Thea interrupted him with the sound of very loud guitars.

"What is *that*?" Crispin stared at the phone, appalled.

Leopold tilted his head and hummed along for a moment before he remembered the title. Then he laughed. "It's 'Smoke on the Water' by Deep Purple. Very funny, Thea. Perfect band for this place."

"But—"

"It's a classic tune, Crispy. Tells a true story. See, the band was supposed to make a record, but then some guy burned the building down, and—"

"I fail to see how this is helpful." Crispin put his hands on his hips and glared at Leo.

Leopold shrugged. *This isn't my mess.* For once he was an innocent bystander simply dragged along for the ride. Anyway, he was totally crappy at fixing disasters, so he'd leave it to Crispin to figure things out. Surely he *would* figure things out, right? Eventually?

While Crispin continued to grumble at the phone, and just as Leopold was on the brink of an anxiety attack, the giant came ambling out of his house. He was pushing a wheeled wooden cart the size of a semi and whistling happily. Crispin and the phone both went silent, but at least this time Crispin maintained consciousness.

"Oh, good!" the giant boomed. "You're awake."

"I.... Yes." Crispin's voice was tremulous, but he was clearly making an effort to calm himself, and Leopold had to admire that.

"I brewed some of Aunt Brogrog's famous tea. It'll cure anything short of death—and even that's debatable, as long as the corpse is reasonably fresh. A cuppa will set you right as rain."

And then somehow all three of them were sitting cross-legged on the soft ground, the giant delicately holding a teacup big enough to double as a hot tub, and Leopold and Crispin with much smaller mugs that may have been made from outsized purple acorn caps. The giant had offered them sandwiches too, but they'd declined politely and were instead nibbling on bits of shrubbery. The leaves were very tasty. The tea, on the other hand, had a strong medicinal flavor, but they sipped it politely anyway.

"We've missed proper introductions," announced the giant. "On account of the swooning and all. I'm Fromlith Flokrion. And yes, of *those* Flokrions, although I come from the poor branch of the family, so don't expect fanciness around here. Not that I mind the relative lack of wealth. If you ask me, the rich Flokrions are far too stuck-up. They think a few gold-covered, jewel-encrusted mansions in the bogs make them better than everyone else, but they're not. Now, who are you folks, and how in Glagglorth's name did you end up tussling with five-footed pleeths at this time of year?"

By now, Crispin had managed to pull himself together. He was sitting straight-backed, his expression earnest. "The creatures simply showed up and attacked us. I don't know why." He brushed his chest fur, as if smoothing his missing tweed vest, and then frowned, looking down at the white tufts as if they had personally offended him. "I am Crispin Eladrin Moss'caladin, and I am a Curator with the Office of the

Lost. I am currently tasked with collecting this person, whose name is Leo—um, Leopold Lane. But there was apparently some kind of mishap and we ended up here instead. I'm terribly sorry for intruding."

Fromlith shook his head. "No, no, it's fine. It's nice to have some company. I moved here so I could work from home with peace and quiet, but sometimes it's a little *too* quiet."

Leopold decided not to ask what kind of work a giant engaged in, although he *was* curious.

Meanwhile, Crispin was nodding slowly. "That's very kind of you. I appreciate your hospitality. There are rumors at OotL about your folk, you know, and now I see that those rumors are entirely slanderous."

"What kind of rumors?"

Crispin shifted uncomfortably. "Erm, about your diet...."

"Oh, you mean that we eat fae?" Fromlith chuckled.

"Yes. Quite untrue I see, and—"

"Oh, no. We eat you guys all the time. You're tasty. Aunt Brogrog makes this scrumptious fae stew. She won't tell anyone what her secret herb blend is, but the meat gets so tender! It's a Flokrion family tradition to have it on holidays. Well, not the hoity-toity Flokrions. Not *fancy enough* for them, of course. They serve their fae roasted over a spit, with apples stuck between their teeth." He rolled his eyes.

Crispin had gone pale, which was an interesting phenomenon when seen on a furry face. Leopold wasn't feeling too secure himself. He considered making a run for it, but with the giant's long legs, Fromlith would catch him instantly. Maybe a better strategy was to convince their host that there was something wrong with Leopold and that noshing on him would make him sick. Leopold squinted his eyes and tried to imagine how a diseased magic deer thing might act. Was it better to faint, like Crispin had, or to stagger around in circles?

But Fromlith was laughing. "Hey, don't worry. You're safe with me. Eating your guests is bad manners, and anyway, I'm vegan."

"V-vegan?" stuttered Crispin. His hand had taken Leopold's and was squeezing it vigorously.

"Yeah. Better for my health—I have high cholesterol. Besides, you never know what the fae have been eating before you catch them. My cousin Dlodlos got a bad one once and spent three days puking his guts out, even with the help of my auntie's tea."

"I am *not* tainted!" announced Crispin, clearly offended.

"Yeah, probably not. But you never know." Fromlith slurped some tea and then set down his cup and rubbed his hands together. "Now then! You were saying something about a mishap?"

Crispin let go of Leopold's hand and made another effort to pull himself together. Leopold had to give the guy credit—he didn't give up easily. Unlike Leopold himself, who rarely found anything worth the effort.

"The device I use to transport between worlds is malfunctioning," explained Crispin. He held up Thea, displaying her cracked screen.

Fromlith squinted at the tiny—for him—device. "Ah. Gotcha. Well, I'd offer you a corner in my cottage since you hardly take up any space, but the truth is that sometimes my relatives come to visit, and I'm not sure I'd trust them around you. My auntie would have you in a pot of boiling water like *that*." He snapped his fingers, a sound like trees being felled, and Crispin emitted a distressed little squeak.

"Yes, well, very kind of you. But I need to return to OotL. Quite urgently, you see. Another reflective surface will likely do. So if I could borrow a mirror?"

"Don't have one. Sorry. My people don't cast reflections."

"I thought that was vampires," interjected Leopold, who'd mostly remained silent until now.

Crispin and Fromlith stared at him as if he'd just claimed that the Earth was flat. "Vampires aren't real," said Crispin in very much the same tone that Leopold's parents had once told him—when he was very young—that there were no monsters under his bed. "Those are just *stories* they tell to frighten children."

Fromlith nodded his agreement.

"But how do you know that?' protested Leopold. "I mean, if there are elves and giants and killer rabbits and magic deer people and… whatever the hell that bird thing on the roof over there is… why not vampires?"

Crispin gave Leopold's knee a patronizing pat. "Yes, but elves and giants and southern minor cockatrices, which is what that 'bird thing' is—"

"*Southwestern* minor cockatrice," interrupted Fromlith. "They used to think it was a subspecies but now it's in its own category."

"Oh, thank you. I'll need to correct the OotL records on that matter." He held Thea out at arm's length, and then sighed, slipping her back into his pocket. "Leo, those things are all real. Vampires are *pretend*." He said it in exactly the same tone as one of Leopold's foster mothers used to say Santa Claus wasn't real.

Leopold ignored the tone. *Well, that's a small relief.* It was nice to get at least one piece of good news today: he wouldn't have to worry about vampires showing up and wanting to suck his blood. Which, when he thought about it, really didn't do all that much to improve their current situation. "Okay, fine. But without a mirror, how do we get out of here?"

Fromlith shrugged. "I'm not big on shiny stuff. The other branch of the family, they could probably lend you a silver tray or something, but not me. Doesn't fit my aesthetic, and honestly, I think it's pretty tacky."

Crispin's shoulders sagged, and for the first time, Leopold felt truly bad for him. The poor guy had just been trying to do his job, and now he was having a crappy day. Leopold could feel his pain, because that was Leopold's story almost every day, and it sucked. "Is there anything else around here that might work?"

Thea began playing Deep Purple again, more quietly this time.

After another long slurp of tea, Fromlith rubbed his beard

thoughtfully. "There's stuff in the city, but with your tiny legs, you'd take days to get there."

"Days!" Crispin wailed.

"Yeah, and it's probably not particularly safe for you to go there anyway. You know. On account of the stew."

Leopold tried to imagine what it would be like to be stranded here forever. He hadn't left any loved ones behind, and the grass here really *was* delicious. But no televisions. Probably no pizza. And his apartment in Sacramento might be fairly shitty, but it was *his* shitty apartment, and his bed was fairly comfortable, and the roof kept him dry. And in Sacramento there were, as far as he knew, no flesh-eating giants. Only flesh-eating viruses, which to be sure was not much better, but he'd never run into one of those yet either.

Thea turned up her volume, and much as Leopold liked the song, he really didn't have it in him right now to care about a burning casino in Switzerland in the 1970s. Even if the chorus was totally catchy.

Wait.

The name of the song was "Smoke on the Water." Water. Which tended to be reflective.

"Is there a lake around here?" Leopold asked.

Crispin gaped at him with surprised admiration. "Yes! If the light shines on still water correctly, that might work very well. Well done, Leo!"

Ignoring the nickname, Leopold preened a little.

Fromlith's face was scrunched up in thought, which was an impressive sight. "Well... not a lake. But if you walk a few hours in that direction"—he pointed—"you'll reach the Pond of Disappointment."

That didn't sound promising. His whole life had been a pond of disappointment, and he wasn't keen on spending hours walking to another one. "Why is it called that?"

"Dunno. Maybe because someone wanted a lake and got something smaller instead. I guess it's reflective enough for you, though."

"Pond of Disappointment." Crispin seemed to be tasting the name on his lips. "Worth a try, I suppose." He stood and brushed bits of foliage off his pants, then looked up at the giant, who still loomed even when seated. "Thank you again. But time is of the essence, so we'll be going now."

Leopold stood as well and stretched his legs a little. He wasn't sure what he thought about having hooves. It was kind of nice not to need shoes or socks, but his hooves were fairly sharp, and he wondered if he might be in danger of injuring himself in his sleep. He wouldn't be a bit surprised, given his luck.

He thanked Fromlith too. He didn't know about the other Flokrions, but this one seemed like a decent guy. "Good luck with your roof repairs. And I hope you have a fun vacation."

"I will. Good luck to you as well. Oh, and one other thing."

Crispin made an impatient noise. "Yes?"

Fromlith pointed behind them. "You'll probably want to watch out for that."

7
CRISPIN

Crispin closed his eyes.

There was only so much a self-respecting desk fae could take. He'd expected—no, he'd deserved—an easy retrieval. All he needed to do was go to Earth, pick up this one (rather slovenly, if he was forced to admit the truth) lost human, and be back home before the clock struck midnight, inside his cozy tree home with Minkis.

Now he was in a strange and apparently very deadly purple world, facing down a vegan giant who would probably still eat him if he got hungry enough. He was stuck with antlers and hooves— *hooves*, for the silver queen's sake!—and probably still bleeding from that damned five-footed adorable pleat. Or whatever the hoary-haired honker himple Fromlith had called it. Oh and his faithful companion Thea seemed more interested in blaring out what he could only assume was some kind of bizarre mating call than in getting him home.

And now he had to worry about *something else*? "What. Is. It?"

Fromlith squinted from under eyebrows that, on their own,

would have made quite convincing hedges. "I can't really tell. It's dark and twisty, though. And it smells like…." He sniffed the air, his inhalations causing the trees around them to shudder. "Like smoked evil."

"I had smoked salmon once." Leo scratched his furry chin. "Never understood what the big deal was."

Crispin's eyes flew open. "Would you please, just for one eternal moment, shut your godsdamned trap?"

His hand flew to his mouth as Leo's eyes went wide and he took a step back, blinking wildly. "I'm so sorry, Leo—Leopold. I don't know what came over me." If his mother ever heard him speak to someone like that, she'd have his hide. Even Minkis would be disappointed, in a sagging tail, dull-eyed squirrely sort of way.

Leo stopped blinking. "It's all right. I mean… it's not. But I figure you're not as used to weird shit as I am."

Which was, well, patently ridiculous. But Crispin wasn't in a position to argue just then.

"Maybe… just maybe… we should look at the dark and twisty thing?" Leo jerked his head in the direction that Fromlith had pointed.

Crispin sighed. It seemed as if it was going to be a long while before he got back to the comfort of his OotL desk.

He looked up and frowned.

The dark and twisty thing was extending a tendril toward them. It was, in fact, a version of the same being that had come after them back in Leo's apartment, though it seemed to have its smoky teeth sheathed for the moment. "We should, um, probably go." He looked back at Fromlith. "Thank you so much for the tea." He set down his acorn-cap mug, which stubbornly refused to stand upright on its pointy bottom and spilled medicinal tea all over the cart.

"So… not a friend of yours?" Fromlith picked up the tiny cup like a grain of sand between his large fingers and put it away.

"Definitely not."

"Well why didn't you say so?" He opened his mouth wide and

bellowed a sound so loud that Crispin was forced to cover his ears with his palms, pressing against them so tightly he feared his head would pop.

Leo did the same, and then vanished from sight.

Crispin blinked and then stared at the place where his collected human had been, but his gaze was pried away by a horrid screeching. It seemed designed to join with the giant's cascading bellow and to melt Crispin's brain out of his ears despite the hand covering.

He spun around and watched the black and twisty thing writhe in midair, captured by the giant's banshee cry. It began to come apart into squirming threads blacker than midnight, each hissing and wailing like a dying bandersploot before popping out of existence. Like Leo had just done. And there were the teeth. They gnashed in his general direction before fading into nothing. *How does smoke have teeth?*

When the noise stopped—as quickly as it had begun—and the dark and twisty thing had been banished, Leo was there again, solid as a bowl of porridge left in the sink all day, looking at Fromlith in abject admiration. "That was badass."

It was Crispin's turn to blink. "Did you... were you...?" He lacked the will to formulate the question he really wanted to ask. Maybe he had hallucinated the disappearance. Zanther knew, he was under enough pressure. "What does 'ass' have to do with it?"

"I think he means I kicked its butt." Fromlith frowned. "Not that it had one. A butt, I mean."

Crispin sighed. "Yes, I figured that part out." Had he imagined the whole *blinking out of existence* thing? Maybe some of his brain *had* leaked out of his skull. He touched his cheek, just to be sure, but it was dry as a bone.

He shook his head. His mind was already on overload. He didn't need another mystery. "I suppose we should be going. We can't find Disappointment without a good walk."

"That's for sure. I hate exercise." Whatever had happened to him, Leo seemed no worse for wear.

"I meant the pond." Why had he been sent to collect this... this waste of space for the Office? Where would they even put him? *Maybe this is all a test.* Efrim Eflin El'Esprin was due to retire soon. Maybe this was all an elaborate ruse to see how he handled himself under pressure. Yes, that must be it.

All he had to do was get them to this Pond of Disappointment in one piece, and they would be able to cross over to the Office at last, and everything would go back to normal.

Well, not totally normal. His perfecality score was probably shot for the year. Theodor would likely snag the prize this year, and lord it over him the way only a dwarf could.

Crispin sighed.

"The grass is really good here," Leo said. "But I wonder if we might have a few more of those... cookie crumbs you brought with the tea?"

Crispin's stomach rumbled in agreement. "Leopold's right. We could use a bit more to eat before we rush off into the forest again." *And maybe something to deal with those... what had Fromlith called them? Gleeth? Pleeth?*

"I'm afraid I can't do that, my little friends." The giant grinned, teeth as big as tombstones, and Crispin shuddered.

He's going to eat us after all. Crispin closed his eyes, determined to depart this worldly plane with at least a modicum of dignity.

Leo, in a surprising act of bravery, placed himself in front of Crispin. Or maybe he'd just tripped. In any case, he drew himself up to his full height, a good three inches taller than Crispin, and stared down the giant. "You can't have him. He's my... my desk fae."

Crispin blinked, and so did the giant. Why did it sound as though something else had been about to come out of the Earthling's mouth?

"You thought... I mean... I already said that..." Fromlith grabbed his belly with both hands and began to laugh, a sound so guttural and deep that it shook the leaves off the closest trees. He slapped his knees, and birds flew out of the forest canopy in alarm, and the sky cleared as the wayward clouds steered out of his way.

"I don't see what's so funny." Leo turned on Crispin. "What's he laughing about?" His eyes narrowed. "This is all your fault, you know."

"I'm laughing, dear friends, because you've apparently misunderstood me. I don't eat things with faces, as delicious as the two of you look. What I meant is that I couldn't feed you here, because I intend to accompany you to the Pond of Disappointment, and we could eat on the way." He chortled again, seemingly amusing himself. "A Flokrion always looks after his friends. Especially those he doesn't eat." He nodded and spun around toward his massive cottage. "Let me just gather a few things and we'll be on our way."

He vanished as nimbly as a thirty-foot-tall creature could into the darkness of his home.

"What was that thing? The cloud thing, with the teeth?" Leo was staring at Crispin as if he would somehow know, his earlier hostility apparently forgotten.

"You were mad at me just two minutes ago—"

"Sorry about that. My blood sugar's a bit low. I get a little..." and he wobbled his hand in a way that reminded Crispin of a three-footed sploot.

"Um... splooty?"

Leo's mouth worked on that a bit, and then he blinked again and nodded. "Sure. Let's go with that." His gaze lifted to the tree where the dark and twisty thing had been. "So what was it?"

Crispin scratched his head. "I have no idea. It looks a bit like the things that chased us out of your...." He'd been about to say "garbage pit," but that didn't sound politic. "Um... your flat. But what they are, where they came from, or what they want"—*could an ethereal being truly want anything?*—"I haven't a clue."

For all this trouble, he was going to ask for a raise when he got back home. And an extra week off. And maybe a pony. He'd always wanted a pony, and he figured they'd owe him if he got this one back safely. "Thea?"

His hopes that she'd maybe found her way back to sanity were dashed when she hiccuped and then belched something green that might have been spores from the invading purple moss.

He forged ahead anyway. "Any idea what that weird dark thing was?"

Her response was to play something that sounded halfway between fingernails on a chalkboard and a dwarf with a head cold. Crispin sighed and started to put the device away.

"Wait. I know this one." Leo mouthed the lyrics. "It's Marilyn Manson."

"Well, she has a perfectly lovely voice." Crispin rolled his eyes.

Leo waved that assessment aside. "It's called 'We Are Chaos.'" His eyes met Crispin's and for the first time there seemed to be a bit of light in them. "Maybe Thea's trying to tell us something?"

Crispin frowned. Thea was broken all to bits, just like his schedule. "I don't think so. I'll have to get a new PTD when we get back." *If we get back.*

"I still think she might be—"

"Here we are." Fromlith appeared from his castle-sized cottage with a couple human/fae sized packs. "This should fill your stomachs."

Crispin took his. It had two straps, presumably for putting over one's shoulders. "Where did they come...." It crossed his mind that the previous owners of the packs had likely become soup, or maybe a delicious spot of tea, so he decided he didn't need to know. "Thank you, Master Fromlith." His mother would have been proud of his diplomatic skills.

"You're welcome, Master Moss'caladin."

Crispin opened the sack, took out a giant cookie crumb as large as his fist, and then settled the straps of the pack over his shoulders.

Leo rolled his eyes but did the same.

"Say," Fromlith said, "your mother doesn't happen to be Cerillia Ailedrin Moss'caladin, by any chance?"

Was it his imagination, or did the giant shudder a bit when he spoke her name? "Why yes, she is." Apparently Crispin wasn't the only one in whom the Mother of Fae inspired fear.

"Ah, very good then." Fromlith clasped his hands and looked down at the ground, over his shoulder, up at the sky—basically anywhere but at him.

"Fromlith."

"Yes, Master Moss'caladin." Still no eye contact.

"You're not looking at me."

"No, sir, I am not."

"Why not?" Was the giant... afraid of him?

"Because your mother has let it be known, far and wide, that no one is to harm a hair on the head of her last-born son. Which is, apparently, you."

Crispin growled. "Why that two-faced, not nice, mother freaking woman."

"Who taught you to swear?" This time there was a definite twinkle in Leo's eyes.

"My mother. Who, apparently, doesn't trust me to take care of myself." No wonder his job had been so easy. The Mother of Freaking Fae had laid down the law. *Does she think so little of me?*

There would be a reckoning when he got home. He promised himself that much. "Fromlith," he said softly.

"Yes, Master Moss—"

"Just Crispin, please, with my friends." *That* surprised him. Had he started to think of this possibly fae-eating giant as a friend? "Let's agree that you've done your bit by not eating me, and move on from there, shall we?"

That wide half-a-cemetery grin split the giant's face again. "Very good, little sir." He knelt and held out his hands. "Might I give you a ride to the pond? It's much faster than if you two walk your tiny people steps."

Crispin shot Leo a look, and Leo nodded.

As the giant lifted them onto his wide shoulders, Thea again broke into song.

Leo grinned. "The Proclaimers. Your little friend there has some dope taste in music."

Crispin frowned. *How long would it take, exactly, to walk a thousand miles?*

"Grab onto the ears, my friends. This is gonna be a bumpy ride."

8

LEOPOLD

When Leopold had been eleven years old, some do-gooder group had schlepped him and a busload of other foster kids to a C-list theme park for the day, apparently believing that a tomato-themed Ferris wheel would somehow make up for not having parents. It wasn't really a fun experience. Rides kept breaking down while Leopold was waiting in line for them and once, memorably, while he was riding a roller coaster called the Zucchini Spiral. The employees had to call in a rescue crew for that one.

Eventually Leopold had wandered off from his group and found a quiet corner of the park where food wrappers and deflated balloons sat in sad little piles along the curb and a boarded-up hut bore a sign promising that an unspecified new attraction was coming soon. There was a single operational ride in that section—the Great Asparagus Escape—and it had no line.

Intrigued, Leopold had checked it out.

A short path set up the storyline, which involved joining asparagus spears in an attempt to avoid a beast that spat Hollandaise sauce. An incredibly bored-looking teenager strapped

51

Leopold into a seat that was suspended by chains from the top of a tall green stalk.

Gears ground and the seat—and Leopold—ratcheted upward in a series of jerks. Leopold would have enjoyed the view if his stomach hadn't started feeling queasy, a situation that didn't improve when the seat began swinging wildly back and forth. Pretty soon it was all Leopold could do to avoid puking up the greasy burger he'd been served for lunch, and the recorded sound of the Hollandaise beast sloshing and bubbling hadn't helped either.

When the ride finally ended, Leopold had staggered right into the search party tasked with looking for him. He'd promptly thrown up on the Head Do-Gooder's shoes.

He'd blissfully pushed that entire incident out of his mind, but it came back to him now as he swayed and lurched through the forest on Fromlith's giant shoulder. Closing his eyes didn't help, and neither did clutching at Fromlith's hair, which had the texture of shag carpeting.

"Why do you look like that?" demanded Crispin.

"'Cause you turned me into a deer." He was annoyed at having to explain himself when Crispin was so clearly to blame.

"I did not. This wasn't my fault. And anyway, that wasn't what I meant. You appear... distressed."

"Motion sick," said Leopold through gritted teeth.

"Ah." Crispin was silent for a few moments and then cleared his throat. "The fac don't experience motion sickness."

"Bully for you." He turned away, pretending to examine the passing foliage. Squirrels—or squirrel-like things—leapt through the branches like little acrobats. He closed his eyes and breathed slowly.

Fromlith had seemed to ignore the entire conversation, and didn't appear at all alarmed to have a nauseated deer-thing perched on one shoulder. In fact, he was humming off-key and glancing around while he walked, as if he were enjoying a pleasant stroll. Occasionally he stopped to admire a plant, or to point at creatures that resembled enormous butterflies but probably sucked people's blood or dined on brains.

The stopping and starting wasn't helping Leopold's stomach, but it seemed fairly rude to point that out.

"Do you want a distraction?" Crispin asked after a while.

Leopold considered before giving a tentative nod. "Maybe."

"Well, we could talk about our families, if you wanted."

That was when Leopold remembered that Fromlith had mentioned Crispin's mother and had seemed impressed by her. "Fine. You start. Who are your parents?"

"Well, I don't know exactly who my father is. There are several possible candidates, and they all helped Mother raise me. All very fine fae." Crispin said this with more than a hint of pride.

If he squinted, Leopold could almost see his tweedy garments. "Ah. So your mom is a free spirit? That's cool." He'd always sort of admired people who could manage multiple relationships, especially considering he'd never been able to handle even one.

"My mother is the Mother of Fae."

Leopold heard the capital letters and understood that it was a title, although he didn't know what it meant. "Is that, uh, like the Mother of Dragons?"

Crispin sputtered, but before he could say anything, Fromlith chimed in. "A pod of dragons lives down the road from my sister. Nice neighbors, but sometimes they accidentally set the hedges on fire. Drives up insurance rates something crazy."

And that got Leopold musing about risks and coverage for various creatures, which was almost interesting enough to take his mind off being sick. But he wanted to know more about Crispin's parentage. "So, the Mother of Fae?"

"She is a... well, I don't think you quite have a term for it. A queen? A goddess? Something along those lines."

"Sounds important."

"She is. And because of that, she had very little time for me and my brother when we were young, but we knew she loved us, and our fathers took good care of us."

A somewhat unorthodox family structure, but Leopold allowed that maybe it was more common among fae than among humans. In any case, he felt a little envious. It must have been nice to be surrounded by a lot of caring adults. "A brother?"

"Aspin." Crispin sighed, and Leopold could hear years of sadness and disappointment in his tone. "He's a hunter. Mother hoped I would be as well, and she wasn't entirely pleased when I chose to be a desk fae instead." Another sigh, this time vigorous enough to tickle Fromlith's ear and make him twitch a little, causing an extra lurch in Leopold's stomach.

Leopold had never chosen a career. He'd simply grabbed whatever jobs he could find and held on to them as long as he could, which usually wasn't very long at all. He'd never really given any thought to what he *wanted* to do. Especially because he knew he'd only screw things up if he tried. "Do you like being a desk fae?"

Although Leopold couldn't see Crispin well on Fromlith's opposite shoulder, he had the sense that Crispin puffed himself up a bit. "I do! It's a little like hunting, in fact, except I don't have to kill anything, and it's entirely satisfying to collect items that I know are important and to file excellent reports. My perfecality score is always at the top of the ranks. Until now, that is." And yep, there came another of those sighs.

They continued onward up a gentle slope to a meadow of lilac-hued grass. It smelled nice, and if Leopold had possessed any confidence that he'd be able to keep the stuff down, he'd have asked to stop and have a snack. But since he still didn't feel well, he contented himself with gazing wistfully at the waving fronds. Ironic to be in a place where he was surrounded by delicious free food but unable to eat any.

"How about you?" Crispin interrupted Leopold's thoughts. "You mentioned something about your parents earlier, I believe."

"They're dead." Leopold said this flatly. It had been years since he'd felt any emotion over the loss. "Freak accident when I was a kid. Camel attack." He'd been there but had luckily been distracted by some goats and so didn't actually see them die. Saying it out loud reminded him how truly weird it was.

"I'm so sorry. Brothers or sisters?"

"Nope. I was adopted. Not a clue who my bio family was. My parents never said, and the paperwork was lost at some point. Anyway, they didn't have any other kids." He'd been more than enough, probably. He'd been a handful.

"Wh-what happened to you after your parents passed away? It must have been so awful." Crispin's voice was thick with sympathy, the kind Leopold usually hated. But coming from the fae, it sounded sincere.

Leopold hadn't expected that. "Foster care. Kinda got bounced around until I grew up." None of his foster parents had been terrible by any means. But none had been willing or able to keep him either, because not long after he'd settle into a new house, disasters would start to happen. He once overheard a social worker referring to him as Bad-Luck Lane.

But feeling sorry for himself was even worse than feeling pukey, so Leopold was almost relieved when he spied something gray and amorphous skulking through the trees nearby. "Um, Fromlith?"

"Yeah, I saw it. Don't worry. I'll roar if it comes too close."

The last time Fromlith roared, Leopold had temporarily blacked out, and he wasn't eager to repeat that. He clutched the giant's hair more tightly. "Do you know what it is? And why it's chasing us?"

"Nope. I've never seen anything like it. But it smells weird. Like the time Aunt Brogrog got tipsy and decided to make scallion-pickle cupcakes."

Leopold's stomach was displeased by that concept and made its displeasure known with another queasy lurch. He shut his eyes tight and tried not to think about bad baking, bad gray monster clouds, bad memories, or any of the day's other unpleasantries.

He might have actually dozed off a little bit. Aside from messing things up, he possessed one additional superpower, which was the ability to nap anywhere under nearly any circumstances. He'd probably developed the knack when he was a little kid, because no matter where he and his parents had lived, they'd always ended up with noisy neighbors. Or maybe he'd picked it up while in foster care, when, depending on his circumstances, he'd sometimes slept on narrow institutional cots, in unfamiliar cars, or even in office chairs.

This time he came awake fully when Fromlith halted. "Is the monster here again?" Leopold asked sleepily, looking around. They were in a small valley with a steep slope ahead of them. The hillside was covered in pebbles and small rocks, all the same dull gray as old concrete. The valley floor was also mostly gray stone, although it was scattered with short scraggly plants in shades of pale periwinkle.

"No monsters here." Fromlith stooped so that Leopold and Crispin could slide off his shoulders. Crispin landed gracefully, as if executing a dance move, but Leopold stumbled and fell, scraping a hoof loudly against a sharp rock and tweaking his ankle.

He scrambled back to his feet. "How do you know there aren't any monsters?"

"No self-respecting monster would come anywhere near here. It's... uninspiring. And nothing you find in these parts tastes good anyway." Fromlith's stomach rumbled as if in agreement, shaking the ground.

"Thus the name," said Crispin, looking pleased with himself for figuring it out. "The Pond of Disappointment."

Fromlith nodded sadly. "Some of my ancestors tried to build a vacation resort here, on account of the waterfront. They came with high hopes, but nothing worked out. The buildings were poorly constructed. The food was bland. The weather was always too hot or too cold. There was nothing to do except swim, but the pond—which started out as a lake, I guess—shrank until it was too cramped for giants. So everyone left."

Leopold didn't say so, but he could relate. On the few occasions when he'd had enough spare cash to go on vacation, he hadn't had fun. The Grand Canyon had been so foggy he could barely see beyond the end of his nose, let alone into the storied depths. His campsite in the Sierras was evacuated due to a forest fire. When he visited a quaint little coastal town, all the shops and restaurants were closed due to a power outage, signs on the beach warned of sewage contamination, and his motel room was infested with bedbugs.

"But where's the pond?" Crispin peered at the sad little valley.

He had a point. There was not a drop of water in sight.

"Over that hill." Fromlith pointed. "But if it's all the same to you, I'm going to say good-bye here. The pond is a real downer."

Although Leopold didn't relish climbing that slope, especially with his sore ankle, he couldn't really ask Fromlith for more. The guy had been more than generous.

Apparently concluding the same thing, Crispin gave Fromlith a courtly bow. "Of course. Thank you for your assistance."

"And you'll tell the Mother of Fae that I didn't harm a hair on your head?"

"I'll tell her that you were a perfect gentleman, and provided... *enormous* assistance."

This must have pleased Fromlith, for he beamed, bent, and clapped Crispin hard enough on the back to send the desk fae flying into Leopold. This time they both fell down, legs and antlers tangled. It took them a while to recover—and on Leopold's part, a fair bit of swearing—and by the time they did, Fromlith was already stomping off into the distance, heading eagerly back to his enormous tiny house.

Crispin brushed himself off. "Let's do this, shall we? My perfe-cality score—"

"Is dropping by the minute. I know. Fine." He was ready to get this nightmare over with. Sore ankle notwithstanding, he started up the hill.

It was hard going. There was a path of sorts, but sometimes it disappeared and they had to find it again. At times the slope was so steep that they both had to proceed on all fours, which at least turned out to be easier as deer-things than in their usual forms, but even then the scree tended to shift beneath them. Leopold thought he'd be relieved when they reached the top, but he wasn't—not when he saw the equally steep downward path to a patch of water with all the charm of a sewage treatment pond.

"Ugh," said Crispin, gazing down at it.

"Agreed."

"There's a lovely little pool near my home, you know. Crystal-clear water surrounded by soft fragrant grasses and tiny flowers. Sometimes Minkis and I go for a dip after I get home from OotL, before I fix dinner." His gaze was unfocused, and a slow smile spread across his face, making him more handsome.

Leopold frowned. "Who's Minkis?"

Crispin shot him a look. "My pet squirrel, of course. He's wonderful. I can show you some photos...." He stuck a hand in his trousers pocket but brought it out empty. "Oh. I may have lost them when we, um, transitioned."

"Bummer," said Leopold, who was relieved. He was in no mood to be subjected to cute pet pictures. He turned away and started his skidding, sliding way down to the water. It was a harrowing journey, but they both made it to the bottom without losing their precarious balance.

For a few moments, they both stood on the shore and looked at the pond. "Well. I suppose it *is* reflective." Crispin looked doubtful.

"Is this gonna do the trick? You know, I have to work in the morning. Cleaning busses, not sitting in an office and filing reports about doodads I've collected. And it'll probably be raining again. And I'll probably do something soon that'll get me fired, and—" He stopped and emitted a sigh as impressive as Crispin's. "Just do the thing already."

Frowning, Crispin pulled out his phone and stared at the cracked screen. "Thea?"

There was no response.

"Thea? We've found the pond. Now if you could— Oh, damn the black eye of Pothos!"

Leopold glanced over to see what Crispin was staring at and wasn't even a little surprised to see an oily gray cloud making its way toward them. It was hard to judge the cloud's dimensions. One moment it looked roughly human-sized and the next it seemed bigger than the hill they'd just climbed. Its edges shifted and its interior swirled, and there was something both sinister and purposeful in the way it slunk forward.

"I thought Fromlith said no monsters," Leopold said tightly.

"It appears our giant friend was mistaken." Crispin looked as displeased as if he'd eaten a mouthful of skunk-sprayed porcupine.

"What does it want? Why is it chasing us?" Leopold's heart raced, a feat it was unused to on any regular basis.

Crispin shook his head frantically. "I don't know! Thea! Help!"

The phone made a series of noises like an old-fashioned modem, played a bar or two of "We Are Family," and spat a volley of greenish sparks that made Crispin yelp. He managed to keep hold of it, though, which was a minor miracle.

There was nowhere to run and no place to hide, and there were no roaring giants in the vicinity. Leopold didn't even have a weapon —not that he knew how to fight a cloud anyway. And Crispin, who held his ground despite looking terrified, didn't seem to know what to do either. Probably desk fae didn't often face death.

The cloud slithered closer. It had a sound, Leopold realized. Or more accurately, sounds. Static like a radio not quite getting a signal. Glass shattering. The wind battering a house. Engines idling and then revving. All of them at once, making Leopold's heart race and his skin feel goose-pimply. And it tugged at him, the way your foster mom tugs at your shirt collar when you refuse to leave the candy store of your own volition.

"Leave us alone!" Crispin shouted. "I am a curator with the Office of the Lost and I order you to stop interfering in my collection duties!"

The cloud didn't seem impressed. Maybe Crispin needed a badge to flash.

It came even closer. Leopold couldn't smell it—maybe only giants could—but he could *feel* it, alternately cold and hot, and with an electrical charge that made his hairs stand on end.

Crispin was holding his phone up like a weapon. "Go away!"

It didn't.

And the weird thing—well, hell, *everything* was weird, wasn't it? —*one* weird thing was that although Leopold was scared, he also felt an urge to walk toward the cloud, to meet up with it, to touch it. It must be the same way moths felt about flames.

"Go away!" Crispin bellowed even louder. Apparently he felt no similar draw.

Leopold took a step forward.

Crispin grabbed Leopold's arm, tight.

And the cloud spoke, its voice filling the air so thoroughly that Leopold could barely breathe. "Giiiiive himmmm to usssss." Foggy teeth gleamed in its depths, gnashing like breaking glass.

Oh, shit. Leopold knew to a certainty that he was the *him* in question. And for a brief time he was afraid that Crispin would simply shove him into the cloud and make his own safe escape. Leopold could hardly blame him if he did.

Instead, Crispin tightened his grip on Leopold's arm and screamed, "Thea! Take us back to OotL!"

And then he dragged Leopold into the pond.

9
CRISPIN

When Crispin was a wee fae, long before he found his calling in the Office of the Lost and first sat down at his neat, perfectly white marble desk—allegedly carved from the stone of Mount Olympus—he'd opened The Door.

The Door was a strange fixture in his mother's house, although Cerillia Ailedrin Moss'caladin's home wasn't a home, per se. There were no real walls, no particular barriers of any sort, although even that depended on the place in which it materialized. It had the odd (and often annoying) propensity of shifting from one world to the next, so that he might go to sleep on Therrin, with her grand castles and well-manicured forests, and wake up to the blood-curdling howls of the ghoulsts of Thauria.

Mother's home was usually a grove of trees—often great oaks, lit by eldritch lights, that reached up into an impossibly tall sky filled with stars; in other incarnations, tall spindly spiral trees with heart-shaped leaves. And sometimes, as when it manifested itself in a casino on Odds, startlingly realistic wallpaper of the grand trees.

No matter how the home manifested, local males were always finding their way in, looking for Mab or the Fairy Queen or the Ecch

Ridah... and his mother always indulged them. She loved playing her little games, telling them they would be stuck with her if they ate or drank a thing in her house. Some immediately imbibed, and were severely unhappy when they were shown the exit the next morning, while others went to great lengths to try to avoid even breathing the air.

But however her house looked or who came to visit, The Door was the one constant.

It sat off to one side of the wide clearing in the heart of the Estate, where one of their ancestors had built the center and focal point of Mother's home: a large amphitheater that looked like a stone bowl, filled with the softest of silk pillows.

One morning, Crispin awoke after a particularly long night of drunken imbibing by the Mother of Fae and her latest paramour—a gray-skinned, single-horned brute from Greebals, their current temporary home. Two of Crispin's co-parents, Aether and Freyis, had called it a rhinsus before they'd stumbled off into the darkness together.

The rhinsus lay flat on his stomach, his horn moving gently up and down, a stubby gray arm thrown over Crispin's mother's torso. This was a tableau he'd seen repeated over and over with various suitors, so frequently that he barely gave the poor wretch a second look.

He liked the world of Greebals. It was lush and green, filled with lakes and rivers and interesting smells. But over the years, he had slowly reached a level of boredom that would make a blade of grass uproot itself and go in search of a cliff to jump off of, just to end the monotony. He was an adolescent fae now, after all. His seventy-odd years ought to count for something. He had grown tired of his mother's Estate, of the boring everyday sameness. Aspin was away on the Great Hunt, and even when he was home, he didn't spend much time with his "weird little brother Elly."

There had to be some adventure that he hadn't experienced before. He'd rejected the idea of sneaking off the Estate. Not only had he already done that, but Mother was overdue for a change of scenery. If she departed Greebals and then had to come back for him from another world, she would be very angry.

Things often *exploded* when the Mother of Fae was angry. Or turned into fish and frogs. Or simply ceased to exist, though he doubted she would visit such a punishment on her youngest child.

His eyes wandered past the Red Dukes of Vespertine—all five of them, collapsed in a pile amid crystal flagons of his mother's cherry wine—and up the slopes of the hollow.

And there it was. The Door.

His mother (and all his other parent fae) had been *very explicit* about it. He was never to open The Door. Bad things would happen if he did, things they never quite explained, which was somehow worse. His imagination had filled in a variety of possible outcomes, none of them good and many of them ending up with that same threat of nonexistence.

He took a seat on a white stone bench carved with cupids—nasty things in reality, no matter how charmingly they were portrayed— and considered The Door for a few moments. He pulled out his omnipresent pad of paper and charcoal stick and began sketching its outlines.

In its Greebals incarnation, a complex intertwining of deep green vines framed a round door of thick wood panels, with a brass handle curled like the toe of an elf's boot. The Door was always red.

Don't open The Door. Ever.

Crispin sighed. All of his life he'd been told all the things he *shouldn't* do.

Never look the Red Dukes in the eyes. Never interrupt the Mother of Fae when she was "entertaining." Never lead a mortal back to the Estate without an adult's express permission.

And never, ever open The Door.

The adults around him were always making up rules for *him* while they did whatever they wanted. Many of the edicts existed to make sure he stayed in his place; he was sure of it.

Maybe the whole Door thing was one of those?

He set down his sketch pad and charcoal stick and crept past the Red Dukes, careful lest any of them have their eyes open. Then he made his way up the wide stairs that surrounded the amphitheater, old gray stone, which although splintered by moss-filled cracks nevertheless seemed flush with strength and dignity and ageless wisdom.

Aether and Freyis had made their way back at some point and were snuggled together on one of the steps, smiles on the two men's sleeping faces.

Crispin repressed his own smile. He'd seen what they did together. Maybe one day he'd be old enough—and ready enough—to try.

He climbed the wide stone steps of the amphitheater and stood on the paved circle that fronted The Door. Up close, the portal looked —strange. Unreal. As if someone, or something, had constructed the *idea* of a door, based on many other doors they had seen in the past. It looked like a real door, mostly. But if you got too close, the details were off. Some of the interwoven vines just ended, replaced by other vines that appeared out of nowhere. The woodgrain was suspect too; in some places it formed what almost looked like words, in others it disappeared as if someone had brushed it away.

He reached out to touch the brass handle. It was warm to the touch. As one, the vines turned toward him like the heads of snakes. Crispin shivered, expecting the vines to attack him, but instead they just moved back and forth slightly, as if blown by a breeze he couldn't feel.

He took a deep breath and twisted the handle, and The Door slipped open with a loud groan.

The vines screamed. Wind howled from the crack between The Door and the frame, quickly scaling up to a wild keen that filled the vale.

Lightning flared and static crackled behind the half-open portal.

Tendrils of dark smoke pushed their way out and quested around the space near The Door.

"Crispin, what have you done?" His mother was suddenly, startlingly awake, her presence a shock at his back.

His face covered with cold sweat, he looked over his shoulder and wished he hadn't. Cerillia Ailedrin Moss'caladin's eyes had gone wide and her mouth was open, moving wordlessly. He'd never seen the Mother of Fae frightened.

A growling roar drew his attention back to The Door. Something huge was on the other side. He could feel it—enormous, twisted, broken—the antithesis of Order. It pushed forward, eager to reach him, to consume him. Although he was terrified, he was perversely tempted to allow himself to be drawn in.

And then Aspin was there, his golden sword unsheathed, looking every inch the conquering hero. He was bright where Crispin was dim, sharp where his little brother was dull, dressed in golden chain mail and shining with his own light, his blond locks swinging in the air as he fought the shadows. He swung at the tendrils of smoke, and they parted like water, oozing something black and foul onto the layers of decomposing leaves, sizzling and giving off a putrid smell, like death and decay.

The thing that had been pushing its way through The Door retracted, and the tentacles of icy cold that had squeezed Crispin's heart released him as well.

Aspin lifted a mighty leather boot and kicked The Door shut with a resounding *thunk*.

The clearing fell silent, save for Aspin's heavy breathing.

A shadow fell across Crispin as something blocked out Greebals' brightest golden moon.

Crispin looked up into his mother's face.

She was calm, her face as placid as the lake on the edge of her Estate where a young man and his wizard friend had once found a fabled sword. As calm as death.

Crispin shuddered and closed his eyes, expecting to be spelled out of existence.

Instead, a cool hand cupped his cheek. He dared to open his eyes and, staring into hers, saw great pools of anger and—surprisingly—concern.

"Don't ever disobey me again."

All of this flashed through Crispin's head in an instant as they ran into the tepid waters of the Pond of Disappointment. He skidded to a halt in the silty sand at the bottom of the pond and turned to face the oncoming cloud. "I know what it is."

"Dude. Gonna need more." Leopold blinked. "If this is the Zima again—"

"It was *never* the Zima." Crispin sighed. Why couldn't they have sent him to collect a crown, or a key, or... even a possum? Possums pretended to be dead when threatened, right? That would be better than the man's constant questions and inane observations. "Here, follow my motions." He took Leo's left hand in his right and turned to face the advancing fog.

It crept across the stubbornly colorless water toward them, as if it were as unsure about the place as he was.

Crispin raised his free hand and drew a square. Blue fire flared in the air where his finger had been, leaving a perfect form. "Hurry, do another."

"That's chill. Definitely not the Zima." Leopold poked at the glowing figure hanging in midair.

Thea chose that moment to break into song again, belting out something about a lake and fire and the sky.

"Deep Purple's 'Smoke on the Water.' Sweet playlist, but she already did that one," Leopold said.

Crispin eyed the advancing smoke cloud. It had shifted shape and now resembled a nasty mouth full of trailing teeth. He remembered that deep rumble. "So sorry to rush you. But if you don't mind? We seem to be running out of time."

Leo blinked again, and something seemed to snap into place in his head. "Oh crap, sorry." He blushed, probably the most color the area around Disappointment Pond had seen in ages. "Sorry. I get distracted easily. My friend Pete says—"

"Squares." Crispin was busy drawing more, each one intersecting another, building a burning wall between the creature and the two of them.

"Sorry." Leo joined him, still holding his hand.

Where the human's hand passed, perfect circles remained, glowing with the bright blue light.

"Oops, you said squares."

"Circles work too. The important thing here is *Order*." If he was right, they could still save themselves.

"Like, from Amazon?"

Crispin had no idea what a nine-foot-tall warrior woman had to do with it. "Just draw." He continued to inscribe squares, this time above them and to the side, and Leo followed in the other direction. They had to turn to complete the enclosure, but soon they had a glowing dome of circles and squares around them on all sides.

Crispin let his hands drop, reluctantly. *It's done.*

Strictly speaking, he hadn't minded holding hands with Leo. It had been necessary, after all, in order for him to share his small magic with his charge.

The cloud slammed into their makeshift protection, but even though the enclosure looked porous, the smoke remained on the outside, flowing past them, crawling up and over them, blocking out the disappointing light of day.

It was absolutely quiet in their strange carved-out space, except for a sizzling sound where the smoke touched the glowing shapes. Even Thea had stopped singing, a relief after the strange cranking sounds she'd been emitting earlier.

"Why can't it come in?" Leo stared at the prowling cloud.

"It's Chaos." He'd seen it once before, behind The Door in his mother's Estate. "Pure Chaos is the root of all magic, but it can't be allowed to roam the world unchecked." His brother had explained, days after what came to be known as The Incident, that The Door—and the pure energy locked behind it—was the key to the Estate's power.

"Chaos." Leo reached toward it as if mesmerized, his hand reaching the barrier and passing through. Sparks flew where his hand touched the cloud, and he jerked it back. "Fuuuuck."

Crispin stared at him. "You've got to be the most...." He took a deep breath. He was not that kind of person.

Leo's eyes met his. "The what?"

"I'm sorry. I'm tired. I didn't mean to say—"

"Spit it out, *desk elf*." Leo's hands were on his hips, and he looked none too happy.

"Not an elf." Crispin swallowed hard. "And not to be coarse...."

"Never."

"But you can be, a little, a wee bit, well, sort of dense sometimes."

Leo stared at him.

Crispin closed his eyes. "I'm sorry. I've gone too far."

Leo burst into laughter.

"What?" The human's reaction puzzled him.

"That's it? I'm a *wee bit dense*?"

Did I say it wrong? "Yes. I'm sorry, Leo."

For once, the man didn't correct him about the name. "Crispy—"

"Crispin." He was not going to let *Crispy* become a thing.

"*Crispin*. I've been called worse than *dense* five times before breakfast. *Moron. Idiot. Nincompoop. Shit trail.* Even *bastard spawn of a Saint Bernard and a pile of rocks.* Rather proud of that one actually. I was filling a gas tank and forgot to put everything back together first, which could have been really bad if—"

"Leo." Crispin put a hand on his shoulder to get his attention.

"What?"

"Look."

Leo's gaze followed his down to the pond. The water beneath them had become as still as a mirror. It was shiny, sparkling, pretty much *undisappointing* in its smooth perfection.

Thea's voice came out of the transport device, suddenly clear as a bell. "Prepare for transfer in five...."

"Where are we going?" The smoke raged above them, trying to break through.

"Four...."

The water flashed black, and then golden, the color of sunrise on half a dozen worlds Crispin had visited.

"Three...."

"This is the best trip I've ever been on." Leo took his hand again and squeezed it.

"Two...."

Maybe things were about to get back on track. Maybe Thea was working again, and he'd be back in the Office in a couple more seconds, none the worse for wear, his perfecality score intact—or at least only slightly dinged up. *A fae can hope.*

"One." Thea's voice changed, becoming deeper, somehow ominous. She continued:

One lethéd hour that duty never brings,
*Oh! one dim hour to drift, Moth Moon, with thee! ***

Then three things happened at once.

The Dome of Order that had been protecting them flashed and disappeared, letting the smoke in.

Someone screamed. It might have been him.

And the world dropped away from under their feet, leaving them in free fall.

* From the poem "Moth Moon" by Florence Ripley Mastin, public domain

https://poets.org/poem/moth-moon

10

LEOPOLD

Wings.

Enormous and white, glittering as if set with millions of tiny diamonds, as delicate-looking and translucent as gossamer silk yet somehow tremendously strong.

"Ooh." Leopold reached out to touch, because who wouldn't want to touch them, who wouldn't want to stroke and see whether they were as soft as they looked, whether they would caress his skin and—

"Hey! No grabbing!" Crispin stepped back angrily.

Leopold blinked and realized they weren't in the Pond of Disappointment. In fact, they weren't even damp. Instead, they stood in a vast meadow of green grass that he felt no desire to munch on. Overhead in the twilit sky hung three moons of varying sizes. He wondered idly if any were made of cheese.

Crispin was gazing around too and looked disappointed. "This isn't the Hall of Mirrors." That seemed fairly obvious due the absence of both *hall* and *mirrors*. Maybe the pond water had gotten to him.

"Then where the hell are we? Did you really expect everything to work right when we were at a frigging disappointment pond? What was the deal with that Chaos Cloud thing and why is it trying to get us? How are you gonna get me home? How can I—" Leopold stopped as a revelation hit him. "Dude. You have *wings*."

The fur, antlers, long muzzle, and hoofs were gone, and now Crispin looked pretty much like a regular person with fairly pointy ears. He wore a sleeveless knitted bodysuit that ended at the knees. It had navy and white stripes and reminded Leopold of a Victorian bathing costume.

Crispin was slowly waving his wings, which were almost as big as he was. "Leo," he said sternly, "will you kindly try to focus?"

"But... wings."

"Yes, of course. You have them too."

"I.... What?" Leopold craned his neck to look behind him, and sure enough, a pair of wings had sprouted from his back as well. They weren't the feathery kind like birds have, but were instead diaphanous and double-lobed like a butterfly's. And he could *flutter* them, which felt amazing, sort of like a really good back stretch. "I have wings!"

Leopold was also wearing a close-fitting bathing-costume thing, only his was made of spandex—or something like it—patterned with random splotches in 1980s neon hues. It could have been sort of embarrassing because his body had none of Crispin's slim strength and because the tight fabric left *very* little to the imagination, but he had *wings*, godsdammit, and that was awesome.

Crispin rolled his eyes. "Of course we do. This is Phaxsi and we have taken the form of awaannisa, who live here. What's more important is that we're not where we're supposed to be—the Hall of Mirrors. And now in addition to being stranded, we have a major problem on our hands. And my perfecality score—"

"Is suffering. Yeah, I got that." Leopold had never held a job that included anything like a perfecality score. Which was probably fortunate, because his score would have been somewhere in the deep negatives. Still, he could understand Crispin's distress.

However, Leopold was certain that his own distress was deeper and more important, given that he'd been collected against his will and whisked off to two different and very weird worlds.

Except on this world he had wings.

He fluttered them a few more times because it felt so damned good, and then, just when he was wondering if he could fly, he *did*. His trajectory was shaky, he rose only a few feet, and he promptly crashed onto his back in the soft grass. But he'd *flown*, and that was amazing.

Lying immobile on the ground, the three moons glimmering far overhead, Leopold smiled. "I've never flown before. One time I had a few extra bucks and the airline was having a crazy cheap sale, so I booked a ticket to Phoenix. Just to see what it was like to go up in the air. But the plane was super late getting in because of a freak storm somewhere in the Midwest, and then after we boarded they found out that something was broken and they made us get off again. They finally ended up canceling the flight, so I just went back home. It sucked."

Crispin had wandered over during the monologue and was staring down at him. "You didn't try again?"

"Nah. They wouldn't honor the sale price anymore and... well, what was the point? Something else probably would've gone wrong anyway. It always does."

That was self-pity, so he shut his mouth. Unless a guy had a guitar and a decent singing voice, nobody wanted to listen to him whine about how the world *done did him wrong*.

"I've never been in an aeroplane either," said Crispin, sitting beside him and folding his wings neatly.

"Do you even have them where you live?" It didn't seem very fae-like.

"No, but I've visited your world a few times before. Once I collected a boot—just one, covered in sparkly silver rhinestones—and once it was an egg, and the other times... well, I'd have to refer to my notes. Anyway, none of those trips involved aviation, but I do find the concept quite interesting. You people claim not to believe in magic, yet you pay money to be locked inside a large metal tube and hurtled through the sky."

Leopold sat up and blinked at him. "Airplanes aren't magic. They fly 'cause of... um... drag? Lift? The air goes over the wing and under the wing and um...." He made some gestures with his hand, but those didn't help; he blew a raspberry instead. "Fine, maybe it *is* magic."

Crispin nodded as if his point had been made. "I'd enjoy the opportunity to try an aeroplane, I think. Perhaps on a future mission. Assuming I'm ever assigned to anything again after this debacle."

"You could get a different job. I've been fired so many times I've lost count, but I always find something else eventually."

Leopold had meant to be consoling, but Crispin's lips thinned. "There *are* no other jobs. Not for me. I am a desk fae." And then he pulled out his phone and essentially begged Thea to beam them up, but she remained silent.

After a while, Leopold got to his feet and made another attempt at flying. It was glorious for about three seconds, at which point he crash-landed again. And again. He was getting bruised, but he figured it was worth it for those three seconds of joy. Crispin just watched, frowning, and didn't use his own wings.

On his ninth or tenth try, Leopold managed to stay aloft long enough to do a barrel roll but then landed with enough force to knock the wind from his lungs. Once he could breathe again, he decided to take a break from flying. He sat beside Crispin, who was staring at his blank, cracked phone screen.

"Nothing helpful from Thea?" Leopold asked.

"Not a word."

"Should we try to find another pond? Or something else reflective?"

Crispin shrugged. "Perhaps. But I don't know where anything is in this place, and I'm not keen on wandering randomly." He looked forlornly around them at the bright grass that stretched to the horizon, decorated here and there with flowers of various types, colors, and sizes.

Leopold followed his gaze. In the distance there was a brown smudge—mountains, maybe? Or given his luck, a giant steaming pile of—

Entirely out of the blue, Thea began playing a country song, which made Crispin yelp with surprise. He seemed to have learned from his prior mistakes, however, and this time managed to keep a grip on the phone.

"Hey, I know this one," said Leopold, surprised. "One of my foster mothers was a Dolly Parton fan." She used to sing along while she cooked dinner, and she hadn't minded if Leopold, who was eleven, warbled along with her. But one day a fire had started in the kitchen and, although luckily nobody was hurt, the house was destroyed. Leopold had been shifted to a different foster family.

Oblivious to this bit of personal history, Crispin was listening to the lyrics. "She's singing about silver and gold."

"Those are reflective."

"Yes, but I don't have any on me. Do you?"

Leopold patted his weird bathing suit thing, but it didn't even have pockets. "Nope."

"Then...." Crispin brightened. "The Temple of the Moons! There are several on Phaxsi, as I recall, and they are plated in precious metals. I wonder where the nearest one is." He looked around as if expecting a shiny building to materialize. It didn't.

Thea stopped singing and refused to provide any additional information, although she did hiccup now and then. Crispin wandered for a bit but found nothing.

"You know," Leopold eventually pointed out, "you'd get a better view from the air. I'd look myself but I can't get much elevation. I bet you could, though."

Crispin frowned and flapped his wings. "But I'm not permitted."

"You're banned from flying?"

"Yes, well, it's part of the Treaty of Hrglethemot, isn't it?"

As if Leopold would have the slightest idea what that was.

Crispin paused and then said, as if reciting from memory: "...*in consideration of which the Fae of the Connected Worlds do hereby pledge and covenant that they shall heretofore and in perpetuity abstain from all flying, soaring, gliding, or hovering, and they shall also....* Well, there are two hundred and twelve other articles, but they're not pertinent to our current situation. Violation of the treaty could result in severe repercussions."

Leopold scrunched up his forehead. "But you said you hoped to fly in an airplane."

"Yes," said Crispin, nervously shifting his feet. "But I believe that may be an exception in that the airplane *passenger* isn't technically flying at all, but rather sitting inside a vehicle that is."

"So there are exceptions to the rule then."

"Well, not exceptions precisely, but—"

"But an emergency should be an exception. It's, uh, *exigent circumstances*." He'd heard that phrase once, in a cop show. "And we're pretty exigent right now."

Crispin folded his arms. "The Treaty of Hrglethemot does not contain provisions—"

"Look, Crispy. Do you wanna stay stuck here forever, or do you want to get home to your desk and your, um, raccoon?"

"Minkis is a *squirrel*." Crispin seemed offended. But he also seemed to be truly considering the rest of what Leopold had said, and eventually he huffed. "Fine."

"Fine what?"

"I'll... you know," Crispin flapped his arms. That action was rather silly since he was in actual possession of perfectly flappable wings. But Leopold didn't point that out. Sometimes the nicest thing to say was nothing at all.

"Great," said Leopold. "You reconnoiter. I'll wait here." He sank down again into the soft grass, wishing it was as delicious as the purple grass on Vlotho.

After another few contorted facial expressions, Crispin handed over the phone, warned Leopold not to do anything to it, and then lifted into the sky as gracefully as a giant butterfly. His wings were probably not big enough to lift something as heavy as a desk fae, but Leopold had already learned that there was no point in relying on silly things like logic and the laws of physics while on this adventure. Instead, he looked upward, more than a little envious as Crispin flew in circles, rising higher with each circuit.

After a few moments, he landed softly beside Crispin. "How was that?" He was a little out of breath.

"You looked like a natural," Leopold muttered, somewhat overcome with envy.

Crispin shrugged. "Many of the fae are naturally capable of flight. My people gave it up in the Treaty of Hrglethemot. It was probably intended to punish us for improperly making use of Chaos, which caused a lot of problems for everyone and, in turn, caused several other peoples to ally and declare war."

Now, this was interesting. "Wait. Your folks were *using* that monster thing?"

"They still are. All of the fae do, and many others besides. Chaos provides the power behind our magic. And that's fine so long as it's carefully contained, but my forebears were…. Well, suppose in your world a human owns a very large ferocious dog, and he keeps it chained up so as to protect his property. A guard dog, yes? That's considered acceptable. But instead suppose he removes its collar and permits it to wander the neighborhood and terrorize everyone. *Not* acceptable."

That did make sense. "So your fae ancestors let the dog loose and—"

"And nearly started a war, which they would likely have lost and which would certainly have entailed enormous death and destruction. After the Almost War, they agreed to keep Chaos leashed, as it were, and also made several other concessions to atone for their poor behavior. Foreswearing flight was one of those. Providing assistance to the Office of the Lost was another."

Oh. So that was how Crispin got his gig. Leopold had probably watched too much Disney and way too many episodes of *The Fairly OddParents*, but he'd always pictured fairies flitting around in forests and granting wishes—maybe occasionally sprinkling magic dust—not sitting in offices collecting stuff. Well, if it had been intended as punishment, that had failed, because Crispin clearly adored his job.

"Did your gang let the Chaos free again? Is that why it's chasing us? 'Cause it seems like that would be a pretty big contract violation right there."

Crispin was silent for so long that Leopold figured he'd clammed up for good. But then he gave a long sigh. "I don't know."

Leopold was going to ask more, but then Thea started playing an old song by Sly and the Family Stone, and Crispin fluttered aloft again.

Soon he was hardly more than a bright spot of light in a darkening sky.

Leopold had read about fireflies but had never seen one, and now he imagined that they must look something like this. He wished desperately that he could be up there too, that he wasn't doomed to bumble about barely a few feet in the air and then crash-land. But it was also nice just to watch.

"Hey!" he shouted. "Crispy! That's really cool! Show me your moves!"

Crispin did a dive followed by a steep ascent and a showy series of twirls. He performed a little ballet with dips and pirouettes and cartwheels. It was amazing. Breathtaking, almost. It was—

Something huge and dark soared across the sky, snatched Crispin with enormous claws, and flapped away.

11

CRISPIN

Oh, what a joy to *fly*.

Crispin rose through the air, free from the clutches of gravity at last, a feat previously denied to him by the ancestors who'd signed that blasted treaty. He could forget almost that what he was doing was banned. But, in fact, that simple thought gilded his flight with a naughty bit of forbidden pleasure.

He wasn't used to naughty bits of... well... much of anything. It had been a long, dry spell since the last time he'd—

Something huge and dark enveloped him like a cloud, and for a brief instant before he blacked out from the pain, he thought it *was* the cloud, come back for him again. *But who will save Leo?*

Crispin sighed, floating in that happy space between sleeping and waking, content to just stay in bed a few minutes longer. Surely Minkis could fend for himself for a bit. There were acorns in the nut bowl, and plenty of water in the glass pipette that hung near The Door.

His bed felt uncommonly comfortable today.

But something was poking him in the middle of his back. He shifted, trying to find a good spot without waking up too much, a delicate balance.

It was rather cool too. Had he left the door ajar when he'd gotten home? If so, that was clumsy of him. *I'm not usually such a half-wit....*

Sharp pain lanced through his shoulder, bringing him fully awake. "Fuuaaaark." He blinked, trying to reconcile what his eyes were telling him with what his brain knew to be true. He was home in bed, safe and sound, and yet—he realized with growing alarm— he was staring at the toe-ends of five gigantic fuzzy baby-blue slippers.

"You finally awake?"

Crispin turned his head, bringing him face-to-face with a creature only a little shorter than he was. The similarities ended there.

It was covered with royal blue fuzz—much deeper in color than the slipper things—which extended partway down a pair of wings that enfolded it like a cloak, ending in bright white edging. It had six legs, two curving antennae, a couple sharp mandibles, and big blue eyes that wouldn't have been out of place in a human face, except for their size—about as large as his fist.

"I... um... yes." It was far from his most elegant response. "I seem to have injured myself." He reached back to touch his shoulder and found crusted blood where his right wing should have been.

"Yes, so sorry about that. Molly snapped it off when she grabbed you." It blinked, but its eyelids closed from the sides instead of from top to bottom, like most creatures.

Molly? At least it didn't hurt too much.

Crispin shook his head. *Where are my manners?* Ignoring the pain where his wing had been, he extended a hand. "Crispin Eladrin Moss'caladin, at your service."

The stranger spit a bit of something black and sticky into his open palm. "Morris Mucklin. Pleased to meet you."

Crispin stared at the goo, unsure if he should wipe it off, or lick it, or…. Staring at Morris, he decided to just close his hand, which made the splooge, well, made it splooge itself out the sides of his fist.

Morris seemed satisfied with that.

Crispin vowed to wipe it off—surreptitiously, of course—when he had the chance. "So… where are we, then?" He turned to look over his shoulder, and wished he hadn't. There was nothing but green sky there.

Above him. Next to him. Below him.

He grabbed the edge of the… what was it? It was made of branches and leaves and clumps of green moss. He turned back slowly to his new friend Morris, the situation slowly dawning on him. "This is a nest, isn't it?" He swallowed, hard.

"Right quick you are. Usually takes the dinner a bit longer to realize its predicament."

"Yes, well, thank you. Mother Fae always said I was…." *Wait, what?* Something stuck in his craw. "I'm sorry. Could you repeat that last bit?"

"Which bit?"

"You didn't say *dinner*, did you?" Crispin stared at the fuzzy slipper tops and finally saw them for what they were. Eggs. Strange blue fuzzy eggs, to be sure. But eggs, nonetheless.

"Ah, right. It does tend to freak out the new arrivals a bit." Morris blinked again. "Molly always leaves the explaining to me while she's out, flitting about. Me wings are a bit… vestigial." He lifted them up, and they did seem far too short to carry his weight.

That's not important right now. Crispin's most urgent goal was extracting himself from his current culinary destiny. He had no desire to be food for anyone. "Well, yes, I can see that. And it has been an absolute delight meeting you and the… children."

Had one of the eggs just shuddered?

"But I really must be going." He turned again to look out over the edge of the nest. Something was happening to his right shoulder where his now-missing wing had been, but he wasn't quite sure what. It felt... squirmy? He didn't have time to figure it out just then. *More important things and all.*

He stretched out over the edge of the mossy branchy surface to look down.

Down down down down down.

The nest was cradled on a shelf along a bright red cliff face, studded with bits and pockets of verdant growth and a few other nests like the one he was currently sitting in. It was a nearly vertical drop, hundreds of feet down, ending in a roiling layer of fog. Or clouds? *How high up are we?*

He turned back to his host, determined to put that long drop out of his mind. "So do you always chat with your... meals?"

Morris shook and wheezed in what might have been laughter. "Oh, I won't eat you. I prefer bugs and berries. Molly always brings me back a bit of something special."

Crispin sighed with relief. "Oh thank the seven gods of solstice." With luck, Leo and Thea would find a way to rescue him, and then they'd all be on their merry way. "I really thought you meant *I'd* be your dinner."

Morris huffed again, flapping his little wings. "Oh, I can see how you would have gotten that."

Crispin laughed with him. "Yes, I was quite worried—"

"My dinner. You. Imagine that." He shook his head, his eyes watering.

Now Crispin felt a little offended. Why wouldn't he make a perfectly scrumptious dinner? Not that he wanted to be eaten—by giants or by giant moths, and why was this becoming a running theme?—but he liked to think that, if someone did actually eat him, he would provide a satisfactory, perhaps even exemplary, dining experience.

"No, you'll be *their* dinner." Morris pointed at the fluffy blue eggs, which were most definitely starting to quiver.

Fear gripped Crispin again, sliding her icy fingers under his world-appropriate onesie. He suddenly missed Leo—as messy and lost, in both senses, as he was—and even Thea, despite her new habit of playing strange Earth songs and not actually doing her job. "I, um, see." He most definitely did not see, but he wasn't going to give his host the satisfaction of noting his fear.

"So, we have a few more moments before the birth." Morris settled in, staring raptly at the eggs. "Life gets a bit boring for a house husband like meself. Why don't you tell me a little more about you and yours to fill the time? Molly should be back soon and will need her frumbles licked clean, but until then I'm all ears."

Crispin refrained from mentioning that he didn't see any ears at all on the strange little creature, and he had no desire to find out what part of Molly a *frumble* was. "What are you, anyway?" He started to work his way around the nest, hoping against hope that there might be a cavern entrance at the back, or even a Crispin-sized crevice he might wedge himself into in a probably doomed effort to keep himself safe from the coming mothpocalypse.

"We're ferykens, often mistaken for faeries from afar. But we are clearly superior."

"Wait, did you say faeries?" Maybe there was an easy way out of this mess. "Do you know Cerillia Ailedrin Moss'caladin?" His mother had explicitly forbidden anyone from harming him.

Morris cocked his head sideways. "Don't know that I do." He watched as Crispin rummaged around the back of the nest. "No way out there, I'm afraid. Wouldn't do to put a nest where food could just run off, after all."

Crispin blinked, conceding the point. "I don't suppose we could work out some kind of trade? Like... maybe you let me go, and I find you some even better food?"

"You know of some better food?" Morris's wings seemed to brighten.

"Well, not here. No." Damn his honest streak. "But once I get home—" He rubbed at his itchy shoulder, surprised to find a bony nub there.

"'Fraid it's too late. The missus has returned. Oooh, and she brought a little something with her."

Crispin looked up to see the dark form that had grabbed him descending on the nest. Mrs. Morris—Molly—was truly an awesome sight, like a cross between a moth and one of the fire dragons of Ferkin Four. No one knew what happened to the worlds of Ferkins One through Three, but it was widely assumed that it was the dragons' fault.

She carried something in her claws.

"Leo!" he managed, just as the human—his human—was unceremoniously dumped into the nest. "Leo, are you all right?" Crispin rushed to his side as the darkness settled over them.

Morris rushed to his mate's side as she perched on the edge of the nest, strangely delicate for her huge size. "Welcome home, my love." He extended a long blue tongue, and Crispin got a wildly unfortunate look at her frumbles before he forced his gaze away.

"Leo, wake up!"

Crispin's human lay there, peaceful as an angel, somehow suddenly beautiful to him. It was like a fairy tale. Unsure what he was doing, he leaned over to kiss... well, maybe not his prince. His human. Their lips met and—

"Hey, what are you doing?" Leo pushed him away, sputtering. "Take advantage of a guy while he's down...." His gaze went to Crispin's shoulder. "What happened to your wing?"

"Molly here broke it." He pointed to the big blue moth thing—feryken—who was apparently enjoying being cleaned, based on her low throaty rumbles and quivering mandibles. "Sorry, Leo. I got caught up in the moment."

Leo blinked. "S'alright. It wasn't half bad." He looked around the nest. "So what's the sitch here? It took a lot of work to get your friend over there to come down and pick me up too."

"The *sitch...uation* is that we're about to become comestibles for the progeny of our fine fuzzy friends here."

Leo stared at him. "What?"

Crispin sighed. "The moth babies are going to eat us."

"Ah." Leo's eyes widened. "Oh. Well, that's not great."

"No. Certainly not great at all." Had he really, just moments before, found this clod attractive?

"So let's get out of here then." Leo pulled Thea from his pants pocket. "Will this help?"

"Oh thank the Red Dukes of Vespertine." And he would, the next time he saw them. He took Thea, cradling her in his hands. "Can you get us out of here?" He waited breathlessly for a response.

A song rolled out of her, catchy and danceable, but not the assistance Crispin was seeking. He sighed.

"Wait, no, I know that one. It's 'Jump' by the Pointer Sisters. One of my foster moms was sweet on them."

"Seriously? We must be a few hundred feet above ground, if not more. And I can't fly, remember?"

"You'll be able to soon."

Crispin stared at him.

"Your wing is growing back."

He reached over his shoulder to touch the growing nub. *And so it is.* He'd forgotten about that part of awaannisa anatomy. Not that it would be wingish enough in time for an escape.

With a small puff of fuzz, the first egg burst open, revealing a white squirming creature with alarmingly sharp teeth.

Molly and Morris had stopped their mildly pornographic activity to avidly watch their progeny.

"Trust me?" Leo met his gaze and took his hand.

Better than being moth food. "Yes." At worst, they'd be instantly killed when they smashed into the rocks below. At best....

He didn't know what *best* looked like in a moth-food vs. smashed-to-pieces situation.

"Come on then, dude." Leo led him to the edge of the nest, climbing onto the rim. "Let's jump!"

Crispin, against his better judgment, tucked Thea away and took Leo's hand.

Was it his imagination or did a spark pass between them?

They jumped, soaring into the green sky and then quickly falling away from the edge.

Molly swooped after them, her form blotting out the sun as the clouds raced up toward them.

Crispin's heart tried to pound its way out of his chest and he prepared to die. He squeezed Leo's hand, strangely satisfied that they would leave the world together—

And then, in a flash, they were somewhere else.

12

LEOPOLD

"Pheromones," said Leopold firmly.

Crispin just blinked at him, so Leopold elaborated. "Those Mothra things were emitting pheromones—and ew, that was way more moth lovin' than I ever wanted to see—and the chemicals affected us too, and thus the kiss."

"The ki— Oh. Yes, of course." Crispin sat up. "But perhaps at the moment we have other, more important, matters to deal with? Such as how you managed to transport us *here*."

Leopold, who was already sitting, scratched his head. "Dunno. I just sorta had a feeling that jumping was the right thing to do, and anything seemed like a better option than getting eaten by those... things, so.... Probably Thea zapped us." He shrugged.

Crispin's face scrunched up, in a way that Leopold was starting to find adorable. "But there was nothing reflective."

"Maybe there was but we just couldn't see it 'cause it was night. Hey, do reflective things still reflect in the dark? That's kinda like that thing about a tree falling in a forest, and—"

"Did you deliberately get taken by Molly so you could rescue me?" There was an odd expression on Crispin's face and Leopold couldn't decipher it.

"I didn't wanna be stuck in bugville all by myself, did I? You're my ticket home." Leopold looked away because he was very much afraid that Crispin *could* interpret his expression.

They were in a park, he finally noticed. A nice one, with carefully manicured lawns and a few stands of tall trees. Children's happy shrieks came from behind one of those stands, hinting at the presence of a playground. A pair of squirrels scampered across the grass. Whereas it had been nighttime in the moth place, here the mellow rays of a summer evening bathed everything in golden light. Off to one side, a rose garden was in riotous bloom. On the other, a row of stately palm trees flanked a street, and ahead of them were expensive-looking houses.

Leopold leapt to his feet. "Sacramento! We're back home!" He whooped and shot his fist into the air.

Crispin, who was considerably slower to stand up, looked around, frowning. "Um. I'm not so sure. Do those people look a bit, er, different to you?" He gestured toward a small group clustered near the roses.

"Well, it *is* Sacramento. We may not be San Francisco, but we have more than our share of weirdness, and...." Leopold trailed off as his mind finally processed what he was seeing. Those people had tails. Long, shiny green tails with a ridge of soft spikes. And their faces....

Crispin grabbed Leopold's wrist hard and spoke quietly but urgently. "A police officer is approaching. I beg you, if you value your freedom and safety, do not speak to them. Not. A single. Word."

Still in Crispin's grip, Leopold spun to see the uniformed police officer. He intended to protest Crispin's orders but then got a good look at the cop's face. "That's a lizard!"

"Not a lizard," Crispin hissed. "Archosaur. Now be quiet!"

Leopold clamped his mouth shut. As the cop sauntered toward them, Leopold noticed that he and Crispin were back in their original forms, in their original clothing. He kind of missed the wings, to be honest. It had taken a bit of effort, but once he'd gotten the hang of the whole flying thing—

"Good evening, officer," said Crispin. He was smiling, but his fingers were bruising Leopold's wrist.

"Evening, sir. Are you enjoying the park?" The archosaur had a surprisingly light voice that Leopold thought might mean she was female, but he wasn't sure. She wore a fairly standard cop uniform of navy slacks and lighter blue shirt, complete with badge, but the slacks were tailored to accommodate a thick tail that was long enough to drag behind her. Instead of a hat, she had a pinkish skin crest on her head and claws instead of fingernails. Her forearms were inset with patterns of tiny jewels.

Crispin's smile broadened a little. "I am, thank you. It's lovely."

"I think maybe you're a tourist—we don't get many fae around here—so you might not be familiar with all the local laws, sir. You can't have your pet ape in the park without a leash. It's pretty cute in its little outfit, though." She made a cooing noise at Leopold. "What breed is it? Ooh, is it one of the hairless breeds? I hear they're good if you have allergies."

Leopold didn't know what part of her speech to object to first, which was probably just as well because it meant he didn't say anything at all. He did have to stifle a yelp, though, when Crispin squeezed even more tightly.

"He's just a mutt. A little stubborn, you know, but quite intelligent. And, er, loyal. And I do apologize about the leash. I was unaware."

She nodded. "Well, I won't ticket you then. Because our little snookums is just too darn adorable, isn't he? Such a cutie pie!" This time she not only made kissy noises but also chucked him under the chin and scratched behind his ear with a scaled claw that was nonetheless quite smooth against his skin. With great difficulty, Leopold managed not to bite her.

"Thank you, officer. I do appreciate it." Crispin reached into a trouser pocket with his free hand and pulled out an improbably long length of rope, which he quickly knotted around Leopold's neck. It wasn't tight enough to choke him, but it wasn't exactly loose. Glaring at them both, Leopold rubbed at his sore wrist.

"Aw," said the cop. "Him's a wittle grouchy about the leash, isn't him?"

"Indeed." Crispin gave a tug on the rope that Leopold interpreted as a warning. "And I do believe it's time for his dinner, so we'll be getting back to the hotel. You know how apes get when they're hungry. Thank you again!"

The cop managed to ruffle Leopold's hair before they escaped.

As soon as they were out of earshot, Leopold growled. "What the *hell*, Crispy?"

"Crispin." His usual protest sounded a little halfhearted. "Do you want to be taken away to the pound? If not, we need to keep the leash on you when we're in public here."

"Where the hell is here?"

"Earth."

"But—"

"A slightly different version of Earth. We'll call it Earth 2, though as far as the natives are concerned, your planet is Earth 2. Anyhow, in this place the dinosaurs evolved to become the sentient species. The apes did not. Otherwise the worlds are quite similar, although I must say that this one is more peaceful. Archosaurs are somewhat less pugnacious than primates, as it turns out. Now hush—you mustn't let others hear you speaking."

They passed several others as they walked. Couples and families out for an evening stroll, apparently. Most of them paused to admire him, petting him and calling him embarrassing names. Which was bad enough, but even worse was the archosaur in the muscle shirt and too-tight shorts who muttered something about germs and told Crispin his pet ought to be muzzled.

Leopold snarled at him. The startled and slightly frightened look on the archosaur's face was reward enough.

They walked for over a mile: out of the park, through a residential neighborhood, and into what was clearly downtown. A lot of businesses were closed because it was now nighttime, but there were also a lot of restaurants that seemed to be lively. Realizing he was hungry, Leopold gazed longingly into the windows as they passed. Somehow the treats gifted by Fromlith hadn't seemed to have transitioned with them. Or Leopold had lost them on Moth World. Or maybe they'd eaten them all. He couldn't remember—his memory was the first thing to go when he was really hungry.

"They wouldn't let you inside," said Crispin quietly. "Sorry. I'll get us something to eat soon."

"Where are we going?"

"It just so happens," and Crispin puffed up a bit, regaining some of his former pomposity, "that I know someone in this city."

"As long as this someone has food. Human eatable food." He felt it was important to specify the last part, lest he get a hunk of raw meat shoved under his snout.

Leopold did not like being a pet. But since there wasn't much he could do about it at the moment, he allowed himself to be led along. A group of what were probably teenage dinosaurs skateboarding by a fountain made monkey noises at him and laughed.

It occurred to him then to wonder how he'd understood everyone no matter where they went. Even the moths. Surely not all worlds spoke English.

It was probably just the magic; best to leave it at that.

They came to a tall glass-and-steel building that wouldn't have been out of place on L Street back home, and went inside to an elegant lobby. A dinosaur in a suit was perched behind a gleaming wood desk. "I'm sorry, sir. We don't allow pets in this building. You can tie it up outside if you like."

"I'm just paying a quick visit to a resident, and it's vital that I take, er, my pet with me. Perhaps you could announce me? I'm Crispin Eladrin Moss'caladin." He said his name with an air of importance.

The concierge straightened his back. "Of *the* Moss'caladins, sir?"

"Of course."

"I'm so sorry, sir! I had no idea. I'll call right away."

Huh. Crispy's mom really was a big deal. *Interesting.*

As promised, the concierge made a quick call and then waved them to the elevators. As soon as the doors closed, Leopold yanked the end of the rope out of Crispin's hand. "What the *hell*?" He'd been saying that a lot lately.

"I'm sorry. It's only, primates here aren't capable of speech. If they heard you, they'd probably cart you off to a lab somewhere to study you, and...."

Leopold was getting some serious *Planet of the Apes* vibes. He shuddered. "Fine. But we're not sticking around here, right? I think I almost preferred the damn moths."

Crispin bit his lip. "I'm sorry, Leo. We'll leave as soon as possible. That's why we're here in this building—we're going to visit an acquaintance."

Leopold let the nickname slide. There were too many things to be unhappy about all at once. And because Crispin didn't sound especially thrilled about this little visit, Leopold grew uneasy. "What kind of acquaintance?"

"He's—well, I suppose wizard would be the closest approximation." Crispin looked away, shoving his hands in his tweedy pockets.

"We're off to see the wizard?" Leopold asked incredulously. "Seriously?"

If Crispin understood the reference, he didn't play along. He just sighed. "Needs must."

The elevator dinged and the doors slid open.

The softly lit hallway had paintings on the walls and little tables holding vases of fresh flowers. Apparently being a wizard paid really well.

Leopold had a thought and came to a halt. "Hey, if this world is so much like mine, how come they have magic and we don't?"

"You do. But there's some sort of damper that keeps it from

manifesting strongly. Nobody knows exactly how, and frankly, nobody much cares. Earth is an anomaly and also dangerous, so we all tend to avoid you."

His feelings unaccountably hurt, Leopold followed Crispin silently to the final door, which was marked with a mysterious sigil instead of a number or letter. The door swung open before there was a chance to knock, revealing a plump archosaur with purplish scales and a royal-blue head crest. They wore a pair of neon-green sweatpants and a T-shirt advertising something called Theropod Airlines, with an image of an airplane soaring over mountains.

"Crispin! I am so honored to have you—"

The wizard stopped and gaped at Leopold, eyes wide. "Oh no! Oh, we can't have *that* here!"

Leopold stared at him. *What, now I've been demoted from pet to inanimate object?*

"It's fine, Juzir," Crispin said smoothly. "I know your building has a no-pet policy, but there are extenuating circumstances. I can assure you that *he's* housebroken and doesn't have fleas."

Leopold shot Crispin a grateful glance for restoring his personhood. Or at least gender. Until now, he hadn't been aware that a dinosaur could look both horrified and terrified, but this one did. "N-n-no! Take it away!" And the door slammed shut with enough force to shake the nearest vase of flowers. Several locks clicked into place.

"I guess he has an ape phobia." Leopold stared at the closed door.

But Crispin was frowning in concentration. "I don't think that's the problem."

"Well, it's not my fault. I didn't say or do anything scary."

"No. But...." Crispin inhaled sharply and paled, staggering back a few steps. "Oh no. No, it's not possible."

"Crispy? What's the matter?" Leopold reached out to steady him, but Crispin only backed away.

And then he spoke in a small, careful voice. "Leopold, you told me that you were adopted. What do you know about your, er, biological family?"

"What does that have to do—"

"Please, Leo*pold*! Answer me."

Fuck. It sounded like Crispin was panicking, and Leopold was clueless as to why. And for reasons he couldn't explain, he didn't want to see the desk fae distressed.

"I don't know anything about my bio parents. Some firemen found me squalling in front of the station as a newborn. I was in a basket, like Moses, only, you know, no Nile. No note either, or anything else. Not even a diaper. Authorities did a little investigating but never got anywhere." He'd always tried not to dwell on it. At least someone had cared enough about him to leave him somewhere safe, and his adoptive parents had taken good care of him. When he was younger, he'd sometimes scanned crowds to see if he could find his features in someone else's face, but he never did.

If anything, Crispin now looked even more upset. "So you could be… anything."

"What do you mean?"

Crispin stared at him a moment. His eyes shone as if he were about to cry. "Oh, Leo. We need to talk."

13
CRISPIN

Crispin hoped he was wrong. He prayed to the Dark Eye of Pothos that he was wrong. But the look on Juzir's face... he hadn't seen the archosaur wizard so scared since he'd had to face his finals in advanced scryology when they'd been dorm-mates at Hastor. And those exams had been potentially deadly.

He needed answers. And he most definitely did not need to think about how Leo's lips had felt, pressed against his own, back on Phaxsi. Pheromones or no pheromones.

"You're kinda freaking me out, Crispy." Leo shut his mouth as a young archosaur couple approached—both male, by their coloring —frowning at the two of them.

"You're not supposed to have that... thing... in here." The taller one, whose crest had been dyed an eye-peeling shade of acid orange, pointed at a sign posted on the tastefully pebbled walls. *No pets.*

Crispin shot Leo a warning look. "I'm so sorry. It was a matter of life and death and there was nowhere to leave him." He reached out awkwardly to pat Leo on the head. "He's very well trained."

Leo snapped at him.

"Doesn't look like it," the other one said, taking his boyfriend's hand and pulling him away. "We'll be back in twenty minutes. Get it out of here before then or we call building security." They disappeared into the elevator.

"I really hate this place." Leo growled.

Crispin nodded. "That's good. Grunt and growl. It will help sell the whole pet thing."

Leo glared at him.

"That's good too." He needed to get them out of sight, and there was one person—only a thin panel of wood away—who could answer his questions.

He pounded on the door. "Juzir, let me in. Look, I know you're scared, and I have an idea why, but if we're both right, it's just as dangerous leaving us out here as it is letting us in."

He could try to magic his way through the door, of course. But first of all, that would be rude, and he tried to never be more rude than the situation absolutely required. And secondly, Juzir had probably set up wards to protect his apartment, and you never knew what might happen when one magic butted up—rudely—against another. "Seriously, Juzir, you owe me for the whole Beckia situation."

Beckia Trönt had been the prettiest ogre Juzir had ever set his eyes on, and Crispin—who didn't get the appeal, but to each their own—had helped set up a clandestine date for his young wizardly friend. It had gone spectacularly wrong, but that wasn't the point. "Come on, Juzir, open the door."

"I don't want to." His old friend sounded just as surly as he had when he'd shown up at the dorm soaking wet, fresh from being dragged into a pond and manhandled by his ogre date.

But he was speaking. That was progress. "Remember that time you got yourself locked into a quadragic equation and I helped you figure out how to get out without losing one of your limbs *and* the ability to say the number nine?"

A long pause. "Yes."

"You trusted me then." Crispin looked up and down the hall,

nervous that the couple would return or that someone else would catch them. "I need you to trust me now."

Nothing. Juzir was stubborn... as stubborn as a Nephraxian oxhound on the hunt.

Crispin turned away, ready to lead Leo—*don't think about the kiss* —out of the building, when the door cracked open, just a smidge.

"Give me a minute." It slammed shut again.

Leo was staring at him. "You two go way back, don't you?"

Thea, tucked into Crispin's pocket, burst into song.

Leo frowned. "Ouch. 'Careless Whisper.' What did you do to him?"

Crispin blanched, "I didn't... it was just one time... we never...."

The elevator chimed.

"Oh crap." Leo slammed a hand over his mouth.

As the elevator doors opened, so did the door to Juzir's suite. His short green arm reached out and pulled them inside, slamming the door shut just before the new arrivals would have seen them loitering in the hall.

"Bring it over here." He indicated a lone wooden chair with a nice-sized tail hole in the back, surrounded by candles and chalk marks on the floor.

"I'm perfectly capable of bringing myself." Leo marched over to the chair and plopped down like a petulant child—which he basi-cally was, if Crispin was honest.

Juzir's eyes went wide. "It speaks?" He stared at Leo, then turned an accusing gaze on Crispin. "*Don't* make me regret this." His tail slashed around angrily, coming close to knocking one or more egg-shaped vases off of wide shelves.

"*It* has a name. And *it* is tired of pretending to be a pet." Leo pulled off the rope and threw it toward Juzir's gray couch, which also had holes for tails. "Hey, that's weird."

The length of cord hung in midair.

Crispin sighed. He was tired. Physically tired. Emotionally tired.

And tired of lying to one of his oldest friends. "Its... *his* name is Leopold. He's not an ape. Well, he's descended from apes—"

"Hey!" Leo glared at him. "Right here in the same room, *dude.*"

Crispin hurried on, because Leo was right; he didn't deserve to be treated like this. "He's from the other Earth. The one where... where archosaurs never evolved. They're called humans."

He expected anger, denial—even to be thrown out into the hall once again, his "pet" with him. But instead, Juzir was clicking his teeth, something archosaurs often did when deep in thought. He made only one comment, quietly, as if to himself. "Fascinating."

"But him being a pet, that's not what scared you, is it?" Crispin had an inkling; the thought had been growing ever since Leo had pulled that disappearing act in front of Fromlith.

Juzir didn't reply. Instead he addressed Leo directly for the first time. "I've placed a protective ward around you. That's what caught the rope." He reached forward with a short arm and plucked it out of the air and out of the spell. It fell to the ground with a thump.

"Protecting me? Or you?" Leo's eyes narrowed. "You sure we can trust this guy, Crispy?"

"Crispy?" Juzir chuckled, a full-bellied archosaur laugh that made the egg-shaped vases on his shelves tremble and showed off his sharp incisors to great advantage, "I rather like that."

"It's *Crispin*," he growled. This whole thing was getting out of hand, and not just the silly nickname part. "And yes, we can trust him. He and I go way back."

"The whole *Beckia situation*, you said. He ate her, didn't he?"

"No, he did not *eat* her." Though that wouldn't have been entirely out of character for an archosaur. Still, the school had rules against that sort of thing—otherwise there would have been chaos.

He turned back to his old friend. "So, can you help us? I need to get him back to the Office, but first...."

"You need to know what he is." He met Leo's eyes, which seemed now to be permanently narrowed.

Juzir scratched his chin with three long, neatly trimmed yellow claws. "You know he's not... what did you call it... *human*, right?"

"Take that back!" Leo sprang to his feet, bumping up against the protection ward and rebounding into the chair. "Ow."

"What do you mean, not human?" Crispin said at the same time. "He's one of the most human humans I have ever met. Bumbling, heedless of the feelings of others, heedless in a way that only a truly magicless species can be...." He trailed off, aware that Leo's gaze was once again directed at him. "Not that I don't find it all rather... charming." A memory of the aborted kiss flashed through his head. *Why did I do it?*

"Just like I find your prissy, stick-up-the-ass, elitist desk fae manner... charming." Somehow he managed to make the word seem more like *maddening*.

Juzir looked as if he'd just stepped into something wet and sticky. He waved his little arms at them. "Gentlemen, no need for insults. What I meant is that he wasn't *born* human. Though he seems to have grown into it."

Definitely not a compliment.

"Thank you... I think?" Leo frowned. "So if I wasn't born human... was I one of those changeling babies? Or maybe more like the Exorcist girl?" He tried to turn his head around to face the wall behind him. "Owww. Guess not."

Crispin shook his head. "See? Totally human." But he'd had his suspicions about Leo. At least twice, he'd been pretty sure that Leo had vanished, only to reappear somewhere else, a talent Crispin was fairly sure was not typically human. "So what is... what was he?"

"I'm not sure. But let me show you something." He fetched a book from one of the wall shelves, using his tail since his arms wouldn't have reached that high. He held the heavy leather-bound volume awkwardly in his little arms.

Crispin hoped it wasn't bound in ape skin.

"Let's see. Here it is." He made a series of growls and grunts as he waved his clawed right hand in the air, and something shifted. The protective ward glowed, shivered, and suddenly collapsed inward, clinging to Leo. The electric lights flickered off and on again.

When things stabilized, Leo looked... different.

"What is it?" He held up his ward-shrouded arm, covered with a sparkling fog that didn't obscure the skin underneath.

"Your true nature."

"Chaos." The word came out of Crispin's throat with the sharpness of a knife. Leo's nature was what he had suspected... what he had feared most. "But how...."

"Wait, you're saying I'm not human?" Leo looked at Juzir. "That I'm like that cloud that's been chasing Crispy and me?" The wide-eyed, drop-jawed look on Leo's face would have been comical if the situation wasn't so serious.

Crispin frowned. *How could Leo be Chaos and be so thoroughly human?*

Leo was nodding now, his eyes back to their normal proportions. "It does kind of make sense. My whole life has been organized chaos." He was staring at his hands in wonder and maybe a little fear. "But what does it mean? I'm... not going to hurt you, am I?"

No "dude" in that sentence, so Crispin deduced he must be truly afraid.

Juzir pulled up a couple more chairs. "The ward will keep you... contained. For now. I don't know if Crispin has told you this, but all of our magic is based on harnessed Chaos. The world needs some Chaos—without it, there would be no magic, no music, no creativity. The world would be flat and boring. In small doses, Chaos is what keeps life interesting."

"But in larger ones?" Leo held his index fingers a few inches apart; an arc of electricity sparked between them.

Juzir frowned. "If raw Chaos were ever to break free from its prison... it could mean the end of everything."

Silence fell over the room as the three men stared at one another, each contemplating what that result might mean.

Crispin closed his eyes. His perfecality score was already shot, but it wasn't really his fault, was it? Bidulla had left quite a lot of important information out of the packet when she'd sent him on what was supposed to be a simple collection mission. Or had she not known? And what about the Oracle? Wasn't it supposed to be all-knowing?

His score no longer mattered. He had to find a way to stuff this Chaos genie back in the bottle. And he had a sneaking suspicion just which bottle—or door—it had come out of in the first place.

He wanted to hug Leo, to tell him everything would be all right, but he wasn't sure it was true.

"We need to go see my mother." When he pulled Thea out of his pocket, she began to hum.

"Is that your transport device?" Juzir held out his green-scaled hand.

"Yes. Thea went a little crazy when I first met Leo and the Chaos Cloud arrived. I'm not sure how to get home." He handed over the phone.

Juzir looked it over. "Yes, a little of the Chaos got inside. Not much I can do about that, I'm afraid. I may be able to help with the trip back to your mother's Estate, though." He handed Thea back. She was now singing something about walking a dinosaur.

"That would be great. Thanks, Juzi." For the first time since this whole sordid adventure had begun, he felt a little peace. Order was being restored, one step at a time. "You okay, Leo?"

For once, Leo didn't correct him. "Just fucking fantastic. Why wouldn't I be? Your friend basically just told me that my whole life is a lie, that I'm Chaos Incarnate, and that I might be a danger to everyone and everything around me. But sure. I'm just *fine*."

Crispin sighed. Leo might not have been born human, but he sure played the part well.

Juzir didn't seem to notice. "I'll help you get home, like I promised. But first you need to tell me *everything*. Then get a little rest while I figure things out. The ward should hold for a while." He got up and put his spell book back up on the shelf. "Anyone fancy a triceratops sandwich?"

14
LEOPOLD

Leopold was exhausted.

Which made sense—he'd been hopping between worlds and running from death for what felt like years but was really just one super eternal day. He'd hitched a ride on a giant, was nearly eaten by Mothra, and had become Crispy's theoretical pet. *Um, and there was a kiss in there too.* But more than that, Leopold was exhausted in part because he'd just found out he wasn't human.

He slumped in the chair while Crispy and Juzir had an animated conversation. It was about him, so he really should have paid attention, but he was too preoccupied.

Not human.

Chaos.

It was insane. But also... it fit. And it explained so very much about the way his life had gone.

"Oh my God!" he shouted as a new revelation hit him.

Crispy turned to look at him, worry clear on his face. "What? What's happening?"

"I think I killed my parents." The realization shook him to his foggy core.

"Pardon me?"

Leopold wrapped his arms around himself and moaned. "My parents. The people who adopted me. I think I killed them."

Crispy came as close as he could without touching the ward. "What makes you say that?"

"Camels. They died in a freak camel accident. Crispy, that's not normal. People don't die that way—at least not in California. But they did, and it's my fault 'cause I cause chaos—I *am* Chaos—and everything goes to shit around me." He was shaking and wasn't sure whether he wanted to cry or puke. Maybe both.

"Plenty of odd things happen to people without any, er, interference from you," Crispin said. "I have an ancestor who died when a roc—the bird, I mean—accidentally dropped a rock—a solid collection of minerals—onto his head." Crispin reached for him, but was stopped by the protective ward. "Even if you did in some way influence their fate, you didn't do so intentionally or even knowingly. You were a child. You can't blame yourself."

Oh yes, I can. And while he was at it, he could feel guilty about all the other disasters that had bloomed in his presence. Thea's malfunction was undoubtedly his fault, which meant he was responsible for Crispin's ruined perfecality score and for the fact that they couldn't reach the Office of the Lost.

"Oh God. I'm evil." Leopold moaned again and hid his face in his hands.

"Listen to me." Crispin sounded unusually forceful. "Chaos is not evil, not any more than... oh, fire is evil, or water. Yes, those things can cause damage, but not because they want to—it's simply due to their nature. And recall what Juzir said: Chaos is also the source of creativity. Without it we'd have no arts, and then wouldn't the worlds be dull places?"

Leopold felt slightly comforted. Not just by what was being said, but also by the fact that Crispin was the one saying them. He was trying to make Leopold feel better. Crispin, who'd kidnapped him and who was the prissiest, most infuriating creature Leopold had ever met. But who hadn't abandoned him when things went south. *There was also that kiss.*

"What are you going to do with me?" Dread sat heavy in Leopold's stomach. "And why is the... the other Chaos chasing after me?"

"I don't know. But I expect that my mother can help."

At some point Leopold got off the chair and curled up on the floor at the edge of the ward, which had expanded to give him a little moving-around space. Soft voices lulled him to sleep.

He woke up covered by a blanket and with a pillow under his head. He wondered how Crispin and Juzir had gotten those items past the defenses. Then he wondered how he'd so easily come to accept desk fae, dinosaur wizards, and magical wards. Maybe that was the upside to being a piece of Chaos—you weren't too shook up when your world turned deeply weird.

Leopold sat up and then slowly stood and stretched. He was sore. The pillow and blanket had been nice, but the floor was still hard. There was no sign of Juzir, but Crispin was curled up on a lumpy piece of gray furniture filled with weird holes that might have been the dino equivalent of a sofa. Asleep, he looked young and untroubled, all his uptight fussiness gone.

They'd kissed, hadn't they? Leopold hadn't imagined it. Possibly due to moth pheromones. Possibly due to Leopold's chaotic influence. Or possibly because they found each other attractive. Hell, maybe all three.

As if sensing Leopold's stare, Crispin blinked awake. For just a moment, he smiled brightly.

And then *wham!* Out came the tight-faced scowl. "We shouldn't have slept so long."

Leopold shrugged. "I dunno what time it is. Pets don't have watches."

Crispin rolled his eyes. "You needn't be so peevish about it. It could be worse. What if archosaurs considered apes tasty, for instance? At any rate, we'll leave here shortly."

"To see your mother." Leopold had gotten the impression that something bad had gone down between Crispin and his mother, but his desk fae—friend?—was being tight-lipped about the whole thing.

"Yes," said Crispin, shoulders slumped.

Leopold was going to ask how they would achieve this feat, but then Juzir entered with a tray. He was clearly still wary of Leopold and avoided looking at him, but he smiled at Crispin. "Breakfast!"

When had Leopold last eaten? He'd lost track of which world it had been. His stomach growled loudly enough to startle their host. *Man, I would sell my soul for a breakfast burrito or a big stack of pancakes.*

But wait—soul. Assuming such things existed, did he have one? It didn't seem as though Chaos would. God, he'd almost forgotten that he wasn't human. But if he wasn't human, why was he so damned ravenous? And also why—

"Breakfast," said Juzir, frowning at Leopold. Then he muttered something else that Leopold didn't understand, and two metal bowls appeared on the floor. One of them contained water. The other had something yellowish with green bits; it might have been scrambled eggs with herbs. Or it might not.

Crispin had a regular plate and some kind of cutlery, although he was struggling with it since it had been designed for archosaur hands. Leopold, however, had dog dishes. But he was hungry, so he dug in anyway, muttering to himself about asteroids and extinction events.

Once the food bowl was empty, a new need became urgent. "I have to use the bathroom."

Juzir wrinkled his nose. "You smell odd but I don't think you need a bath."

"I am housebroken, but I won't be much longer if you don't get me to a toilet."

Comprehension dawned on Juzir's face, but he still didn't look happy. "I can bring you a... bucket."

"No. Absolutely not." Leopold might have only a shred of dignity left, but by golly he was going to hang on to it. He crossed his arms.

Then, to his mild surprise, Crispin intervened. "Juz, let him go. Surely it couldn't hurt to release the ward for just a few minutes. He'll do his business and then hurry back, you'll find a way to whisk us out of here, and we'll be out of your, erm, scales."

Looking a bit dyspeptic, Juzir waved his arms for a few seconds. Something made a loud *pop!* And Leopold suddenly felt... freer. Sort of like when he took off a pair of really tight skinny jeans and pulled on baggy sweats instead. He was going to ask where the bathroom was, but Juzir pointed down the hall and Leopold dashed there with as much decorum as he could manage.

The bathroom was large, with one of those rainforest shower-heads he'd always coveted. There was also a small sink, and a weird bristly thing attached to one pale-blue wall. He peered at the bristles in confusion until a few trapped iridescent green scales gave him a hint of its probable use: to help Juzir shed. Ugh.

But since archosaur personal grooming was not his immediate worry, he examined the toilet, which, unfortunately, wasn't well suited for human anatomy. It was still better than a bucket, though, and Leopold did the best he could. He felt better immediately... until he went to flush the thing and was stymied. An electronic control panel displayed a dozen buttons, each with a different incomprehensible symbol. It was worse than one of those fancy Japanese bidets.

He pressed a button at random—then winced when music blasted from hidden speakers. At least it might have been music. Or it could have been a recording of someone being tortured. Another press turned the cacophony off, thank gods. The next button made the entire toilet glow violet; he had no idea why. A third released puffs of eucalyptus-scented steam from the ceiling.

Frustrated, Leopold pushed them all, repeatedly, pounding out the Darth Vader tune from Star Wars. *Baam baam baam bam-bam baam bam-bam baaam....*

The toilet flushed. Hooray! But Leopold's exhilaration was short-lived, because now the toilet started to shudder, jets of water erupted from the bowl, the music intensified, and, somewhere deep inside the building, something rumbled.

Leopold did what any sensible person would do under these circumstances: he ran.

In the living room, Crispin and Juzir were deep in conversation, apparently about Thea, who was clasped in one of Juzir's hands. "Get back on the chair," ordered Juzir. He must not have noticed whatever was going on in the bathroom. Leopold, sensing that wasn't going to last long, scurried to his chair and sat down. The ward was up again in a jiffy.

"So," said Juzir to Crispin, "I can repair it, but the incantations will take several hours to set. Would you like to go to the movies while we wait? *Iron Stegosaurus 2* is playing. I'm not sure it's as good as the first one, but I hear it's lots of fun. It's about this billionaire inventor who—"

"I'm not leaving Leo," said Crispin, which earned him a point in the tally that Leopold was keeping. Then he cocked his head as if listening to something, his eyes widened, and he shot Leopold a quick, panicked look before turning back to Juzir. "I think we ought to move things along. Is there a faster way? We've been using reflective surfaces."

"Well... maybe. But it's not very precise. You could end up back home or you could end up in a tar pit. Look, we could pick up some pizza and—"

Juzir sounded lonely. Leopold wondered when he'd last gone out on a date. If at all.

Crispin shook his head decisively. "I'll risk the tar pit."

Leopold wasn't sure he agreed, but now he was catching the noise that had Crispy so uneasy. An ominous gurgling rumble that might be due to unhappy plumbing. "I'll risk it too," Leopold said loudly.

Although Juzir looked a trifle offended, he shrugged. "All right. But don't blame me if you end up neck deep in sticky pitch. I lost a cousin that way. Crispy—"

"It's Crispin!"

"Crispin, take your transport device and stand close to the ape. On the count of three, I'm going to lift the ward. You'll need to grab him and imagine your destination as clearly as possible. Details matter. The taste of your favorite meal there, the feel of the carpets under your feet, the color of— Do you hear something?" Juzir cocked his head.

"Just my pet's stomach." Crispin closed his eyes in thought. "Let's see… my mother's floors are usually carpeted in meadow-grass and chamomile. Now can we please move this along?"

Juzir hummed, wiggled his fingers, and started chanting something that sounded a lot like the bathroom's torture music. Then he huffed. "One. Two." The rumble grew louder and the floor began to subtly vibrate. "Three."

The ward popped away. With Thea in one hand, Crispin grabbed Leopold's elbow with the other. Somewhere in the distance, an alarm began to sound.

"Now, Juzir!"

Clearly distracted, Juzir started chanting again. A noise came from the bathroom—something that sounded suspiciously like a large porcelain vessel shattering. The floor shook so hard that some of Juzir's vases wobbled off the shelves and crashed onto the floor.

There was an explosion loud enough to deafen Leopold.

And then the universe tilted.

15
CRISPIN

Crispin blinked and immediately closed his eyes again.

His head hurt, as if he'd imbibed an entire tankard of Bidulla's homemade Ogre Ale the night before, the especially strong variety she made for Ogre Solstice. No, *hurt* didn't do his head justice. More like *screaming pain*, as if his poor tender brain had been subjected to a prolonged banshee-chorus Christmas concert.

He lay still for a while, hoping the pain would recede and feeling perplexed. It wasn't like him to go on a bender. That was more Aspin's style. Crispin's older brother was the son Cerillia had always wanted: tall, strong, handsome, handy with a bow, unafraid to face down either a band of marauding trolls or a twelve-course state dinner.

Where am I? The pain ebbed, little by little, lessening to sword-in-the-gut level before dropping to that of ten painfully stubbed toes. At last, he dared open his eyes.

To nothing.

He blinked again, but the nothing stubbornly refused to become something. Next time his boss offered him a drink, he'd have to beg off—politely, of course.

He sat up, his hands slightly sinking into the soft emptiness that held him up. After a little more thought, he realized that it wasn't nothing, exactly. More like a distinct lack of something. The world around him was a sort of annoying white beigey gray, a nondescript color that seemed to mutter *don't look at me; I'm not interesting.* Even the air had a strange not-there quality to it, though there must have been air, because he was still breathing.

He tried to remember what had happened just before he'd ended up here, but his memories seemed just as amorphous as this strange un-place. He did a sudden sharp intake of breath.

"That's what this is!"

He was in the Un-Place. The place between worlds.

Crispin shuddered. He'd heard stories about people who had been trapped here, when the *zip* between places didn't work. It was fortunately rare, or else no one would travel by mirror, but it happened.

Sometimes they were found weeks, months, years later. Sometimes they were never seen again.

There was a groan behind him, and he snapped his head around.

A man lay there. A human male with disheveled hair and with clothing that was nearly as messy. "Leo?" Crispin's memories snapped back into place. "Leo!" He crawled over to the poor hapless man.

The leash was still around Leo's neck, the one Crispin had fastened when they were on Earth 2. Just before the explosion. Something had happened in Juzir's apartment as the archosaur wizard was about to send them home.

Leo blinked. "Crispy?"

For once, Crispin let the annoying nickname stand. "Are you all right?"

He didn't look all right. His skin was decidedly gray, but not a normal kind of sickly gray. It was more like his body was filled with gray sparks, just under the skin.

"I feel sparky." Leopold's whole body shook, as if he were having a seizure. "What's wrong with me?"

Crispin took his hand, and the hum of electricity ran through him. "I don't know." *Think, Crispin, think.* If his theory was right, Leo wasn't really human. Or at least hadn't been born that way. He was a bit of Chaos magic loose in the world.

Maybe it was better that they were stuck here in the Un-Place. Because realistically, how much damage could Leo even do if he lost control in a place like this? Probably nothing.

Or he could break all the mirrors, all the passages between the connected worlds. That would be catastrophic for billions of entities; probably for Leo too. And somehow Crispin had gotten rather attached to the cantankerous, messy human during their long journey across worlds.

He squeezed Leo's hand. "Tell me what you're feeling."

"It's... like I'm liquid, sloshing around inside my skin. Like something wants out." His eyes met Leo's. "Should I let it go?" His brow was slick with sweat. "I'm not normal, am I?"

Crispin snorted. "No, don't let it go." He touched Leo's forehead with his free hand. "You're running a bit hot." He wished he had a bit of water to give to his... friend. Yes, that term sounded right. "And you're one of the most boringly normal people I have ever met. Almost as boring as I am."

A ghost of a smile played across Leopold's lips. "Boring? *Boring?* You're a goddamned elf, dude."

Crispin laughed. "A fae. A desk fae. Can't get much more boring than that."

Leopold shook his head. "You travel between worlds. In just the time we've been together, we've been potties—"

"Piwati."

"...and seen mirkins—"

"Feryken."

"...and giants and even a whole world filled with arkysores."

"Archosaurs." If they ever made it out of this bland place, he'd have to work on Leo's language skills.

"My point is that you are anything but boring! Seriously, Crispy, you make it really hard for a guy to get a word in edgewise." During his speech, his pallor had been slowly changing.

"Look!" Crispin held up Leo's hand. "Your skin."

Leopold sat up and peered at his arm. "It looks like skin."

"Exactly. The more boring and human you act, the more human you become."

"Like Pinocchio?"

Crispin racked his brain. "Oh, yes, the story from the wooden world of Geppettoso. They always did take a shine to your kind."

"You mean Pinocchio... he was real?"

"Of course he was. But that whole claptrap about him becoming human was just a story."

"I'm not though, am I?" Leo's eyes were wet.

"Not what?"

"Human." His lanky brown hair fell over his eyes. "That's what the arkysore was saying."

Crispin sighed. *Close enough.* "Listen, maybe you weren't human to begin with. I wasn't fae to begin with, either, just a small magical cell that divided and divided again to make me the stunning example of office faedom that you see before you today. You didn't start out that way, but you are as human a human as I've ever met. Maybe that's what counts."

Leo reached up, gently pulled Crispin near, and kissed him. Crispin gave in, the warmth of Leo's lips melting his insides.

He allowed himself—just for a second—to imagine a life with the strange human... waking up in bed with him in the treehouse, feeding Minkis together, taking quiet walks in the forest under the scintillating canopy of the Greatwoods... even coming home after work to recount stories of his long day at the office—

He pushed Leopold away. "I... we... can't."

Leo's eyebrow arched. "Why not? Is it 'cause... I am what I am?"

"Yes." Crispin regretted it immediately, seeing Leopold's crest-fallen look. "Oh, not that. Like I said, you're as human as anyone I've ever met."

"Then what?" His eyes widened. "You're a virgin!"

Crispin barked a laugh. "I most certainly am not. I've played in the berry bushes with my share of men before." Though not many, and not for a long time. Not since Qyl. The ache in his nethers reminded him of that. Their affair had been both short-lived and disastrous.

"Then what?"

Crispin sighed. "You're a—" he had been about to say "a recover-able," but that didn't sound right. "A client." He'd never hear the end of it from Bidulla if he got too involved with the merchandise.

"Oh." Leopold lay back on the white beigey gray nothing and stared at the white beigey gray sky. "So you can't but you want to." A grin teased the edges of his lips. "I can work with that."

Crispin huffed. "I never said I wanted to."

"Your lips did."

He sighed. He almost preferred Morose Leo to Smug Leo. He got up, casting about for something, anything, to get them out of there. Intentionally taking a few steps away from Leo. Just to check out the area. *I can't trust myself being close to him.*

He pulled his portable transport device from his pocket. "Thea, can you get us home now?"

It was a long shot, but maybe here in the Un-Place, the bit of Chaos she'd ingested might be muffled? Or maybe pulled out of her altogether?

She whistled softly, but then, nothing.

Crispin abruptly sat down, out of ideas. He'd long since given up on his perfecality score. Now he just wanted to go home.

He shuddered and started to cry—something he never did, espe-cially in front of others. Not since his brother had teased him merci-lessly for crying over his last pet, a raccoon named Echo, who had wandered away from home one night just before his mother's Estate had changed worlds.

He put his head in his hands, trying to hide his sobs.

Leopold was beside him in an instant. "Hey, I'm sorry, dude. I didn't mean to hurt you. I was just joking." He put his arms around Crispin.

Leo's response was so different from Aspin's teasing jabs. *He really does care about me.*

In an instant Leo had somehow erased the space between them. This time Crispin was sure of it. "Wait. How did you— You were over there, and then you were *here.*"

Leopold shrugged. "I don't know. I just knew you needed me. So I was... here." As he said it, he frowned. "Hey, that *is* kinda weird, right?"

Crispin stared at him. "Has this ever happened before? I mean, I think you did it when we were with Fromlith, but it all happened so fast, I wasn't sure. And then when we fell out of the nest...."

"I guess?"

"But before that. Before you met me?"

Leopold frowned. "I... don't know. Maybe?"

"How can you *not* know?"

"Well, there was this time when I crashed my car, only I was outside of it, you know? Like, I figured I just got thrown out on impact. But the paramedics said it was strange that I didn't have any injuries."

Crispin nodded. "Because... you decided to be somewhere else?"

Leopold blinked. "I guess? But people can't just decide to be somewhere else and... do it. Can they?"

"Not people. *You.*"

"Ouch, dude. That's harsh. I thought you said I was as human as anyone you knew?" The hurt look on his face wounded Crispin too.

He frowned. "I didn't mean..."

Leopold's grin stretched slowly across his face. "I know. But you are *so* easy."

Crispin shoved him. "I need you to be serious for a moment."

Leo mock-saluted him. "Yes, sir."

Crispin got up and took a few steps through the nothingness and turned back toward Leo. "Come over here."

Leopold started to get up.

"Not like that. See if you can wish yourself here."

"Oh, okay." He closed his eyes and his whole face scrunched, as though he was trying to force something out of himself.

Nothing happened.

"All right. Let's try something else. Close your eyes, take a few deep breaths, and visualize yourself next to me." Deep breaths were always helpful when one was stressed, and they were both certainly under a lot of stress.

Leopold did as he was told. His face slackened, making him look almost childlike, and he took five slow, deep breaths. "Did I do it? Am I next to you?"

Crispin sighed again. "No. You can open your eyes." He needed this to work. He had to get home to see his mother. She would be able to set things right, even if she cut him down to size for being such a "huge disappointment" and "nothing at all like your brother."

"Leo…" He blinked. Leopold was standing right next to him. "You did it."

Leopold looked down and around himself. "I did. What did I do different?"

Crispin bit his lip, thinking. Both times, he'd needed Leopold's help. It couldn't be that simple. Could it?

Were they connected somehow?

"I have an idea. Take my hand."

Leopold obeyed, his palm warm in Crispin's and pulsing with life. For not being human, he did a really good impression of one.

Crispin found himself wondering what it would be like to touch Leo's naked chest, to lean into him and smell his neck, to…

He shook himself. *This is not the time.*

"I have to tell you something." Leo looked suddenly very serious.

Is he blushing? Maybe he feels the same way too. "What?" Crispin held his breath.

The world seemed to stop. Not that there was anything going on around them, but somehow time froze for an agonizing moment while Crispin awaited Leopold's next words.

"I think I broke Juzir's toilet."

The world resumed its movement. It may have grumbled under its breath about *so much ado for nothing.*

Crispin stared at him. "You...." It was so not what he was expecting. "So that's what the explosion was?"

Leopold nodded miserably. "Tell him I'm sorry, next time you see him?"

Crispin chuckled. It started as a little thing but then expanded into his belly, and soon he was laughing out loud. "You broke his toilet!" Somehow it was the funniest thing he had ever heard.

Leo grinned, picking up his mood. "Yeah. I flushed it, and it started to gurgle and shake, and then... *boom.*"

"Boom!" Crispin lifted his hands into the air. They laughed together, falling into each other's arms, and a weight lifted from Crispin's shoulders.

Sure his perfecality score had probably cratered by now, but what other desk fae would have been able to get them this far, safely? Certainly not Theodor ur Deepmountain, or any of the other curators. He had done it, with Leopold's help. Together they could do anything, he was suddenly sure of it.

And what would happen when he finally delivered Leo to the office? Bidulla would want to squirrel him away somewhere safe, maybe even study him.

I won't let that happen. But first, he had to get them both home. Needed to get them home. "It's okay, Leo. They have good plumbers on Juzir's world."

Leopold's tentative smile was genuine. "Are you sure? It must have made an awful mess."

"I'm sure." He'd see about sending Juzir some restitution once he made it back to OotL. They had a fund for such things, issues caused in the line of duty. "But right now, I need you to take us to see my mother." It was true. As much as he fretted about having to deal with Her High Fairyness and her usually pointed jibes about his life and career, he needed to see her. "Can you do that?"

Leo nodded. "I can try." He threw his arms around Crispin and squeezed him tight.

Crispin hoped Leo couldn't *feel* how much Crispin needed him in return.

"Take us to the Estate," Crispin intoned.

The Un-Place faded around them, and then with a snap, they were somewhere else.

Leo let him go, his eyes widening. "What the...?"

Crispin blinked in dismay. "Oh dear."

16

LEOPOLD

Prior to meeting Crispin, Leopold's knowledge of fairies and elves and such was... limited. And pretty much based on cartoons, Keebler ads, Tinkerbell, and *Lord of the Rings*, for the most part. He'd had the general impression that Crispin's mother's home would be a magical forest with giant mushrooms, or maybe a charming grassy glen with a fairy circle of stones.

Instead, they ended up in Las Vegas.

Okay, it wasn't Vegas, *exactly*. It was more acid-trippy, which honestly Leopold wouldn't have thought possible. He and Crispin stood on a sidewalk alongside a busy street lined with enormous, flashy buildings. The street traffic consisted of non-motorized vehicles: chariots, unicycles, and.... Jesus, was that lady riding a *unicorn*? The buildings were either shiny and sleek or had themes. Only instead of Paris or ancient Rome or pirates, these places apparently celebrated spaghetti, lawn mowing, and Des Moines. The restaurants were themed as well; the closest one had a giant neon sign proclaiming that it was *Marie Curie's: Home of the Glowing Rib-Eye!*

Just as in Vegas, many of the pedestrians clutched oversized plastic cups displaying bar logos, and many of the pedestrians seemed at least a little tipsy. But none of them were human, exactly. They were lots of other things though, most of which Leopold couldn't identify.

"Come on," said Crispin, his voice sounding resigned. "She's this way." He started marching down the sidewalk.

"What is this place?"

"The Estate. My mother's home." He paused. "Well, technically, it's where the Estate is, at the moment."

"You grew up here?" Leopold couldn't picture that.

Crispin shook his head. "No. It doesn't work like that. My mother's Estate—her court—is wherever she wants it to be. I think she's even made some brief visits to your world now and then, just for variety. However, this place is one of her favorites. Unfortunately."

"What's it called?"

Crispin made a sound like a brook burbling over stones.

"What?"

"It means Place Where Tourists Believe They'll Get Rich But They Won't Because Odds Always Favor the House. Hardly anyone but fae can pronounce it correctly, so most people just call it Odds."

Well, that was fitting.

And hey, at least the frigging leash was gone.

They walked at a brisk pace past a gigantic store called Nothing But Pickles and a nightclub in which one could pay to watch ogres doing ballet. *That I'd like to see.* He imagined elephants on tiptoe wearing pink tutus....

The front display at one hotel, instead of dancing fountains or an erupting volcano, involved giant numbers swirling around in apparently complex math equations, none of which Leopold understood. Other visitors, however, seemed delighted. There were also buskers, singing what Leopold assumed were supposed to be songs or wearing costumes and encouraging people to take selfies with them.

Leopold was intrigued and would have liked to explore, but Crispin turned off the sidewalk and onto a sweeping ramp that led to the entrance of another hotel. Leopold was a little disappointed that it wasn't the one extolling Des Moines; he'd been curious to see what the theming entailed. This hotel was called Prickles, which made sense because the décor centered on cactuses.

They'd barely stepped into an enormous lobby when Leopold dragged Crispin to a halt. "Hey, Crispy. All these cactuses. Um, do they sort of look like...."

"Penises." Crispin heaved a heavy sigh. "Yes."

There were a lot of them, some small and some large, some in planters on the floor, some on large pedestals, some displayed on elaborate hanging shelves. They came in different colors and with varying degrees of spikiness. But every one of them was phallic.

"*Why* are there cactus dicks everywhere?"

"Because it's Prickles."

As if that explained everything.

"Come *on*, Leo. We need to find my mother before she decides to decamp to another world." Crispin firmly grasped Leopold's hand and tugged him past a registration desk and a couple of restaurants and then onto the floor of a vast casino. Mercifully, the theming was lighter here, showing mainly in the carpet pattern and some of the light fixtures. Other than the multi-species customers, this could easily have been any of the high-end Vegas joints, complete with card tables, slot machines, and a sports book, although none of the sports looked like anything on Earth. One of them seemed to involve kangaroos juggling hedgehogs.

Leopold had to hurry to keep up with Crispin's pace. "I went to Vegas once. I'd been fired from my job at a copy place after a couple of the Xerox machines exploded, and I figured I could find something decent-paying there. I liked all the noise and flashing lights and how there were people stumbling around any time of night. It's fascinating how people lose track of time and discard all sense of caution."

"Did you find a position?" asked Crispin, who was now leading them toward a curving escalator.

"Briefly, yeah. I had to sweep and mop the floors in one of the big casinos. Normally I hate cleaning, but this was sort of fun 'cause I'd find all kinds of stuff. Money, unredeemed winnings receipts, jewelry, phones, clothing.... Once I came across a wedding cake just sitting on the floor behind a blackjack table. I turned everything in—I'm not a thief. But it was interesting."

Crispin gave his hand a gentle squeeze. "I wouldn't think that you'd take things that didn't belong to you."

That warmed Leopold's heart. People rarely believed in him. "But I'm Chaos."

"Chaos isn't evil. It's like... like fire. I told you. It can be very dangerous, but it can also help create valuable things. Think of how terrible food would be without fire."

Not evil. That was a surprisingly big relief. Leopold had caused a lot of bad things to happen in his life—maybe even his parents' deaths—but he hadn't intended to.

They were on the escalator now, experiencing a leisurely rise, spiraling around several gigantic glass phallic cactus sculptures. They were sort of pretty if you didn't think about them too hard.

"Leo? If you liked the position, why did you hold it only briefly?"

"Same reason as always. Things blew up. Um, not literally, in that case." Leopold frowned at the memory. "I was working near the quarter slots when suddenly all hell broke loose—everyone who was playing won a jackpot, all at once. And that continued for a good ten minutes until security came and cleared the area out. The bosses figured it was some kind of weird technical glitch. But then the same thing happened the next day when I was nearby, and then again the day after that. So they fired me."

Actually, first they'd dragged him into an office in which some extremely scary men interrogated him about how he was fixing the machines. Leopold, frightened half to death, had insisted that he had nothing to do with it. They'd held him for a while longer, but when the security cameras showed him doing nothing more sinister than sweeping, they had to let him go. Not without threats, however, and a clear warning to never return to that casino or, for that matter, anywhere else in the city.

"That's not fair," said Crispin.

"In retrospect, maybe it was. Now I know I probably was messing things up somehow."

"Injecting chaos into probabilities."

That made sense, Leopold thought as they got off the escalator and strode down a long, wide corridor lined with shops selling clothing and jewelry, most of which wouldn't work well on human bodies. However, he did spy a suit that might fit him perfectly but would undoubtedly be out of his budget, even if he had whatever currency this place used.

"What?" asked Crispin when Leopold lagged in front of the display window.

"I'm a jeans-and-tee kinda guy. But I always wondered what it would be like to afford nice duds. Not that I'd have anyplace to wear them."

Crispin looked thoughtful. "Well, meeting royalty would be an appropriate occasion to dress up."

"Yeah, well, I'll remember that if I ever have lunch with a king."

"Leo, you're about to be presented to the Queen of the High Holy Fae."

Oh. Leopold had forgotten who Crispin's mom was. He looked down at his clothes, which weren't exactly fresh at this point in the adventure. "She's just gonna have to deal with me like this."

"Maybe not. Come on." With an odd little smile, Crispin dragged him into the shop.

The salesclerk looked more or less like a very handsome human, only with slightly iridescent bluish skin, deep green hair, and no nose. He glided over immediately. "Can I help you beings?" As he spoke, Leopold noticed what looked like several rows of tiny sharp teeth.

"That suit in the window, for my friend here," said Crispin.

The clerk grinned a sharp smile. "Excellent. Just a moment, please." He hurried away and disappeared behind a door.

"I can't afford that," protested Leopold in a stage whisper.

"Not a problem. I'll put it on my mother's account."

"But I—"

"She has more money than she knows what to do with, and I feel as if you're partially her responsibility. She can pay."

Before Leopold could protest, the clerk was back. "Follow me to the fitting room, please."

They entered a large room, and both the clerk and Crispin seemed to think it was appropriate to stand there and watch as Leopold tried on the outfit. Well, whatever. Pretending to be blasé, he stripped to his underwear and then donned a black silk shirt and wool trousers and jacket. From a distance, the suit looked dark brown, but up close it had a subtle leopard-spot pattern. Everything fit him perfectly, as if it had been tailored for him. *Fae magic, probably.*

"I bet I look dumb," said Leopold, suddenly self-conscious.

But his audience shook their heads firmly. "You look wonderful," said Crispin.

"Delicious," agreed the clerk.

When Leopold finally braved the mirrors he saw... a man with messy hair and a really awesome suit. "Wow."

"Shoes!" announced the clerk, as he produced—seemingly out of thin air—a pair of shiny black oxfords that fit as if custom-made.

The clerk stuffed Leopold's old clothes into a fabric bag adorned with the shop logo, and then the three of them walked to the sales desk.

"Put it on Cerillia Ailedrin Moss'caladin's account, please," said Crispin. "She's my mother."

The clerk frowned. "But you're not Aspin. Oh! You're the *other* one."

Crispin looked distinctly unhappy about that but didn't say

anything. Moments later he and Leopold were back in the corridor, now moving at a much faster pace.

"What was that clerk?" asked Leopold, slightly breathlessly.

"A merman, of course."

"But he didn't have a tail or fins or...."

"He's one of the amphibious kinds."

Leopold didn't know what to make of that.

A few seconds later they turned down another hallway, this one with thick carpeting and gold-colored lighting fixtures that continued the phallic cactus motif. In front of a set of double doors stood a large person in a dark suit. He had tusks and a long snout like a boar.

"Crispin Eladrin Moss'caladin and guest." Crispin sounded slightly imperious.

The guard gave a little bow, stepped aside, and held one of the doors for them.

"Where are we?" whispered Leopold into Crispin's pointed ear.

"The high rollers' lounge."

It didn't look like Leopold's idea of a lounge, more like the type of casino that James Bond or Cary Grant might hang out in. Everything was luxe and glittery, including the people, who wore what Leopold assumed was designer clothing on their worlds. Waitstaff in tuxedoes or cocktail dresses glided around with trays of drinks and food, and there was also a large bar at one end of the room. No jangling slot machines here, and the conversations, although steadily flowing, were quiet, as might be heard in a fancy restaurant.

"Oh, Oberon's golden balls." Crispin was staring across the room, but Leopold couldn't tell at what.

Leopold blinked. By *balls*, did he mean parties, or...? He scanned the room desperately, certain the Chaos fog was about to start chasing them again. Although he didn't know what would happen if the fog caught him, he was certain he didn't want to find out. But there was no sign of it, and nobody but Crispin seemed alarmed.

"What is it, Crispy?"

Instead of answering, Crispin squared his shoulders, muttered something unintelligible, and took a few deep breaths. He marched forward as if to certain doom, shoulders squared, Leopold trailing behind him.

Their destination soon became clear: a large table at which about a dozen people were playing a game involving twelve-sided dice, a deck of cards, and jewel-toned beetles that toddled along the arcanely-marked felt. Leopold assumed that this group was all fae because they resembled Crispin: slender, pretty, sharp cheekbones.

At the center of this crowd stood a woman with a distinctly regal air. She wore a black leather motorcycle jacket over a short black dress, and her auburn hair was arranged in an elaborate braided bun inset with what were probably rubies. She was stunning.

To her right stood an unusually tall man with piercing eyes and lush lips. His long tresses—the color of butterscotch—were drawn back from a perfectly chiseled face and tied behind his back by an engraved leather thong. Beneath the tuxedo was an obviously trim, athletic body. He looked as if he'd stepped straight off a romance novel cover: a roguish duke, perhaps, or a naughty billionaire.

The entire group stared at Crispin and Leopold, and then the woman spoke. "Crispin Eladrin Moss'caladin. *What* are you doing bringing a *human* here?"

"He's not, um, exactly human. This is Leopold Lane." Crispin's face had flushed slightly.

The Queen of the Fae visibly blanched, becoming, if possible, even paler than she had been before.

Leopold didn't know what to do. Should he bow? He settled on an awkward nod instead. Man, that guy in the tux was gorgeous. It was hard not to drool.

Crispin turned to look at Leopold and frowned. "Leo—uh, Leopold Lane. Please meet Her Majesty, the Mother of Fae, Cerillia Ailedrin Moss'caladin." Then he added, rather quickly, "And my brother Aspin."

17
CRISPIN

As Crispin stared at his brother, a complex stew of emotions worked its way through his gut *and made him fear he'd throw up*.

He had always harbored a curious blend of feelings toward Aspin, the *perfect fae* who was everything their mother expected Crispin to be.

"Aspin." He nodded at his sibling rival, but Aspin's attention was tightly focused on Leo.

"I know you." Aspin walked over to them with the grace and implied danger of a panther, stopping before the hapless human.

Leo, for his part, seemed much less impressed with Aspin's image of refined masculinity. "This one's your brother? I would have guessed that one over there." He jerked his thumb toward a corner of the room.

Crispin followed the gesture to where Uncle Epilen snored in a gilded chair, thick glasses resting on the bridge of his overly long nose, hands clasped over a bulbous belly.

The rest of the courtiers were staring at the newcomers, the room suddenly gone silent.

126

"Um, thank you? I think?" It was certainly a mixed compliment. Epilen was very smart and handled all of the family finances, but he was *not* the most attractive of the family fae.

"Oh, you're much more adorable." Leo pecked him on the cheek, making him blush and earning a shocked gasp from the crowd. Humans rarely entered his mother's Estate, and when they did, she was usually the object of their affections.

His mother, for her part, wore an expression Crispin had rarely seen—genuine shock. Whether due to her unexpected human guest or the prodigal return of her son, it wasn't clear.

Crispin wiped his cheek, as if he could just rub out what had happened, and then straightened his rumpled vest. He was glad he'd taken the time to spruce Leo up a bit, but now he wished he'd done the same for himself. He felt every inch the desk fae among these fancy folk, and worse, a somewhat disheveled and grimy desk fae, likely confirming everything they already thought about him.

"You look *so* familiar." Aspin was still staring at Leo. He reached out to touch his cheek and jerked his hand back when a spark stung him. "What in Hades' dark halls?" Aspin glared at his own hand as if it had offended him.

This was going to escalate fast if Crispin didn't find a way to shut his brother down and get Leo somewhere private.

The lights flickered, and Thea unexpectedly came to his rescue, blaring out a strange "song" that sounded like a mix of car horns and electric guitars played by zombies on acid. Crispin had collected just such a song once, for work.

"Sorry. I broke my transport device." He pulled out his damaged electronic best friend and glared at her, though he was secretly glad for the interruption. "Not now, Thea."

The screen went black, and the music cut off abruptly.

Before Aspin could recover, Crispin grabbed Leo by the elbow and dragged him past his brother and over to the glorious, all-knowing, world-enchanting Queen of the High Holy Fae. "I need a moment with you alone, *Mother.*" He knew just the tone that would push her buttons.

She blinked and sighed. "Of course you do." She turned to her adoring courtiers. "I am so sorry, but a familial matter has arisen that requires my immediate attention." The look she gave Leo told him she knew exactly what he was. "I will return anon."

Crispin grinned. He'd startled her into an anachronism. She'd always been fond of young Shakespeare, who had somehow escaped —mostly unscathed—from his two-week visit to her realm. And had gone on to write an entire play based upon it.

She waved her hand and the room and the rest of the casino dissolved. All of her guests disappeared, except for Leo, Crispin, and Aspin.

Leo gasped. "Are the rest of them... dead?"

Crispin gave a low chuckle. "They only wish they were." Being in the presence of the Queen was like a drug for mere mortals, and her sudden absence hurt like the worst kind of withdrawal. "They will be fine when she returns." He looked around, surprised to find himself in her private bower.

This version of it fit with the fancy casino theme—a huge suite, wall-papered in a shimmering pattern that recalled cottonwood trees, their leaves shifting as if blown by a breeze. He recognized it as an enchanted wall covering, of course. In the middle of it was the omnipresent Red Door, which Crispin avoided looking at. Too many implications there.

The Queen's bed was held up by four massive oaks which disap-peared into the sky—or was it just a ceiling?—where clouds shifted slowly across the plaster. He'd never been able to decide if they were actual clouds or just a fancy painted illusion. Neither would have surprised him.

"Why did you bring *that* here?" Cerillia was staring at Leo with a combination of fear and distaste. But it was her appearance that startled Crispin. She looked... older.

Cerillia Ailedrin Moss'caladin *never* looked older. She was *ageless-*

ness personified, an ethereal being who made all others around her feel old and inferior. But now he saw fine lines around her eyes and mouth, skin pulled so tight across her cheekbones that it was almost translucent, and silver hair that looked more leaden-gray than the color of freshly refined ore.

Aspin frowned prettily. "What is it?"

"You don't recognize it?" She patted her older son on the head as if he were five years old. "You dragged it off to Earth all those gods-forsaken years ago." She turned away to pour a fine sparkling brandy into a crystal goblet and then swallowed it entirely, without offering any of them even a drop.

"Leo... Leopold is not an *it*." Crispin slipped his arm around Leo's waist and pulled him closer, eliciting a *yip*. "He's a human, regardless of how he was...." He'd been about to say *formed*, but that would just make his mother's point. "Born."

Leo turned to look at him. "Thank you, Crispy."

Light dawned on Aspin's face. "You're that bit of Chaos Elly here let out of The Door." He gestured at the red portal, which seemed to grow a little.

Crispin Eladrin blushed at the nickname. But although Aspin had tortured him mercilessly with *Elly Elly Elephant* as a child, Crispin had seen too many scary things across a thousand worlds to fear a bully as petty as Aspin Vellain Moss'caladin—or as Crispin had named him, Velly Ugly.

"The Office sent me to collect him, so he must be important," he said.

Leo pushed away, breaking contact. "About that. What happens to me when we get to Oodle?"

Crispin frowned. *I've never collected a person before.* "I'm... not sure. They'll probably find a nice place for you to live—"

"Without you?"

The Queen was watching them with narrowed eyes. "You've become enamored of him." It was a statement, not a question, and sent a shiver up Crispin's back. It was almost never a good idea to draw the Mother of Fae's attention.

"What I may or may not feel is—"

Aspin leered. "Elly's got a boyfriend. Elly's got a —"

A single smoldering look from his mother shut Aspin up.

"He's not my boyfriend. He's just..." Crispin stared helplessly at Leo. What were they to each other? There was a spark, to be sure, but was it any more "real" than the one that had stung Aspin? They'd had no time to sort things out between them.

Leopold's eyes were fixed on his as Crispin said, "He's just the thing I was sent to collect." It wouldn't do to confirm his mother's suspicions. "I need your help to get him back to the Office. When the Chaos Cloud attacked us in Leo... Leopold's apartment, I dropped Thea and a little Chaos got inside, I think, and ever since then we've been jumping from world to world, trying to get home. Minkis must be worried sick, and...."

Leo's shoulders sagged. "He's right. We don't mean anything to one another." He chewed his lip until he drew blood. "I am just a *thing*, after all."

Oh, Leo, I didn't mean it.

Then his mother's cold hand was on Crispin's cheek, the full weight of her attention upon him. The rest of the room—Leo included—faded from his awareness.

"It's good that you brought him here. Left to run about in the world, he could become... quite dangerous."

But you're the one who put him there. Well, Aspin did. Still, no point in dredging up the past. It could wait. "So you can help?"

She nodded, every bit of her presence urging him to trust her.

He blinked. *She's trying to glamour me.* He twisted away from her touch, and the bower returned with a crash that sounded like glass breaking. "Don't try to get inside of my head, Mother."

It was her turn to blink. Another emotion she rarely displayed moved across her face. *Surprise. And perhaps just a touch of respect.* "You've grown into a man since the last time I saw you."

"Elly's no man—"

"Quiet." She turned a fierce gaze on her elder son, who literally froze in mid-protest.

"Whoa." Leopold stepped forward to touch Aspin's cheek, apparently forgetting momentarily to be angry at Crispin.

Aspin didn't move, though Crispin swore his cheeks reddened.

"This place is trippy." Leo stepped back, and his gaze returned to Crispin. He clearly remembered he was mad, because his eyebrows re-knotted themselves like a pair of angry yarn socks.

Crispin sighed. "So, will you help us, or not?"

A slight smile ghosted his mother's lips. "Of course I will help." She turned back to the bar, suddenly filled with a selection of the finest crystal decanters from a thousand worlds—neat trick, that— and selected three of them seemingly at random. "Your... *friend's* presence here represents a substantial danger to the Connected Worlds. So much Chaos in one place... and up until now, it has been contained in this vessel. But something must have happened to loosen its hold."

"Why didn't you just... send him back through The Door? When... when I opened it?"

She poured a sparkling green liquid into a crystal glass trimmed with gold that was probably worth the economic output of a small planet.

"If we had re-opened The Door at that time... Chaos ebbs and flows, like the tides under the moon. You're lucky Aspin was able to close The Door at all. It was at its strongest then."

Crispin frowned. He hated owing his brother for anything.

"It wasn't your fault, you know." She poured a bit of blood-red something into the green liquid.

For all Crispin knew, it might actually *be* blood. "What do you mean?"

"You were always drawn to that Door, even before you could speak. I think the Chaos was calling to you. It's why I sent you away to the Office." She swirled the liquid around in the glass.

"*You* sent me?" That's not at all how he remembered it. He had departed after a horrible argument with his mother over the way Aspin treated him. His mother had wanted him to follow in Aspin's hunting-booted footsteps, but Crispin had refused, had opted for a more orderly career. "I left—"

"I pulled a few strings for them to take you." She poured the final ingredient from its decanter into the potion, a deep blue liquid capped in white foam that reminded him of the sea. The mixture bubbled and foamed.

It was a blow to his ego. "You... made them take me?" It had been his proudest moment, his act of rebellion, walking away from his family and all their power, finally earning something on his own merits.

"Holy shit. I'm so sorry, Crispy." Leo's eyes conveyed comfort.

This strange human, this bit of Chaos embodied in a clumsy man from a sleepy Earth city, somehow understood him better than his own mother.

"You're a horrible woman, Ms. Cladin," Leo concluded.

"That's Cerillia Ailedrin Moss'caladin. Seriously, Crispin, why do you allow it—*him* to address me that way?" Her arched eyebrow was sharp enough to cut cloth.

Crispin fought to restrain his runaway emotions. So what if her influence had helped him win the job of his dreams? She'd had nothing to do with his once-pristine perfecality score. She hadn't gotten Leo halfway across the connected worlds safely. She had never even had to leave her protected little Estate.

His mother lifted the potion to look at the now-white mixture inside. She nodded, satisfied, and leaned in to blow on its surface. "Earth, fire, water, and air."

The glass flashed with an intense silver-blue light, like lightning, and the liquid turned black as the darkest night.

"Here. Drink this, and all your troubles will be gone." She handed it to Leo, who, mesmerized, put it to his lips.

Earth, fire, water, and air.... "No!" Crispin leapt forward with an athletic prowess that would have done Aspin proud and knocked the glass out of Leo's hand. It shattered against the wall, the dark liquid immediately eating a hole through the phony trees and exposing the stone behind them. The gap in his mother's manufactured reality grew rapidly larger, as if consumed by a hungry beast.

"Elly, what have you done?" Aspin was frozen no more and stood staring at the transformation of the queen's bower.

Crispin ignored him. *What would that potion have done to Leo?* "Do you trust me?"

Leo's mouth hung open. "What in tarnation was that?"

Crispin had no idea where Tar Nation was, but that didn't matter at the moment. "Nightsmaiden. It would have undone you, permanently."

"Holy guns and roses."

Crispin risked a glance over his shoulder. His mother was glowing with a golden light, her eyes closed, as she fought the spell her own actions had unleashed. He hoped she would get it under control—he really did—but she was dead to him now.

He took Leo by the shoulders and shook him. "Do. You. Trust. Me?" They had one place left to go, somewhere Cerillia Ailedrin Moss'caladin couldn't—or wouldn't—follow. And if he was right, they might find the answers they sought.

"Of course I trust you, you pointy-eared idiot." Leo looked as though he wanted to say more, but there was no time.

"Then come on." Crispin took Leo's hand and dragged him toward the wall.

"Elly, don't! You'll kill us all, you stupid little goblin-get!" Aspin started toward him, but he was too late.

Crispin grabbed hold of the doorknob and flung open The Door to reveal a sea of writhing nothing. Caught up in the moment, he kissed Leo hard, eliciting a surprised yelp that Crispin hoped sounded at least a little pleased. "Come on, then!"

He dragged his human charge through the opening and into, at this point, a technicolor soup. The Door slammed shut behind them.

18
LEOPOLD

Did all fae taste like honey and strawberries when they kissed you, or was that just a Crispy thing? Leopold hadn't really noticed the flavor after the first kiss, but there had been Mothra pheromones involved at the time, so that probably interfered. This time, however, there had been no moths, and Crispin had tasted like the world's most delicious dessert, and—

"You saved me!" Leopold suddenly exclaimed, grabbing Crispin's shoulders. "Oh my God, your mother was going to *kill* me and your brother is a colossal douchebag but you stopped them and you *saved* me and your lips have the most amazing flavor!"

Crispin stared at him, eyes wide. "Leopold," he whispered.

"You know what? Call me Leo. It's fine. Anything is fine as long as you keep kissing me." A sobering thought hit him. "You wanted to, right? It wasn't a spell or something? You seem to be, well, into me and you care enough about me to go against your mother, who's Queen of the frigging Fairies and—"

"Leopold."

The second time, Crispin said his name more firmly. And Leopold realized that what he was seeing in Crispin's eyes was genuine shock mixed with a healthy dose of terror. Which was maybe understandable, given what had just happened to them, but Leopold would have hoped there would be some other stuff there too. Like lust or affection or pride. Because Crispin *should* be proud, considering he'd just defied parental authority and fae royalty and saved Leopold and dragged them both into—

Oh.

Dragged them both *here*.

Still hanging on to Crispin, Leopold took a good look around.

They were in a large room that looked a fair amount like his Sacramento apartment. No—it looked a fair amount like *everyplace* he'd lived during his adult years, as if all the details had been mixed up, thrown in at once, and intensified. The walls were painted in patchworks of varying colors, with old band and movie posters tacked up crookedly here and there, and even a bit of Sharpie graffiti from the time he'd thought a wall decorated à la Keith Haring was a good idea. Which it would have been, had he possessed any skill as an artist.

The floor was a patchwork too, of scuffed wood, 1970s vinyl, shag carpet in technicolor hues, and threadbare rugs. The furniture—couches, chairs, tables—looked like a Goodwill clearance sale, the large kitchen had mismatched cabinets and was cluttered with pizza boxes and potato chip bags, and all across the floor lay articles of clothing as well as empty packaging that might someday make it to the recycling bin.

Also, there were no windows and no doors.

"Crispy? Where are we?"

Crispin took a few steadying breaths. "I brought us through The Door. This wasn't what I expected."

"What door?" Leopold had a sense that he should know this, but his brain felt about three steps behind. And the nearest couch looked awfully comfy. Maybe he should sit down.

"The Door you came out of, all those years ago—the Door to Chaos."

Oh. That door.

Leopold let go of Crispin and really did sit down. The old light-pink couch was squishy in the best way, as if he'd been sitting there for years, letting it mold itself to his body. Crispin remained as he was, standing in the middle of the immense room and looking stunned.

"This is Chaos," Leopold managed. It wasn't quite a question.

"Y-yes." Crispin was hugging himself, as if he were cold.

"I mean, I know it's messy. I'm not much of a clean freak. And there's sort of a lot of different stuff here, but I've never had much money, so I've stayed in all kinds of places, and...." He let the words trail away because a portion of one wall was transforming from splotchy pinkish paint to faded 1960s vintage wallpaper depicting wagon wheels and bucking broncos. A light fixture descended from the ceiling nearby, like rapidly growing fruit. It had three pendant lights with orange glass shades, one of them cracked, and two of the bulbs were burned out. The effect wasn't as disconcerting as it should have been, because the changes felt as familiar to him as the original décor, even if he'd never lived anywhere with precisely those details.

"This place feels like home," he said. And it was true. For him, it wasn't scary at all. And yeah, something gray and sort of roiling-cloudish was hovering in one corner, but it didn't seem any more threatening than the house spiders he'd so frequently ignored.

"It is your home," replied Crispin in a tiny voice.

No denying it. "Yeah. This is where I come from. I can feel it. But wait, I thought Chaos was a thing, but now I guess it's sort of a place? I don't get it."

"It's neither. Chaos is a... a concept. It can—*you* can—take physical form. You can manifest in lots of different ways. Some of them are really good, remember? Art. Magic." He managed a faint grin. "Um, sex and procreation and things like that. They all have some

Chaos mixed in, like a spice. And Chaos has a home, a center, but that home may exist physically in a number of locations."

"Like your mother's home."

Crispin nodded eagerly, apparently impressed with Leopold's insight. "Yes! Exactly. Mother's been keeping your home enclosed within hers for some time in order to protect, well, everything. But I opened The Door that time and a little of you escaped." Now Crispin winced. "I'm not sure whether to feel guilty over what I did or sad that you've mostly been imprisoned."

Leopold took a few moments to think this over and then shrugged. "Don't do either. You can't be blamed for opening my Door—you were a kid, and jeez, you kinda had some difficult family issues, didn't you? Anyway, I'm glad I got out. But also, you know, this place isn't bad. It's cozy." He patted the arm of the couch, and when he did, the fabric changed from 1980s pastels to 1970s brown velour. When he patted again, the couch became scuffed black leather that looked as if a dog might have gnawed on part of it. His seat remained equally comfortable no matter what.

"Thank you." Crispin gave one of his patented sighs, but at least a little of the tension seemed to leave his body.

"No, thank *you*. You saved my life. That was incredibly brave."

"Oh, I'm not the brave one. That's Aspin. I just do paperwork, mostly. And it turns out I only got that job because of my mother." His brow furrowed.

Leopold leapt from the couch, ran to Crispin, and grabbed his shoulders again. "You are incredibly brave. Look at what you've faced in the past two days, and you've never given up. You also never abandoned me." His throat almost closed at that last part. Nobody had ever stuck with him once things went bad. Maybe his parents might have, if not for the camels, and he couldn't blame them for that. But everyone else—foster parents, social workers, co-workers, acquaintances, short-term lovers—as soon as it became obvious that he was trouble, they ran off.

"I was daring with my mother," Crispin said thoughtfully, his tight grip around himself loosening.

"You definitely were. Crispy, if not for you, I'd have been eaten by moths or kept as a pet by dinosaurs or... or probably a lot of other awful things. But I wasn't, and I'm here, and I'm alive. And you *kissed* me." He couldn't resist that last reminder.

Crispin lifted his chin. "I did." Then he sagged a little. "But you saw my brother. He's more handsome. He's much more—"

Leopold snorted. "He's an asshat. Seriously, Crispy, I spent just a few minutes around him and that was way more than enough. How do you think he would have behaved if he'd been in your shoes?"

"He wouldn't be," Crispin scoffed. "He's not a pencil-pusher. He's a—"

"A snotwaffle. And if he *did* work for OotL, what would he have done?"

"A *snotwaffle*?" Finally a smile. "That's a... unique way to describe him."

"It really fits, though, right?"

"It really does." For a moment, Crispin frowned as if seriously considering the original question. "If Aspin had my job, he would have abandoned you as soon as he could. And if that wasn't possible, he would have helped Mother poison you."

Aha! "But *you* didn't."

Leopold could watch the full realization slowly sink into Crispin's brain. As it did, Crispin's back straightened and his eyes brightened until he was—absolutely no lie—a zillion times more beautiful that his dickweed brother. He was, in fact, more gorgeous than any human or mythical creature had ever been—and that included Orlando Bloom as Legolas, which was saying a whole lot.

It was a little unclear who initiated the next kiss. Maybe they both did it at once, which would explain why they bonked their noses together sort of painfully before managing to lock lips. It was a spectacular kiss anyway, and Crispin still tasted sweet. Leopold felt as if fireworks were exploding around them.

"Leo?" Crispin managed a word.

"Yeah?"

"Is something... exploding?"

Oh. There really *were* fireworks exploding around them. The really pretty sparkly ones and the big bright ones that made those satisfying *boom* noises, and the whole room was sort of shaking, clothing and boxes and wrappers sliding and furniture shifting and posters falling off the walls. All very thrilling, Leopold thought, until he realized that Crispin was clutching him more in fear than passion.

"Um, Leo? Could you perhaps tone things down just a bit?"

"I'm not—" Oh. Wait. He *was*. This room was his home, was *him*, and that meant he controlled everything that happened here.

Grinning wildly, Leopold stopped the pyrotechnics and replaced the fallen posters with giant photographs of windswept beaches—with the big waves actually moving because he could do that and it was pretty darn cool. He took Crispin's hand and led him to the couch, where they both sat down. A little gingerly on Crispin's part, so Leopold rolled his eyes and turned the fabric into a modern, stain-free navy polyester.

As Leopold settled in, he noticed that the gray cloud in the corner had expanded. It wasn't threatening. In fact, it looked soft and comfy, like a giant wad of cotton, and he imagined wrapping himself inside it for a long, cozy nap. Later. For now, he was focused on Crispin, who still seemed a little jumpy.

"Are you hungry? I can find us something to eat, I bet. There's this Swedish pizza I really like. Well, I dunno if it's really Swedish, but that's what they call it. It has bananas and chicken and curry and jalapeños, and it's amazing. We could have one of those. Or not—we can have whatever you really like. What's your favorite food?" It occurred to him how little he truly knew about his new friend.

"I'm partial to a fresh-baked loaf of bread and some zoucberries, when they're in season." Although Crispin answered the question, he did so a little absently, as if his mind were on something else.

"Sure. We can do that. Maybe if I go poking around in the cupboards...."

Leopold started to get up, but Crispin pulled him down. "In a little while, perhaps. We have important matters to discuss."

"Like... kissing?" Leopold asked hopefully. That was pretty important. "I can tone down the fireworks if you want. Or you can pick the colors. We can pick them together! That would be fun." It was sort of like a date activity. Ooh, a date. Maybe he should switch to better mood lighting in this place and add some music. What was good making-out music? He hadn't really done much dating, per se, and was somewhat at a loss.

Although he hadn't yet thought of a song, one started up, which surprised him until Crispin pulled Thea from his pocket. "Oh, you're here too." Crispin had perked up a bit.

"Wait, I know that song." Leopold flipped through the dusty playlist in his brain. It was from an old 80s movie about... pilots. "*Danger Zone!*" he announced triumphantly. "Thea, that's not really mood music."

She turned up the volume until Crispin gave her a little pat. "Yes. I understand. Thank you." Once she was quiet again, he tucked her away before turning to Leopold. "We need to *talk*, Leo. And not about kissing."

That was disappointing, but Leopold figured conversation would be nice too. "Sure. We could... ooh! We could share what shapes we see in the gray cloud. That's kind of romantic, right?" And he pointed at the cloud, which had grown bigger still and sort of resembled a rabbit in a tutu if he tilted his head just right. Except one ear was off. Maybe he should get up and adjust it.

Crispin held him in place, face grave. "I'm afraid I may have left a mess in... other worlds."

It was hard to concentrate, but Leopold tried because Crispin clearly felt deeply about this. "Yeah, maybe. But no biggie. We're here, and nothing is going to eat us or try to kill us. We're safe." He looked around at the state of his room and knew it was probably nothing like what Crispin was used to. "I can change up the place. Just tell me what you want it to look like. Hell, we can rotate through different themes whenever you want. It'll be great. We'll be home."

His voice broke on that last word, which surprised him. He'd never realized it before, but he'd spent his entire life feeling weird and out of place, and now he didn't. This room *was* him, and if he could share it with someone who cared about him, that would be perfect. More than he'd dreamed of.

Crispin took Leopold's hand and gave it a gentle squeeze. "You're being very thoughtful. But I can't stay here."

"Why not? Is it me? I can change. I'll be whatever you—"

"It's not you." Another squeeze. "And to be frank, you're changing already. Did you know that your hairstyle and clothing have been shifting since we arrived? And so has the color of your eyes. They're gray now."

Leopold put his free fingers against his own eyelid as if he could somehow sense the color beneath. "I.... No." His heartbeat increased and he felt a little dizzy.

"You've spent your entire life among humans, thinking you were one of them, and you became very human yourself. But here I think... I think you're going to lose that. I think you're already starting to."

Leopold tried to wrap his mind around that. "To become just... Chaos?"

Crispin gestured toward the gray cloud, which had crept closer and now... now looked an awful lot like a person, although the features were indistinct. It was holding one arm in Leopold's direction, and a part of him really, really wanted to go over and let the cloud embrace him. But Crispin was still holding his hand.

He gripped it tightly, as though it were one of those lifelines on that TV quiz show, except wasn't that a telephone call and not really a line at all?

"It's not *just* Chaos," Crispin said sadly. "Chaos is an incredibly powerful force. And Leo, if you feel that Chaos is your true nature, the you that you want to be, then I can't tell you not to. Everyone should be their true self."

Leopold swallowed. "Okay?"

"But I can't stay here with you. It would destroy me—it's not my true self. I've always been more inclined toward Order. And back home, oh, there's Minkis who will miss me, and I'd miss him. And there's the damage I've caused. I need to try to fix it."

"Damage?"

"I opened your Door again. We slipped in, but I don't know what may have slipped out. Into my mother's court. And there's the fact that OotL wanted you collected to begin with, which generally means they have need of you somehow, or will eventually, and I haven't brought you in. So there's going to be an issue to deal with there, as well."

Leopold firmed his jaw. "It doesn't have to be your issue. You didn't cause it. And as for your mother's court—"

"I know. She tried to kill you, and my brother, well, we know about him. But they're still my family." Crispin looked as if he might cry.

Leopold took a few deep breaths and tried to weigh his options.

On the one hand, there was that tempting gray cloud reaching for him. He could be happy here, he thought. Powerful. No longer the screwup who got fired from every job, evicted from every cruddy apartment, rejected by every friend and lover.

But on the other, there was Crispin. Who was the best friend he'd ever had and could, Leopold hoped, be even more.

He could keep Crispin here! That would solve everything. Sure, Crispy would complain at first, but he'd come around eventually. Leopold would make sure to cater to his every whim, to treat him like the prince he was, to make him fall so deliriously in love that he'd forget the rest of the worlds and he would—

He would be a prisoner, and Leopold would be his keeper.

The thought horrified Leopold so much that he shuddered and almost vomited.

Shaking and unsure of whether this was the right thing to do and whether he wanted to do it, Leopold stood and urged Crispin to his feet.

"Let's see if we can fix the mess together," Leopold said.

Crispin's expression transformed again, first into surprise and then pure joy. "Together? Are... are you sure?"

"Let's go, Crispy."

Leopold kissed him again, but just a peck on the lips this time because they had shit to do.

19
CRISPIN

Crispin savored the strange feeling that shimmied through him like an electric charge, trying to identify it. It was… *Happiness.*

He was so used to his day-to-day routines, feeling satisfied when he accomplished all his tasks at work. Feeling content when Minkis snuggled up next to him at night. Feeling… all sorts of things that were a pleasing color, more peach or brown or warm gray than black. Or white. *But not like this.*

This was the brilliant yellow of a fresh-bloomed sunflower. The shocking fuchsia pink of a sand flamingo from Oobert Prime. The deep, vibrant blue of the waters around a tropical isle on Earth. It suffused him with pure joy.

"So, what do you think?" Leo was staring at him with those puppy-dog eyes. But somehow they weren't so much puppy-dog as… well… somehow he had become more *Leo,* more certain, taller?

"What?"

"I said, where do we go first?" Leo frowned. "Did you hit your head on something? Or did that kiss screw with your brain? It did with mine."

Crispin blinked. "I don't know. Maybe if we...."

"Um... Crispy?" This time, it was Leo's eyes that went wide.

What now? He turned to follow Leo's gaze, fixed at a point over Crispin's left shoulder. Another Leo stood there, just like the first, but... different. His clothes were a mishmash of Leo's, bits of the various outfits he had worn. "Don't go. We miss you."

We? "I'm so sorry, but we have important things to do." Crispin spoke primly despite the fact that he was kind of unnerved.

Another Leo had appeared next to the first, this one with antlers. "Don't go. We miss you." The two mouthed it in almost perfect unison, but there was a slight dissonance in the voices.

"Leo, what's happening?" He turned back to Leo... *his* Leo—what a wonderful thing that was to think, even in these strange circumstances—who shook his head, his mouth open.

Three more of the strange apparitions appeared behind Leo, one with wings. The third one, strangely, had slitted cat eyes. "Don't go. We miss you."

The walls of the room billowed outward, as if pushed by a stray breeze. As if they were no more solid or real than fog. Or tinsel.

More and more of the Leos appeared, each one different from the next, each one pushing out the walls. Suddenly there were ten. No, twenty... no, a hundred of them now, each muttering his own version of "Don't go. We miss you."

And then he noticed his Leo. "You're... melting!"

Leo stared at him for a second before looking down at his own body.

It was, well, not so much melting as evaporating, like a thin layer of snow on the branches of Crispin's home tree when the spring came. Wisps of Leo's clothing were trailing up into the air, disappearing into it like so many tendrils of smoke.

"It's.... I can feel them. They want me back." Leo didn't sound scared.

Why aren't you scared?

"Don't go. We miss you. Don't miss. Go. We you."

The words were jumbling together in a chaotic way, which totally made sense, or at least he would have thought it did if he hadn't been overcome by a sudden panic. *I'm losing him.*

"Leo, you have to fight it!" He reached out to touch his charge's... his friend's... his lover's face, but his hand passed through it as if it were made of air.

Leo's gaze flickered to him, his eyes widening in recognition for just an instant. "It... feels so good. They want me to come home."

Maybe I should let him go. Leo was back where he belonged. This *was* his home. To the seventeen hells of Arcturus with what everyone else wanted.

Only he wouldn't be Leo anymore. He would just be another strand of Chaos. Not the charming, bumbling, unaware of how handsome he was human who Crispin had gotten to know. To care for. To....

"Leo, I love you!" *Where did that come from?* Only, as soon as he said it, he knew it was true. It had burst out of him from the depths of his soul, fully formed, something that had been growing there for days.

The room went deadly silent.

"You... love me?" Leo stared at him, his tone flat, and Crispin's heart fell to the ground with a wet, squishy thump.

He doesn't love me back. He must have imagined it all. The stolen glances, the kisses—no, those had been real, he was sure of it. But Leo wasn't like him. Leo was a literal force of nature. Who was Crispin to think he could hold on to Chaos? Even such a handsome and confounding piece of it as Leo? *I'm such a fool.*

"You love me." This time it was said with more force. The color came back into Leo's cheeks.

"Don't go. We miss—"

"Quiet!" Leo's whole being shuddered. His body firmed up, drawing the mists back in. "If we do this, we do it my way." He glared at the thousands of other Leos that surrounded him.

Crispin stared at his Leo. "What's... what's happening?"

Leo met Crispin's gaze, and this time Crispin felt as though he was the one who was melting. Leo was himself again, the lovable dolt Crispin had fallen for. "I love you too, you hidebound idiot," Leo said as he knelt and picked Crispin's heart off the floor—apparently this was quite a *literal* place—and gently pushed it back into his chest.

It started to beat again, and Crispin's world lit up. *He loves me too.*

No matter what happened next, that was enough. It filled him with wonder.

Leo frowned. "I have to deal with my... siblings." He turned away, and it should have been like the sun setting, but instead a steady warmth popped and crackled inside Crispin like a cheery fire. "On my terms, not theirs."

Leo spread his arms. "I miss you," he said, his words creating a fog in the air. "Don't go."

The thousands of Leos around them began to shudder, to lose cohesion. One by one they evaporated into gray smoke once more, but their essences—sparkling like a technicolor rainbow—drifted in streams toward Leo. He held up his arms as the first of the essences transfixed him like a spear, his hair rising into the air and filling with golden sparks.

Crispin stared.

The influx intensified. The other Leos fed their energy into him, and his whole body shifted, sometimes having antlers, sometimes wings, sometimes becoming something else entirely. But he was always recognizably Leo.

Then even the walls melted away, the whole world shuddering and fizzing and bubbling around them as it rushed to become part of Leo. Soon they were in a blank white space. Or maybe it was black, or gray? It was impossible to tell.

As the last of the essences slipped into him, Leo shivered and then collapsed, his eyes closed.

"Leo!" Crispin leapt forward, or whatever happened. Motion in an empty place was as uncertain as color. He was at Leo's side, cradling his head in his hands. "Leo, are you all right?"

He looked like Leo. He smelled like Leo. But what if he wasn't really Leo anymore?

Leo remained stubbornly unconscious, a bit of drool slipping down his chin.

He's not dead, is he? Crispin felt for a pulse. There was none. "He's... gone." *He killed himself, for me.*

His heart shattered in a million pieces. Leo was gone. Chaos was gone. He was trapped in this awful, empty place and Leo was gone and Chaos was gone and he had probably just destroyed everything and Leo was gone—

"Hello?"

Crispin's heart raced at that single word. *He's alive!*

Leo's eyes opened wide. But now they sparkled with rainbow hues instead of the dull gray that had come before. His eyes fixed on Crispin. "Who are you?"

Crispin's heart threatened to drop out of his chest again. "You... don't remember me?"

A grin spread across Leo's face. "Of course I do. I was just messing with you."

"But how? You were dead. I checked your pulse—"

"This place isn't real, remember?" He reached up and rested his fingertips on Crispin's neck. "You don't have one either."

Crispin touched his own neck, and sure enough, he seemed as dead as Leo. He grinned.

Leo pulled Crispin's face to his.

This time, there were no fireworks.

In any case, they didn't need them. As Crispin discovered over the next few... minutes? Hours? Time seemed meaningless here. He and his love became one in a way far more meaningful and beautiful than whatever had transpired with the Chaos creature moments before. And it was better than momentary pyrotechnics.

When it was over at last, they lay side by side in the nothingness, panting.

"I could stay here forever, just like this." Crispin had never felt so glorious. So at ease. So right.

Leo's home reminded him of the Un-Place. Were they one and the same?

Leo shook his head. "Damage to fix, remember?"

He sighed. "I know." He stared at the blankness—what would be sky in another world—and wondered at such a perfect moment. A stray thought occurred to him, dragging him back to the present. "What did you do? Just before...?"

A lazy grin on Leo's face told Crispin he knew exactly what "before" meant. "I made them come to me. To become a part of Leopold, and not the other way around."

"So you're now...?"

"Mr. Chaos?" He grinned. "Yeah, pretty much." He shook like a dog, and a whole world of riotous colors exploded out of him, spreading out into a great open field of flowers under a blue sun. "Pretty neat, huh?"

Crispin sat up, hugging his knees, concern impinging on his pure ecstasy. "But are you really still *Leo*?"

Leo thought about it for a moment. "I think so. I can leave the rest behind. It's like... swimming in an ocean, maybe? I can dry off, but I'll always have a bit of it with me."

"You'll carry some of it with you?"

"I guess." His face scrunched up in that adorable way. "Are you sure you want to be with me? Things tend to be a little... unpredictable with the LeoMonster."

"After all that happened, and you ask me that?" Crispin laughed. "I... I think we're *meant* to be together. I can't explain it any better than that. You're the missing part of me." Maybe it had happened the first time he'd opened the Door, when he'd been brushed by what had become Leo. Maybe it didn't matter *why*.

A flight of butterflies in a thousand colors exploded out of the vast nothing, surrounding them in chaotic color.

Chaos wasn't something to fear. He understood that now. "Of course I want to be with you."

Leo smiled, and the butterflies vanished, leaving just the two of them. "So, how do we get started fixing the damage we caused?"

Crispin was grateful for that shared pronoun. "Well, we need to fix Thea. Can you take us to a particular place and time?"

Leo closed his eyes. "Like where?"

"The Office of the Lost. Early in the morning, before everyone else is there."

"Not sure. It feels... I think if I concentrate on what I want, I can take us where we need to be. Maybe. But it may not be what you expect, and I will be... limited once we get there."

Crispin frowned. "Limited how?"

"I can do anything here." He held up his hand, and clouds gathered above them, thunder clashing with rain. He waved again and they disappeared. "But in the real world, not so much. I'm still figuring it out. I've never been corporeal for this long, before... well, before being Leo."

Crispin kissed his cheek. "And you have no idea how glad I am of that." He stood, dusting off his pants. Well, of course there was dirt in... Chaoslandia? He held out his hand. "Let's go. Are you ready?"

Leo grinned. "Thought you'd never ask."

Their hands touched, and the world dissolved around them.

20

LEOPOLD

eopold's head was swirly.

That was pretty excusable, given what he'd been through lately and what he'd discovered about the universe in general and himself specifically. He had an odd duality going on in his head, where on one side he was Leopold Lane, screwup and loser. And on the other he was an ancient, mighty force of nature. That was enough to make his head spin.

He was also a guy who'd just had a beautiful, ecstatic, sexy experience with an elf—excuse me, a fae—who loved him. And whom he loved back.

It was that final factor—the amazing new *Crispiness* of his existence—that made him focus enough to open his eyes and see where he'd brought them.

And then he sighed because it was a lot less interesting than his home. "It's an office."

Crispin, still holding his hand, gave him a look. "Yes. Office of the Lost."

"Right. But you know. Fae and transporting and alternate universes and magic. I was expecting something more... weird."

The vast room in which they now stood looked like a very ordinary workspace, like a call center. There were neat rows of identical heavy white desks, most with neat stacks of paper in one corner and little plastic cups filled with pens. Some had something that resembled a large electronic tablet, and others had little arrangements of framed photos or knickknacks. Each desk was paired with a chair that looked ergonomic but likely wasn't all that comfortable.

It wouldn't have been out of place as the offices of Boring, Large, and Corporate LLC back on Earth.

The floor in this room was shiny and white while the ceiling, far overhead, had built-in light fixtures softly glowing. The white walls were hung with reminder posters about workplace safety and reporting requirements. "Why do you have to submit Form 242GH-X2 when you collect items from Methezuno City?"

Crispin blinked at him. "What?"

Leopold pointed at the sign where he'd just read that.

"Oh." Crispin shrugged slightly. "Because if you store them too close to anything from Xaunas they'll explode. Leo, is that relevant right now?"

"Guess not." Crispin was in a mood, Leopold thought, which was understandable. No one liked going to the office. "So this is where you work? Which desk is yours?"

Now it was Crispin's turn to point. His spot was near the edge of the room beneath a large banner reminding everyone that *Every Lost Item Is Important*. His desk had no photos or knickknacks, no screen, not even a pile of paper. There was, however, a tiny pile of nuts on one corner of the desk.

"Acorns?" Leopold asked.

"Sometimes Minkis hides them in my pockets, and I discover them after I get to work." He sighed, feeling a tad nostalgic, and then shook himself slightly. "I've never seen the place this quiet. Usually there are people bustling around, which can actually be a little distracting if I'm trying to get things done. But I don't really mind. It makes me feel as if I'm a part of something important."

"You are."

Crispin made a face. "I was. Now... I doubt I still have a position here. Don't get me wrong, though. I'd rather have you than my old job."

Leopold smiled, and then Thea started playing Etta James singing "At Last," which reminded them both why they were here. "How do we get Thea fixed?" Leopold asked.

"Not in here. We need to go to the Necessary Room."

"The bathroom?" Leopold remembered the one he'd accidentally exploded at Juzir's apartment and felt a pang of guilt.

"What? No, the Necessary Room." A patented Crispin Sigh. Leopold was falling in love with those too. "It's where we get items that are necessary for our missions."

"You're not going to just replace Thea, are you?" Leopold had grown rather fond of the little device's periodic musical outbursts.

Crispin clutched the phone protectively to his chest. "No! Of course not. Come on."

Leopold followed him across the room. In his wake, desktop items shifted around and lost their perfect alignment with the edge of the desks they sat upon. Leo snickered. *A little creative chaos.*

They came to a door with a sign asking, *Have You Maximized Your Perfecality Score Today?* Crispin blew a raspberry at it. Leo grinned and said, "I'm rubbing off on you."

Crispin opened the door and led them down a dim corridor that reminded Leopold of one of the elementary schools he'd attended, where he'd often been sent to the principal's office due to some mishap he'd caused. This place even smelled like chalk and that weird floor cleaner the janitor had used. The stuff came in an enormous white bucket that, it turned out, did not make an adequate footstool for an eight-year-old who tried to reach the top shelf in the cleaning closet simply because he wondered what was stored up there. That eight-year-old never did solve the mystery, because the lid had cracked, the bucket had tipped over, and—

"Leo? Are you doing this?"

Snapping back to the present, Leopold realized that the OotL now looked *exactly* like that school corridor, complete with posters urging Kindness, Diligence, and Respect, and a poorly done mural featuring the school mascot, Beverly Beaver.

Leopold blinked, and everything snapped back to the original OotL. No beavers. "Sorry."

Crispin was staring at him, wide-eyed. "You can affect the OotL HQ building. That's impressive. Your powers must be...."

Leopold was going to apologize again, even though the strength of his powers wasn't within his control, but then Crispin kissed his cheek. "Impressive," Crispin repeated.

Smiling widely, Leopold grabbed Crispin's hand and they walked some more. And more. They passed closed gray doors, all of them stenciled with a series of numbers and letters, but didn't stop at any of them. "What's in those rooms?" Leopold asked.

"The Collection, of course."

"There are a lot of rooms."

"Oh, this is only one wing! You can't even imagine how many items are here. OotL has been collecting for millennia, from thousands of different worlds and timelines across the Connected Worlds. I'm not even sure how big the Collection is—we have Auditors who keep track of that—but it's enormous and growing every day."

It reminded him of that old movie—the one where they hid the Ark of the Covenant in some dusty old warehouse at the end, so no one would ever find it. He was also reminded of how much Crispin loved his job and how proud he was of what he did, and that made him sad because now it seemed likely that Crispin would get fired. Well, you know what? If Leopold was so all-fired powerful, he ought to be able to do something about that. He had no idea what, but maybe it would come to him. For now he should be concentrating at the task at hand. Except... those doors were intriguing.

"Can I open one and peek inside?" What wonderful things must be behind those doors!

"No!"

"Just one?" Leopold fluttered his eyelashes in what he hoped was a seductive way, but he'd never actually tried that before and probably just looked as if he had something in his eye.

"Not even one. Leo, the items we collect are kept in special environments that are unique to them and suited to their preservation. You could open a door and have an ocean gush out, or you could fall into the deepest reaches of space, or—"

"Yeah, I got it." Honestly, he was sorely tempted to open one anyway, but he restrained himself. Which, he thought as they continued to walk, was almost a first for him. He rarely controlled his impulses. But maybe part of being really powerful was learning to use your power... well, carefully. Chaos didn't have to be everywhere all at once. He could just sprinkle some in now and then in ways that were interesting or even helpful. As Crispin had told him, Chaos was the root of magic and of art. Maybe other things too. Like what about genetic mutations? Didn't those happen sort of haphazardly? He remembered seeing a TV show about that once, how mutations were the source of evolutionary change. Without him, everyone would be just a single-celled bacterium floating around in the ocean.

"I'm glad we're not bacteria," Leopold said.

Crispin gave him a quizzical look before shrugging. "Me too."

They passed a grand atrium that looked like a giant post office, filled with side halls containing thousands of tiny doors, each with a lock—probably where they kept some of the smaller objects. Crispin turned left, and they passed into another hall of doorways.

After another minute or so—how frigging long *was* this hallway? —Leopold asked, "What would my special environment have been?"

"Pardon me?"

"If you'd collected me and brought me back here as planned."

"Oh." Crispin frowned. "I have no idea. We have other fae in charge of Preservation. I'm on the Collection side."

"Of course."

The question kept Leopold occupied for a while, long enough for them to reach a door that was different from the others—much larger and appearing to be made of thick metal, like a bank vault. The symbol in the center of the door looked exactly like an enormous eye. It even blinked, which was disconcerting.

"Is this the Necessary Room?"

Crispin shook his head. "It's the Oracle."

"Oh, the one that gives orders to go collect stuff. What does the Oracle look like?"

"No idea. I've never seen them and I don't know anyone who has. There are messengers who convey the Oracle's auguries."

This OotL place was a lot more bureaucratic than Leopold had imagined. He wondered if there were opportunities for upward mobility or lateral transfers. Before he could ask about that, though, they reached another door, this one made of what looked like ancient wood. And it had a helpful sign announcing that it was, in fact, the Necessary Room.

Crispin pushed the door inward—there was no knob—and they stepped inside.

It looked like... Target on an acid trip. Rows of shelves and racks stuffed with clothing, weapons, odd-looking machinery, fishing gear, shovels, baskets, nets, seashells, rocks, protective gear, books, kitchenware, sacks of coins, and a lot of other things that Leopold couldn't identify. Each category of items came in a mind-blowing variety.

"Oooh... I love this place," Leopold breathed. He could have spent years poking around, assessing what things were and how they worked. Like that reddish thing just to his right. Was it a sweater? If so, it had three arms, and he couldn't tell—

"I tend to find it a bit overwhelming." Crispin was blinking, apparently taking in the disordered order of it all.

Maybe it was the disordered order that appealed to Leopold. "It's... a lot," he acknowledged, trying to see it from Crispin's point of view.

"You never know what you might require. When I was sent to

collect the sap from the last qebhe tree in the Swamp of Lullan, for example, I had to— Well, it doesn't matter right now."

Leopold smiled warmly at… his lover. "You know, later, when we have time? I'd be thrilled to hear about some of your collecting adventures."

The tips of Crispin's ears turned bright red when he blushed, which was adorable. "They're really not that interesting."

"I don't believe that," replied Leopold with complete sincerity. What he really wanted to do was lick those ear points, or maybe nibble on them, oh so gently. But again, he was practicing self-control. Master of his own domain, and all that. "So how do you find what you need in this place?"

"Usually I walk in and it's just there. Right in front of me. But now there's nothing in front of me but you, and you're amazing. I like you in front of me. Or behind me. Or under me—that one's pretty good—or…." Crispin cleared his throat. "But right now we need something to fix Thea." He looked around, frowning.

Gently, Leopold took the phone from Crispin's hand and stared at the screen. It was now cracked so badly that the entire thing was opaque. If they were back in Sacramento, they could take her to a cell-phone repair shop, but Leopold wasn't sure they'd be able to deal with this big of a mess. Besides, it wasn't just broken glass that was the problem. Hadn't Juzir said that some Chaos had gotten into her?

Wait. Chaos. That was him. "Crispy? I don't think we need to fix Thea at all."

"But look at her. And if we're going to move between places—"

"I can do that for us, remember?" Leopold smiled at the phone. "Hey, Thea? I'm thinking that maybe you and I could work together to help fix some of the mess I've made."

"*We've* made," Crispin muttered.

But Leopold ignored him and addressed Thea again. "Do you think that would work? Without us needing to repair you, I mean?"

Thea buzzed happily, emitted a shower of sparks like a Fourth of

July sparkler, and began playing a song. "Is that Donny *Osmond*?" Leopold listened and recognized the song. One of his foster mothers had been a big Osmonds fan. "We Can Make It Together," he announced triumphantly to Crispin.

Crispin reached over to give Thea a gentle pat. "All right, then. I suppose our next step is to clean things up, and probably the best place to do that is at my mother's court." He didn't look remotely enthusiastic, and Leopold didn't blame him.

"No sweat. We can do this, Crispy. I know it." A slight stretch maybe, but sometimes a pep talk was called for, and he'd never had the chance to give one before. "The three of us are a formidable force. Like something out of a Marvel movie, but better. With Thea's brains, your courage and organizational skills, and my, um, Chaos, we can accomplish anything."

"I'm not sure that's true." Crispin took a few deep breaths and straightened his shoulders. "But we're sure as heck going to try. Guys, please zap us to—"

The door slammed open behind them, and they spun to see an enormous person with yellowish skin, tiny eyes, and a couple of tusklike teeth staring at them. There was a badge on a lanyard around their neck, and their houndstooth suit had actual teeth—fangs, really—instead of buttons.

"Curator Moscow!" Her bellow caused items to fall from the nearest shelves. "You've finally completed your assignment. It took you long enough." She gave Leopold a once-over, her gaze dismissive, as if he were no more important than a hat rack. "Make sure you submit the paperwork promptly and properly. Your perfecality score is already in the toilet."

Crispin swallowed audibly, mouthing "sorry" at Leopold and then stepping in front of him. "Hello, Supervisor Krönk."

21

CRISPIN

This time it was Crispin's head that felt swirly.

He'd already given up on his perfecality score—and oh how that hurt just to think it. He'd been the top curator in the department for three quarters running and had the somewhat sad but still significant blue ribbons to prove it.

And now Bidulla—he refused to think of her as his supervisor, and when in the mincing munchkins had that happened?—was about to take his beautiful bit of Chaos and stuff him into a room somewhere for all eternity. Or at least until he was needed.

Wait, that's it! It was so obvious, he wasn't sure why he hadn't seen it before. He stepped in front of Leo. "I... can't let you take him, ma'am."

She stared at him through her huge gold-rimmed cat-eye glasses, which did nothing to soften her fearsome appearance.

"Excuse me, *Curator* Moscow?" She somehow managed to imbue his title with the exact same intonation she might have used for the word for *excrement.* Or *chocolate.* Bidulla Krönk hated chocolate.

Crispin stood firm, though his voice hemmed and hawed a bit.

Have to take it out behind the woodshed and show it who was boss, later. "Well, you see, actually, he's my necessary."

She frowned. "Your *what?*"

She might as well have said *Your double dark chocolate ice cream with chocolate drizzle on top?*

"My *necessary.*" He tried to pull himself up to her height, aware that poor Leo was practically shaking with fear behind him. "I came here to find out what I needed for the next part of my mission, and nothing appeared. Except him." Poor Leo. He was—

Laughter burst out behind him.

Laughing. He's laughing. Maybe it was some kind of nervous breakdown. Bidulla had inspired those in the past, on occasion, driving more than one curator out of the job sobbing and—at least once—rending their own garments. But laughter? "Um, Leo? Trying to make a point here."

"It's just... she looks... have you ever seen Bugs Bunny? When he dresses up like an opera singer with that Viking helmet and the long blond braids?"

And indeed, Bidulla was changing, her skin turning a fluffy gray with patches of white, her tusks shrinking and her two front teeth elongating, her long brown braids turning a cheery yellow.

"Leo, stop it," Crispin whispered out of the side of his mouth. "*Not* helping."

Leo grumbled and Bidulla snapped back to her old, ogreish self.

Crispin wondered whether the changes Leo made to the world were permanent or if they would wear off when he went somewhere else. *What if he changes me? What if... he already has?*

He'd been part deer, part moth, maybe part dinosaur, and he'd assumed it was caused by the strange journey they were on. But what if Leo had done it? *What if he changed how I feel, too?*

It was not something he had the luxury of worrying about right now.

Bidulla, distracted, stared at her once-again-brown tresses. "What in the Dark Eye of Pothos was that?"

Crispin took advantage of her distraction, shoving Thea into his pocket and grabbing Leo's hand. "Take me home." He'd scooped up the pile of acorns on his desk when Leo wasn't looking, and now he just needed to be somewhere safe. Somewhere familiar. "Can you do that?"

Leo's eyes met his. "I... think so. Can you picture it, really hard, in your head? If you do that, I think I'll have less chance of screwing it up."

"What are you two up to? Crispin, it's not safe to let this little piece of chocolate run around unhindered...."

She'd actually said "chocolate" that time. He was sure of it. "I'll file all the reports when I get back." That was all he could promise, and it would have to do. "*Now*, Leo."

"Buckle your seatbelt."

Crispin pictured his home, the beautiful old oak tree with the little round windows spilling out golden light, and a big blue door, welcoming him home.

The world dissolved as the Necessary Room lost shape and color, and the last thing he saw was Bidulla's face. "Curator Moss'caladin, stop that at once, or I'm filing a Form 739w on your sorry little desk fae a—"

Then everything was gone, including Leo.

Consciousness came back to Crispin in dribs and drabs. First he heard birdsong, little *tweets* and *powits* somewhere far above.

Next, he felt something hard and sharp—and cold—poking into his back.

He moaned and shifted, trying to find a more comfortable position, only to encounter something equally annoying pressing into the other side.

He blinked, his eyes adjusting to the green filtered light.

A forest. He sat up quickly, then wished he hadn't. His head swam, little butterflies cheerfully making the rounds just at the edge of his sight.

He took a deep breath, taking in the familiar wet, loamy scent of the forest. *My forest.*

His stomach settled, followed in short order by his head, and he looked around, finding the source of the sharp pointy things that had bedeviled his back. The toes of Leo's boots.

"Leo!" He scrambled over the moldering leaves that comprised the forest floor. His earlier worries that Leo might have changed him felt petty now, contrived. Ungrateful. Leo had saved him again. Saved them both. Why *shouldn't* Crispin have feelings for his Chaos Man?

Leo's eyes were closed, his face pale. "Leo, are you all right?"

No response. Crispin checked his pulse. It was strong enough, but clearly something was wrong.

He looked around. He knew this place; he was home. Not inside his tree house, but close. To the left was the babbling brook whose soothing sounds put him to sleep at night. To his right, the tiny meadow where the fairies danced under the silver moons. And that meant....

A delighted chittering greeted him.

"Minkis!"

The gray squirrel approached cautiously, sniffing at him as if he wasn't sure whether Crispin was real.

Small wonder. I've been gone for days. He reached into his pocket and held out an acorn.

Minkis stood on his hind legs, took it greedily, and dashed back toward the giant oak tree they both called home.

Crispin breathed a sigh of relief. He got his hands under Leo. *Why couldn't you have wished yourself a bit lighter?* Still, he managed to lift Leo's unconscious form. With a mighty huff, he started toward home.

Crispin whistled merrily, and Thea, perched on a little wooden table next to his wash basin, hummed right along with him.

He'd managed to get Leo onto the bed without too many of the leaves that had accompanied him from the forest floor, and his... paramour, he decided, was now in what appeared to be a blissful state of sleep.

It felt good to be home.

Around him, the cozy walls of his tree abode exuded a welcoming warmth, surrounding the wide living space inside. He'd engaged the services of a local dryad when he'd first moved in, and the rather handsome young creature had coaxed the tree to put out a variety of helpful branches, forming cabinets, hooks and wooden towel racks, and even a platform of roots which was now the base of his bed.

He'd furnished the place with colorful bits and pieces that he'd collected during his travels, a practice that was sometimes frowned upon although there was no actual rule against it as long as they were unimportant things, ones that weren't needed by OotL. And he always paid the locals a fair price. There were the forest-green curtains from Phraxis, a very cuddly semi-animated shaggy brown rug from a dragon weaver on Ferkin Four, and the glorious multicolored quilt from Methezuno City, each panel hand-quilted by a family of ogre nuns, on which Leo was currently resting comfortably.

He finished washing his arms and neck and face. It felt magnificent to be clean again, even if only from the middle up.

He'd need to check his cold stores next to find something to whip up for them to eat.

He was so fixated on the task, looking over sealed satchels of venison and wild blackberries and a whole container of zorfnen from —where else?—Zorf, that he failed to hear the rustling behind him.

"Hey Crispy, why is there a cat on my chest?" The bleary voice brought Crispin to full awareness, like a hoarbear after the first of spring.

He strangled a scream. Minkis was peering back at him from the aforementioned chest perch, his eyes decidedly slitted and catlike, his fabulous bushy tail now a long, gray snakelike thing.

Crispin bounded across the room and picked up Minkis, who looked at him with a disturbingly catlike feral cunning. "Put him back!"

Leo stared at him, confused. "I don't have him. You do." He looked around. "This is a crazy place. I once had a dream about a place like this after I had too many of Joey Taylor's edibles. Am I dreaming?"

"No, you're awake. This is my house—" Crispin sputtered to a halt. "You... did something to Minkis. He's *not* supposed to be a cat." His former squirrel squirmed around in his arms, freed himself with the magical prowess of a shapeshifter, and dropped to the ground, landing feet-first. Satisfied, he started licking his soft gray coat with his tongue.

"A squirrel? Oh. I just... when I woke, he was staring at me, and he reminded me of this cat I had at one of my foster homes. His name was Blackie, which was weird because he was entirely gray, except for his toes, which were—"

Crispin put his hands on his hips. "Change him back, *please*?"

"You get really grumpy when you're at home." Nevertheless, Leo closed his eyes, creased his brow, and with an audible pop, Minkis's tail fluffed out, his ears shrank, and his eyes moved back onto the sides of his head. The little creature shuddered, looked up at him with a clearly betrayed look—whether for being turned into a cat or being changed back, Crispin couldn't tell—and scampered up a branch into the dark recesses of the ceiling.

Crispin sighed. He knew that Leo couldn't help it. He should be grateful that his whole tree house hadn't transformed into—what did they call them on Earth?—a trailer.

He sat on the edge of the mattress, which was stuffed with astral down from Rigel 3, and put a hand on Leo's forehead. It felt normal —warm, but goodish warm. "It's not your fault. But we'll have to help you get a better handle on your Chaos. Can't have you changing the world willy-nilly and causing...."

"Chaos?" The smile Leo gave him lit a spark of pure joy in Crispin's heart.

He snorted a very un-desk-fae-like snort. "I suppose a certain bit of that is inevitable." And it would certainly keep things interesting between them. "You don't seem sick." He leaned over and kissed his paramour.

But he wanted to do more. They were alone with a bed in the place he felt safest, after all. That nagging doubt about whether Leo had changed him resurfaced, but he ruthlessly pushed it down.

Maybe he could strip Leo, one piece of clothing at a time, and wash his delicious body with a warm, soapy sponge....

Minkis made a sudden reappearance, chittering wildly, at the same time that a loud knock sounded at the tree house's only door.

Leo sat up, exposing his beautiful, even if not muscularly impressive, chest. "Are we expecting someone?"

Crispin sighed. Drop-ins were unusual but not unheard of. This part of the forest was rather sparsely settled, but sometimes Mrs. Dollywip would send one of her nineteen children over for a cup of this or a bowl of that, and old Meeser Crowflup occasionally needed help with something above the dwarf's reach in his own subterranean den.

He just hoped it wasn't his boss. *Should have set the wards.*

With one last longing look at Leo's mostly-supine form, he got up and followed Minkis to the heavy round door. "Coming!"

"You sure it's safe?" Leo's voice sounded uncharacteristically worried.

"You can always *Chaos* them into a pumpkin, or something."

Leo laughed. "Why is it always a pumpkin? And hey, we're using *Chaos* as a verb now?"

Crispin ignored him and opened the door a crack. Only to find the absolutely last person he ever expected to see again.

22

LEOPOLD

Leopold had planned to advise Crispin to sue Keebler for cultural appropriation—if that was a thing in the... Connected Worlds? Was that how the Mother of Fae had referred to her realm? Crispin's home looked like something right out of a cookie advertisement, only larger and better. Leopold would have preferred more clutter, maybe a few precarious piles of things here and there, but he liked the place nonetheless. Even better, he enjoyed lying in bed with Crispin stroking his face and kissing him, and he had been hoping things would progress satisfactorily from there... when suddenly the not-cat raised a fuss and someone knocked on the door.

Crispin had simply sighed in response, but Leopold was in absolutely no mood for peopling. Or for ogreing or elfing or anything but alone time with Crispin followed by a long sleep in a good bed. And maybe a shower. He seriously considered zapping whoever it was to somewhere far away. But then a man stepped inside the treehouse, and Leopold reconsidered.

The guy was... godlike was probably the best description Leopold could think of. God as in Greek god, or maybe Thor as played by

Chris Hemsworth. Well over six feet tall, with broad shoulders and a bodybuilder physique. Waist-length hair that shone like spun gold, amethyst-colored eyes, and a square chin with a genuine goddamn cleft. He wore what appeared to be an expensive custom suit and pale pink shirt with the top buttons artfully undone.

He was a romance-novel cover come to life, and Leopold was suspicious of him at once. Crispin's extremely nervous expression didn't help one bit.

"Uh, Qylzryd, this is, my Leo—um, Leopold Lane." Crispin managed a weak smile. "Leo, this is Qylzryd Wolfsword."

They shook hands, and of course Qylzryd's paw dwarfed Leopold's hand, and his grip could have compressed iron. "A pleasure to meet you," he boomed. Ugh, his smile looked like something from a dentist's billboard.

Crispin was doing a nervous twitching thing. "Um, Qyl? Nice of you to drop by, but we were kind of busy—"

"I can see that." Qylzryd waved at Leopold's bare chest.

What happened to my shirt? Leopold had obviously lost track of some recent details.

"Look, Qyl. Now is not a good time for whatever—"

The man talked right over him. "Remember that wonderful restaurant we went to? The one that served wild game I hunted myself? Well, yesterday I shot a huge gamjeebeast—probably a record-breaker—and that restaurant is going to have some gorgeous gamjeebeast steaks tonight. Come with me. My treat." He waggled his eyebrows suggestively.

Before Leopold could work up an appropriate response—like turning Qylzryd into a pumpkin—Crispin intervened. "Leo, Qyl and I—"

"Are lovers," Qylzryd interrupted.

"*Were* lovers. I mean, barely even…. It was a two-night stand. Three years ago." Crispin narrowed his eyes. "And you weren't that great. Why are you here?"

Leopold realized he didn't look very scary, especially shirtless and… god, in his underwear. He wasn't tall and didn't have abs of steel. But he was Chaos Personified, dammit, and that should mean something. Like that this ex had better skedaddle, pronto. "We were busy," Leopold said with what he hoped was a cold glare. "Get lost before I do something you'll regret."

"You?" Qylzryd scoffed. He took a step closer, towering over Leopold and bending his arms to flex his biceps.

Okay, not even a pumpkin. Squashhood was too good for this jerk. Leopold was going to turn him into something disgusting, like a hunk of cheese that had been sitting in the back of a refrigerator for a couple of years. Or maybe that weird pinkish slimy stuff that sometimes appeared near the shower drain in one of Leopold's former apartments.

Before he could make a decision—and he did note that Crispin was doing nothing to deter him—there was another knock at the door. Crispin threw his hands up in annoyance, stomped over, and flung the door open.

This time it was someone Leopold did recognize. Juzir the archosaur rushed inside, almost knocking Crispin over, and threw something that looked like a Super Ball at Leopold. When the object hit Leopold's chest, it disintegrated into a little puff of sparkly powder.

And suddenly Leopold couldn't move. Like, at all. Well, his lungs and heart still functioned, which was good, and he could roll his eyes and blink. But otherwise he was as motionless as a marble statue. He couldn't even make any sound except a slight groan. And when he tried to muster his Chaos powers… zilch.

Crispin gave an angry roar. He ran to Leopold, shouting, and shook him, but all he succeeded in doing was to knock Leopold to the floor. It hurt when Leopold's shoulder landed, but at least his stiff neck kept his head from conking against the wood.

"What in all seven Dicharthian hells!" Crispin yelled. He tried to get at Juzir, possibly to physically attack him, but Qylzryd stepped between them and kept Crispin away.

"I am really sorry," said Juzir, peeking out from behind the big man.

Crispin roared again, quite capably. "What did you do to him?" His voice had reached a volume Leopold never would have expected from a well-behaved desk fae.

"Nothing bad, don't worry. It's an immobilization spell combined with a damper hex so he can't do anything... unwise."

"He didn't mean to blow up your bathroom!"

"He blew up your bathroom?" Qylzryd started laughing, and Leopold found that, yes, he could hate him even more than he had initially. Then Minkis dropped down from a branch, bit Qylzryd hard in the shin, and darted away. Although it didn't make Qylzryd drop his guard, his laughter turned into a muttering growl as his expensive suit pants were marred by a growing bloodstain, which Leopold found gratifying.

Juzir had his three-fingered hands up. "This isn't about the bathroom, Crispin. Your employers called and asked for some help. You can't have something dangerous like that"—he pointed at Leopold—"just running around!" Leopold very much wished he could at least call Juzir some choice names. He couldn't even scowl properly.

Crispin was still furious. "He's a *he*, not a *that*. And I love him."

"That's not even a real person, buddy. That's Chaos Incarnate, and the damage it could cause.... The damage it's *already* caused! I've heard a couple of reports about your mother's court, and they don't sound good."

At this point Leopold was ready to turn everyone but Crispin and Minkis into the stuff you scrape off your shoes after walking through a cow pasture. But he couldn't, and when he strained his hardest to use his powers, it *hurt* as if someone had dumped ground glass into his chest cavity.

"You can't do this!" Crispin's face was bright red with anger. "I thought you were my friend."

Juzir might have blushed, but how could you tell with a

dinosaur? Anyway, he should have blushed. "I am. But this situation's just too dangerous. I'm sorry."

A small chaotic scene followed, unfortunately none of it induced by Leopold's now-deactivated powers. Qylzryd hoisted him up and over his shoulder as if Leopold were a length of tree trunk. Crispin surged forward in an attempt to stop him, but Juzir threw a rubber ball at *him* this time, and then Crispin was frozen in midair, his face fixed in an expression of horror and rage.

Minkis bit Qylzryd again—this time on the other leg—and then Juzir froze him too.

Crispin made desperate grunting noises, which Leopold knew from personal experience were the equivalent of trying to bodily throw himself at Juzir to claw his neck out. He'd never loved his fae more.

"Don't worry," Juzir said to Crispin. "The spell will wear off soon." He marched out the door with Qylzryd hard at his heels.

Leopold caught one last glimpse of the Crispin-statue suspended some feet above the floor before Leopold was hauled through the door.

23
CRISPIN

Crispin's rage burned white-hot—stronger than the sun that peeked through the windows as it settled toward the edge of the world—but to no avail. He was trapped in Juzir's spell, and there was no way out until the abominable thing wore itself out.

It gave him time to think. And to stew in his anger.

He'd given his whole life to service at the OotL. He'd done everything they asked, and done it exceptionally well. His former perfecality score said as much. So what if he'd had his mother's help getting the job? He'd made it his own, and he was proud of that.

And this was the thanks he got. They'd sent someone into his home to take away the one person he cared for. His anger surged anew, molten lava on the shores of an acid lake. He'd been to Hellvin once to collect an incendiary fungus, and the visit hadn't been pleasant.

Think, Crispin. Think. If only there was a way to free himself from this spell sooner. Every second counted.

All magic is based on Chaos.

It was something his mother and tutors had pounded into him as a child. And yet he'd never been able to draw on it like the others. Instead, he had an almost pathological sense of order, a trait he'd shown early in life, being nearly obsessed with keeping things in place. In a human, Leo might have described it as OCD. In a fae, it was just strange.

His obsession with Order was part of the reason his brother had always hated him, he was sure, and why his mother had sent him away.

It was also why he was so good at his job.

Sometimes he could manifest it in the real world, as he had done at the Pond of Disappointment on Vlotho, saving them both—so he'd thought—from the attack of the Chaos Cloud.

Order was the natural enemy of Chaos. *So where does my power come from?*

Maybe if he imagined himself imposing Order on the spell that confined him....

He pictured himself drawing perfectly square boxes in the air, one after another. They were all exactly the same size, each one a replica of the first, gradually creating a circular cage on all sides of him.

Searing blue squares appeared around him, lighting the tree house in an eerie glow. *It's working!*

He held his concentration, creating Order with the skill of an artisan, connecting one box to the next until they finally surrounded him. As the last box was completed, the very air around him shimmered, the world shook, and the force that had been holding him up dumped him unceremoniously onto the floor, forcing the air from his lungs in a sharp *ooof.*

Blue lines shattered and dissolved into the air.

When he could breathe again, Crispin grinned. "It worked!"

His eyes fell upon poor Minkis, who had played a hero's role, if unsuccessfully, in the Great Raid on Crispin's Tree House. He scampered over to his best friend's side and repeated the exercise, this time using his hands to draw the squares, and soon Minkis was free too.

The squirrel leapt onto one shoulder and danced, merrily and manically, between the left and right one, his furry tail tickling Crispin's neck and ears.

"Happy to see you again too, my little friend."

Crispin's mind was abuzz. Without Leo, he was stuck here on Torevor, unless he could find a way to summon help.

Why had Bidulla sent Juzir and Qyl—not one of the other curators—after him? It was not unheard of to use off-the-books help, just rare. Maybe she'd foreseen the need to have someone with Juzir's ability to contain Leo. His wizarding abilities were far stronger than the average curator's... in fact, Crispin didn't even know the full extent of his strength.

Or maybe she didn't want the Office to know about it.

Out of habit, he reached into his pocket for Thea.

Her cracked screen lit up, and he recognized the Earth song she played. He'd heard it on a foray to London, retrieving the Crown Jewels and replacing them with exact replicas.

"God Save the Queen?" Did she mean his mother?

He had no intention of returning to the Estate. He'd been burned there more than once, and his mother was just as bad as Bidulla. Besides, he had no way of going there, unless....

He slapped his head. Why hadn't he thought of it before? *I am a bumble-footed idiot.*

"Thea, I'm going to try something."

She emitted what he hoped was a pleased sound.

He set her down on his table and pulled up one of the hand-carved oak chairs.

Minkis scampered up another chair to land neatly on the far side of the tabletop, his little nose twitching and his head darting back and forth.

"I'm going to try to fix Thea." He closed his eyes, working to remember what her magical circuit board looked like. He'd seen them before in the Production Room. With his memory as a guide, he began to draw an intricate and very orderly series of squares and circles and squiggly lines in the air above her. The details were important, and he could see them in his head as clearly as if he'd noted them only yesterday.

It took longer than he anticipated, but soon enough he had the outlines finished. He looked it over one last time, satisfying himself that it was as accurate as he could manage. "Wish me luck."

Minkis chittered.

He pushed the construct down onto Thea's rectangular form, where it settled in and vanished with a sizzle.

Nothing happened.

Minkis edged toward the phone, sniffing the air.

Damn it all to Hellvin. "I'm afraid I've failed. Again." Crispin sighed as he pushed his chair away from the table.

He was just starting to get up when a strange sizzling sound issued from Thea.

He sank back down with a thump and stared at the little mechanical-magical creature.

A sharp crackling accompanied a blue shimmer of light that started at her base and crawled up her broken screen, healing the glass into an unbroken smooth surface once again. Old dents and scratches disappeared, and there was another sound—like steam escaping a kettle—as something dark and smoky poured out of her speaker holes.

Chaos—a little bit of Leo, left behind. It resolved itself into a miniature cloud as Thea's healing completed, leaving her looking as shiny and new as the first day Crispin had bonded with her, before his initial mission. He stared at her and then at the little, angry, roiling cloud.

"Thank you, Crispin." Thea's voice was as clear and strong as he remembered it. "I was wondering when you'd figure out how to fix me. I was running out of songs that you knew."

"Oh thank the seven gods." Relief flooded through him, at least until he noticed the tiny bit of Chaos hovering forlornly in the air over Thea's screen. "But what do we do with you?"

He reached toward the puff of cloud, but Minkis was faster. The squirrel leapt at it, consuming it in one bite as if it were a particularly scrumptious acorn.

"Mink!" That little bit of Chaos had been the only piece of Leo he had left. And what would it do to the insides of the little creature?

Minkis belched, then patted his stomach, looking quite pleased with himself and so far seeming none the worse for wear.

"Are you all right?" Crispin peered at his friend. "Nothing... feels weird?"

It was Thea who piped up. "He says he feels fine, and could he have some of those acorns in your pocket?"

Crispin blinked. "You can *talk* to him?"

Thea whirred a bit before responding. "I can hear him. I think it's something to do with the Chaos he consumed that used to be inside of me, maybe? Wait, no. He says he's always been able to talk."

Crispin blinked three times. "So why has he never spoken with me?" The idea was as believable as the zoucberry bush outside the tree house wanting to pop in for a spot of tea.

Minkis shrugged. "Never the right time. Acorns?" His voice was adorable, just how you'd imagine a squirrel would talk.

"Oh yes, of course." He'd forgotten about the nuts he'd scooped up from his desk at OotL. "Here you go." He dumped them unceremoniously on the table. "Wait... you're talking to me now, too?"

"Sure, Acorn Man." Minkis picked one up and began to nibble contentedly.

Crispin had always had a bond with the squirrel, ever since he'd found Minkis on the forest floor with a broken leg. Mrs. Dollywip fixed him right up—she was an herbal witch in addition to a house mother—and he and Minkis had been thick as thieves ever since. Not that Crispin would ever condone thievery.

He'd known that Minkis was special but not that he could talk. How that would have eased his loneliness, all those nights alone in the tree house after work. "You and I are going to have words about this, my friend." He couldn't help but suppress a smile.

"Minkis has a lot of words."

Was it his imagination, or was the squirrel grinning at him? He was starting to get used to Minkis's voice, which made him worry just a bit for his sanity. He turned his attention back to the matter at hand. "Thea, are you now... fully operational?"

"I believe so. You have an excellent memory for circuitry."

Crispin blushed. He'd always been able to remember things. *Maybe it's a part of my gift.* "Why did you want me to go and see my mother again?"

"Did I?" Her screen flashed again, a bewildering combination of colored lights. "Oh, I did. I think that was the Chaos talking."

Leo. Did Leo want me to go home? Crispin thought back on their conversations. They'd talked about repairing the damage they'd caused, and Juzir had dropped a hint that his mother's Estate was in poor shape. And he *did* need someone's help to find and rescue Leo. Not that useless brother of his, but his mother knew more than she was telling about Crispin's gifts. "Thea, can you get us to the Estate?"

"Yes. Are you sure that's a good idea?"

"Not even a little bit." His old self-doubt resurfaced. *Can I do this?*

Leo needed him. If he didn't do something, and soon, his love would be sealed away in one of the countless rooms at OotL—or might meet a worse fate—and Crispin would never find him.

"All right, take me to the Queen."

"Take us too." Minkis got up on his hind legs, his bushy tail waving back and forth in an agitated fashion.

"What?"

"Go with you, find Chaos Man."

"It's better if you stay here. I don't want to see you get hurt." *Again.*

"Know where he is. Little cloud talks to me."

Crispin's jaw dropped. "You... the cloud... what?"

"I believe Minkis has established a connection with Leo." Thea's voice this time.

Just when I thought things couldn't get any stranger. "Can you take us there?"

Thea's screen flashed. "Not clear yet. But I can take you to your mother."

Crispin sighed heavily, as one does when one's shoulders are weighted down by all the cares of the world. "Yes, take me to Her High Holy Fairyness. But first, let me grab a few things."

He threw some supplies into a carry sack, along with a few other items he thought might come in handy, and in a few moments was ready to go. "You coming, my little furry friend?"

Minkis dropped the acorn he'd been working on and scampered up Crispin's sleeve to perch comfortably on his shoulder. "Minkis ready, Acorn Man."

Crispin frowned, then decided he'd been called worse. He scooped Thea up and held her out before him. "Let's go!"

Prickles—the hotel of the cactus dicks and the sometimes-home of The Estate—looked like something out of a war zone.

Minkis's tail shot up. "Bad."

Crispin's eyes had gone wide. "Bad indeed, my friend."

Fire engines lined the streets, red lights flashing, illuminating a building that was half missing, eaten away by the poison from the chalice and by the Chaos Leo had unleashed.

Some of the walls—those that were still standing—ended in a strange gray nothingness, and a crowd of people stared numbly at the remains.

Crispin sometimes forgot that the places where his mother's Estate appeared were real, not just backdrops for her social games.

"We're gonna need a new hotel." Thea's matter-of-fact voice brought him back down to... well, Varth, which was the home of

Odds, the gambling metropolis where the Mother of Fae had most recently set up camp.

He cast around for signs of his mother and brother. As much as he'd never wanted to see them again after that last charming visit, neither did he want them to come to harm. They were family, after all.

"Forest is better." Minkis sniffed the air, looking back and forth at the devastation. "No Leo here."

From Crispin's vest pocket, Thea chimed in. "Squirrel's got you there."

Crispin nodded. He'd have been very surprised if the quest had been that simple. He started to walk around the disaster scene, gently pushing past the refugees and onlookers. No one seemed to notice that he had a squirrel on his shoulder. Of course, in the free-wheeling city of Odds, that was way down the list of strange things you were likely to see.

The world beyond the hotel seemed startlingly normal. *Is the Chaos contained, then?*

That's when he found his mother standing in a side alley with his brother Aspin. They were surrounded by a group of wizards in long flowing purple robes, whose hands were extended toward what used to be Prickles. A lone police officer was speaking with her. He was nearly human save for his forehead horn—which looked disturbingly like the cactus pricks at Prickles, and didn't that explain a lot?—and the fact that his legs ended in wide, black, cloven hooves. The cop was gamely trying to take a statement from the Queen of the High Holy Fae.

"... a goblet of poison? Ma'am, have you been drinking?"

"Yes, but that's not the point." She sighed heavily, and Crispin realized with a start that she looked different. While she remained beautiful, the small telltale signs of aging that he'd seen on his last visit had spread. Wrinkles emphasized her features, and her hair was still the flat gray it had changed to during his last ill-fated visit. Even her shoulders slumped in their finery, and the delicate beauty of her silver dress—where had she gotten that in the midst of all this literal chaos?—looked as if it had seen better days.

"Mother?"

"Crispin!" Her eyes met his, and some of the old sparkle returned. She touched the policeman's cheek gently. "You will remember none of this. Now go."

He blinked. "Ma'am, I'll ask again. Are you drunk? Maybe we should have this conversation down at the station."

She frowned and touched him again.

His eyes went blank, and when they refocused, he managed a dopey smile. "Of course, ma'am. Thank you for your time." Then he turned and walked away.

"Losing your touch?" Crispin maneuvered around one of the concentrating wizards to come face-to-face with his mother and his arch-nemesis brother.

She made a cute little moue that would have been charming before she'd lost most of her magic. Aspin stepped forward, looming belligerently. "It's your fault. You and that half-breed human you brought here—"

A wave of their mother's hand cut Aspin off as neatly as if she'd choked him.

Crispin expected a scathing remark from her, possibly accompanied by a threat that would sear the flesh off his bones. He braced himself and closed his eyes.

Instead he felt her arms around him, smelled her familiar perfume—one-third toadstool, one-third moonlight orchid, and one-third rainbow.

"I'm so glad you're alive." She hugged him tightly, and for the first time in years he found himself speechless in front of his own mother.

Minkis twittered. "She smells nice."

"I... that is... you really shouldn't...." He took a deep breath. This wasn't the time for recriminations. He needed her help to find Leo, and it seemed as if she needed his too. "Thank you."

She let him go, her eyes narrowing at the sight of the little squirrel, as if she'd just seen him. "We've created a frightful mess, you and I." Her anxious gaze over his shoulder reminded him that the hotel was in ruins, just as another wall collapsed with a resounding crash.

He raised an eyebrow. "We?" He wasn't used to seeing her like this. Vulnerable. Almost mortal.

She had the grace to blush. "Fair enough. You may have precipitated it with your arrival, but if I hadn't listened to your supervisor—"

"Bidulla put you up to it?" Crispin frowned. His mother was never manipulated by other people. She was the one who did the manipulating.

"Yes. *Handsome* woman, that one." A little of the old Cerillia showed though with that taunt. "She was insistent that the Chaos fragment—"

"Leo."

"Right. That *Leo* be recaptured, before he could do more harm."

"And the poison chalice—"

"Was specially formulated for him. It would have knocked him out. Not killed him. I'm not a monster, whatever else you may think of me."

Manipulator. Liar. Corrupted by your own power. But he said none of those things. "So how did it cause all of this?"

She sighed.

She'd just lost everything she'd ever owned. *Have a little compassion, like Leo showed you.* "Tell me what happened."

"She's hiding her acorns," Minkis said.

Thea's voice followed. "He's not wrong. She's hiding something."

"Why is your pet rat talking about me?" She pulled back, staring at Minkis and then at Thea's glow emanating from his vest pocket. "And how?"

"*Squirrel.* And he swallowed a little bit of Leo. He might be able to lead me to him." He frowned. "Enough evasion. Tell me everything. And then maybe I can help you fix this."

Another crash, and something heavy hit the street behind him, making him jump.

A toilet bowl, being slowly dissolved by a random bit of Chaos.

One of the wizards stepped forward and thrust his hands toward it, and the creeping, sizzling nothingness stopped in its tracks.

Aspin frowned. "They're not making any progress. It's getting worse."

"I know." His mother seemed to make up her mind. "They can hold it off for a while yet, though." Her voice cracked, just a little.

This was not the strong woman, self-assured to the point of absurdity, that he had grown up with. He felt pity for her. Which in turn made him feel very strange indeed—as if all that he had always assumed was *up* was now actually *down*.

"Come with me, both of you. It's time I let you in on *all* of my secrets."

24
LEOPOLD

Leopold had been a lot of things over the past few days—a deer creature, a butterfly thing, a pet, and of course Chaos personified—but his least favorite incarnation was his present one: a statue slung over the shoulder of a guy who looked like he'd just stepped off a romance-novel cover. Oh, and Leopold was wearing nothing but a pair of discount-store boxer briefs.

Qylzryd was carrying Leopold face down, which meant that the captive couldn't see much except the ground. First it was green and foresty-looking, then Juzir said something and *zap!* Now the floor was gleaming white tile.

Dammit. He recognized that tile. He was back at the Office of the Lost.

He'd been struggling desperately to Chaos his way out of this mess, but it wasn't working. He couldn't move. He couldn't even make any sounds except for very muffled groans, and those sounded so pathetic that he gave up. He simply had to let Qylzryd schlep him down that endless hallway.

Jeez. If Juzir could zap them here, why hadn't he taken them straight to... wherever their destination was? Leopold could have lived without the extra indignity of a long haul. Plus, this gave him too much time to think. He was worried about what fate OotL had in mind for him, and so he tried to distract himself with other topics. Like Crispin's treehouse, for example. Leopold had liked it quite a lot, even if it was too tidy for his taste. And really, that was nothing a few piles of laundry and some pizza boxes couldn't fix. *Did they even have pizza places in the... what had Crispy called it... the Grapewoods?*

No, that couldn't be right. That was more like the place where Fromlith lived.

Greatwoods. That was it. He savored the small victory of remembering something important.

He could imagine himself staying there with Crispin, maybe finding some sort of job to pay his share. It would be cozy. But cozy in the best way, not in the real estate agent way that really meant *super tiny*.

But maybe Crispin was better off without him. Before they'd met, Crispin had been content with his job, his home, his squirrel. His perfecality score. Leopold had messed all of that up. Not on purpose, but it was his fault nonetheless. And the mess he'd made of Crispin's family relationships? Leopold especially regretted that. Sure, Aspin was a turdbucket and their mother was... terrifying. But family was family, and Leopold knew how miserable it was to not have any.

This wasn't improving his mindset, not one whit. *And what is a whit, anyway?*

"This guy's heavy," Qylzryd complained. As if Leopold had asked to be carried.

Juzir made a grunting sound. "You should have brought a cart."

His porter huffed. "Nobody said anything about needing a cart."

"Well, how did you think we were going to get him here?"

"I don't know. I wasn't the one planning things. I'm just hired muscle."

"Exactly." Juzir sounded smug. "Which is why you're carrying him."

Qylzryd didn't seem to have an answer to that. Leopold was

getting the impression that the guy wasn't especially bright, which made him wonder why Crispin had dated him. Crispin didn't seem like the type to go for pretty but empty-headed. After all, he was falling for Leopold, who was never going to grace the cover of a romance novel.

But wait. Leopold wasn't exactly Mensa material either. What *did* Crispin see in him? After all, Crispin was handsome, skilled at a lot of things, and had a mother who was genuine fae royalty, which probably made Crispin some kind of prince. He was someone who could date and reject hunks like Qylzryd. And yet here he'd been, claiming that he loved Leopold. Nobody had ever done that before.

Oh no. A thought had occurred to him, and it was so awful that he groaned again, not that it made any difference to his captors. He also felt a little queasy, and not just from the motion of Qylzryd walking. What if he had *made* Crispin fall for him? Not by being charming or irresistible, but by manipulating him with his Chaos powers. Not that Leopold had intended to do so, but he also hadn't intended any of the messes he'd made throughout his life. He hadn't, for example, intended to kill his parents.

Maybe he didn't always have the best moral compass, but he was absolutely certain that magicking someone into falling in love with you was capital-w Wrong.

"My leg hurts," Qylzryd complained. To Juzir, presumably. "Where that rat bit me."

"He's a squirrel," said Juzir.

"Well, that *squirrel* bit me." He sounded like a five-year-old.

"He's very small. He couldn't possibly have done much damage."

Qylzryd grumbled under his breath, and Juzir either didn't hear or ignored him.

Leopold, for his part, hoped Qylzryd's leg would fester and then fall off. He would have bitten the jerk himself, if he could have managed it. Chaos bites probably weren't healthy for anyone.

At long last they stopped walking. Juzir knocked, presumably, on a door, and a muffled voice ordered them to come in.

Leopold recognized the voice, so when Qylzryd walked into the room and set Leopold upright on the floor, leaning against a wall like a roll of carpet, he wasn't at all surprised to find Bidulla Krönk staring back at him.

They were in an office, it seemed. Bidulla sat behind a metal desk roughly the size of Rhode Island, in stark contrast to the heavy white stone desks in the main office.

There was a single neat stack of papers on the desk, along with an aluminum pen holder, an enormous mug, and one of those desk toys with the swinging metal balls. She was smiling, which didn't make her any more aesthetically pleasing.

"So," she purred. "That was easy."

"Crispin's rat bit me!" Qylzryd sounded like a petulant toddler.

"Squirrel," Juzir muttered.

"Whatever."

Bidulla wasn't impressed. "You're lucky the Chaos creature didn't turn you into a slug. Or simply dissolve your atomic structure."

Qylzryd scrambled far away from Leopold, looking terrified. "He can do that?"

"Not anymore," said Juzir. "Not as long as the containment spell holds."

Leopold wondered how long that would be. It had already been some time since Juzir zapped him. Maybe his captors had lost track. Maybe in a minute or two he *would* be able to turn Qylzryd into a slug—*thanks for the suggestion, Bidulla, that was a good one*—and do something equally appropriate to Juzir and Bidulla.

But neither Juzir nor Bidulla looked concerned about this possibility, which Leopold found disconcerting. Bidulla was signing and stamping some paperwork on her desk, slamming the stamp down with extra gusto. Seemingly pleased with her efforts, she scooted the papers across the expanse of metal. "Take these to the Exchequer's Office on the fifth floor. They'll process them for you, and you should receive payment within sixty working days."

Qylzryd grabbed one of the papers, gave Leopold a final horrified look, and ran out of the room. Juzir, however, straightened his back. "I didn't do this for the money. My concern was the damage this... being could cause."

"Yeah, yeah, you're a hero," said Bidulla, flapping a hand dismissively. "Do you want payment or not?"

Juzir deflated a little. "Well, I do have to completely rebuild my bathroom." He took the other paper and didn't even glance at Leopold before leaving.

Bidulla spent a moment staring at him, her thoughts opaque. Finally she hauled herself upright. "Well, it wasn't the cleanest retrieval effort, but at least we succeeded in the end." She seemed to be speaking to herself more than to Leopold.

After staring a little longer, she shuffled over to the wall and touched it, revealing a closet behind a hidden door. Leopold wasn't at a good angle to see what was inside; he just caught a glimpse of a broom and a mop. Bidulla stepped partway inside and, after a bit of crashing and banging, emerged with a wheelbarrow, which she stuffed Leopold into. Since he didn't bend much, she had to do a lot of prodding and wrenching to get him to fit. He added *non-consensual touching* to his list of grievances against her.

Humming to herself, Bidulla pushed the Leopold-filled wheelbarrow out of her office and down the hallway. This time he was mostly on his side, so he could see more than the floor, but that didn't help him any. There was just a long procession of doors. The only interesting thing he spied was the Oracle's door, but Bidulla didn't pause there.

Who was this mysterious Oracle, whose dictates had turned his life upside down?

Leopold was still frozen several minutes later, when Bidulla stopped in front of one of the doors, opened it through some process he couldn't see, and unceremoniously dumped him onto the floor, as if he were a bag of cement mix.

He landed face down on thin planks of worn wood.

"If it was up to me, we'd just destroy you." She sounded conversational, like a person discussing the weather or what they might have for lunch. "But the Oracle says no, so here you are. Some of the items in our collection have been here for millennia. Maybe you will be too."

He heard the wheelbarrow wheels squeak a little, and then the door closed with a bang. The lock engaged with a *clunk* of finality.

Leopold lay there for a long time. It wasn't very comfortable, especially when his nose began to itch. And he wasn't especially grateful that he hadn't been killed, because now he was left with all of his doubts and regrets. And seemingly ample time to contemplate them.

He worried about Crispin because, okay, maybe it was possible that Leopold had inadvertently magicked Crispin into loving him, but Leopold hadn't magicked himself. He cared about Crispin. He *loved* Crispin. He'd never been in love before and had sort of given up hope he ever would be, so under different circumstances he would be relieved and happy.

But not now.

Eventually Leopold's muscles began to cramp. Then he developed spasms in his arms and legs, like really bad charley horses, and found that he'd recovered enough to howl in pain. After way too much of that, the agony subsided. He groaned, sighed, and rolled onto his side, finally able to take a look at his new prison.

He was in a studio apartment not too different from many of the ones he'd lived in. No kitchenette, but there was a bed, a couch, a table, and a single wooden chair. There was a television—one of the bulky wooden console types with built-in speakers, like people owned back in the 60s. It was switched on and showing *The Brady Bunch*.

Greg was in trouble for something, but Leopold couldn't tell what because there was no sound. The room had a couple of shag throw rugs scattered on the floor; the walls were painted off-white, as was the ceiling. Leopold couldn't see any light fixtures, but the room was moderately bright.

There were no windows, and he couldn't see a door.

Still aching, Leopold managed to get off the floor and onto the couch. It didn't much improve his perspective. And when he repeatedly tried to flex his Chaos muscles, nothing happened. He couldn't even change the channel on the TV without getting up and turning the knob, and even then, the same show was on all five channels. *Only five channels! What is this, a gulag?*

Defeated and exhausted, he made his way to the bed and curled up, slipping into a dreamless sleep.

He woke up, and everything was the same. Except now *Gilligan's Island* was on TV.

Leopold wasn't hungry or thirsty and didn't need to pee. Maybe that was part of the magic of being in the archive. He would miss food, but when he followed his thoughts to their logical conclusion, he nearly panicked. If he didn't need food, then there was no reason for anyone at OotL to enter his prison. *Ever.* He would be locked in here without ever seeing another living being.

Although he didn't panic, he did enter a sort of frenzy of screaming, running around, and scratching and banging on the walls.

All of which was fruitless. As far as he could tell, there was no way out. And nobody came to investigate the noise. He remembered how eerily quiet the OotL hallway had been, and how there had been no clue about what was behind each door.

When he was completely worn out, he collapsed onto the couch and had a good cry. Eventually that subsided and he settled for staring numbly at the water-stained ceiling.

"Hey! Little buddy!"

Leopold froze and looked around. Still nobody there but him. And also no Kleenex, which was a shame because he didn't even have a sleeve to wipe his nose on.

"Little buddy!"

It was the TV. The TV was talking to him. Well, not the set itself, but the character on the screen, whom Leopold recognized as the Skipper. He was sitting on a downed palm tree, wearing his nautical cap and bright blue shirt, and looking straight at Leopold. He was also smoking a joint, which Leopold was fairly certain had never happened on the show.

"Uh, hello?" Leopold winced. He'd only just been locked up and already he was losing touch with reality.

But the Skipper seemed pleased that Leopold had greeted him. "You've sure got yourself in a pickle, haven't you?"

"I guess. How do I get out of here?"

"Beats me. I had three whole seasons and still couldn't get myself off that damned uncharted island."

Leopold leaned back against the couch cushions and groaned. Couldn't he at least have been given a helpful vintage television visitor? MacGyver, maybe?

"You remind me a little of Gilligan," said the Skipper. He sounded fond. "Poor guy was always getting into trouble. Of course, *he* was an idiot. We all were—even the Professor. If he was so smart, couldn't he have rigged us a seaworthy boat out of coconuts or something?"

"Am I doomed to listen to critiques of TV shows that were cancelled thirty years before I was born?"

The Skipper chuckled. "Nah, little buddy. Anyway, in a few minutes *Bewitched* comes on. I just wanted to give you a little friendly advice."

"Check the weather forecast before booking a three-hour boat tour?"

The Skipper removed his hat and waved it around, clearly wishing he could swat Leopold with it. "Listen up. We might not have escaped the island, but we survived. And you know how? Ingenuity. We found new ways to make use of what we had. A few vines, a little bamboo, some brainpower... *boom*! Now you've got a Geiger counter... or maybe a sewing machine. Where's your bamboo and coconut shells, little buddy?"

Leopold stared at the screen for a long time. "I have no idea."

The Skipper shrugged. "Well, maybe you should."

Then he dissolved into a fuzz of gray static that was replaced by a cartoon witch, flying sidesaddle on a broom.

25
CRISPIN

Crispin's mother led the two of them down the alley and around a corner, past a few drunks snoring loudly next to a bright yellow dumpster. Almost all truly civilized worlds seemed to have dumpsters—though their specific design and color varied wildly—and squirrels, which was a weird stray thought probably inspired by Minkis chittering away on his shoulder.

The sleepers seemed blissfully unaware of the chaotic event unleashed just steps away from their uncomfortable sleeping place, and Crispin sighed, torn between compassion for their plight and disgust at their inability to control their baser impulses.

Then again, look who's talking. You fell in love with a lumpy bit of human Chaos. He hoped Bidulla—or whomever had taken Leo—was treating him right.

Aspin gave Crispin a wide berth, barely disguising his own disgust at his prodigal brother.

Where did we go wrong? When they'd been children, Aspin had watched over him, not just an older brother in name only.

"Through here." The Fae Queen opened an old, creaky metal door

—when had she ever opened a door for *him* before?—and ushered both her sons inside.

It was a sleazy dive bar—as typical a sight on multiple worlds as the dumpster outside—and probably the place where the two sleepers had stumbled out of, after drinking their fill of watered-down beer. The tables were Odds's version of some weird blue plasticy stuff Crispin had seen in old Earth diners, but so old that the once smooth and shiny surfaces were now cracked and faded. Pendulum lights in the form of some kind of prickly round sea creature failed to shed enough illumination to reach the floor, which no doubt, from its sticky feel, was better off for not being seen.

The walls were covered with layer upon layer of posters and fliers, with only an occasional glimpse here and there of an ancient wallpaper that once might have matched the tables. A neon sign on one wall flickered a sickly green *Himpel's Beer—The Best Money Can Buy*. Apparently.

The only *almost* luxe part of the place was along the back wall: a gleaming goldenwood bar with neat shelves of alcohol behind it, as if some enterprising soul had bought the place with dreams of turning it into a new hot spot but had run out of money halfway through the project.

The place was only a quarter full. At this time in the morning, only the most determined drunks were still at it. As one, they turned bleary eyes toward the newcomers.

"Hey lady, this isn't your kind of place. You'd best move along." That was from the barkeep, the only other being fully upright in the dark, dingy place. He was well-dressed in a crisp white shirt and purple suspenders, with the strange prickly horn particular to his people. Perhaps the once-optimistic entrepreneur himself.

Cerillia ignored him. "Out." She pointed at the door, and despite her comedown in the world and her less-commanding appearance, the men and women gathered themselves up and scurried out like so many rats running from a giant cat.

"Hey, those are my paying customers." The barkeep tried to

muster some indignity, which in this place was probably far easier than managing actual dignity.

The Fae Queen strode to the counter and pulled three gold coins from her pocket. "Bring us three"—she glanced at the wall—"Himpel's, please. I trust that will cover your cost?"

The man's eyes had gone wide, as if ready to pop out of his skull. He was probably scared silly; the Mother of Fae often had that effect on mere mortals. Crispin had seen it his entire life. "I'm so sorry. Mom can be intimidating. Will that cover the cost?"

The barkeep nodded vigorously. It was probably enough to finish his long-delayed renovation, and then some. "I'll bring your drinks straight away, ma... um, miss." He shuddered at the look she gave him and hastily turned away to pull down three glasses from the shelf and draw their beers from the tap.

Minkis chittered. "Hungry."

Cerillia raised an eyebrow. "It speaks now?"

"Apparently." Crispin turned back to the barkeep. "And a bowl of nuts?"

The man didn't turn around, but simply held up a thumb in the universal gesture for "I got it."

"Please, follow me." Cerillia led her sons to the far corner of the bar, choosing a table that seemed to be the least dirty and cracked of the lot. She pulled out a chair, stared at it distastefully, and snapped her fingers. It spun merrily around on one leg, awash in sparkling magic, and when it settled down again, it was clean and shone like new. Satisfied, she sank down into it, shrugging off her leather jacket and heaving a contented sigh. She pointedly did nothing about her sons' chairs or the poor long-suffering table.

With a sigh of his own, Crispin sank down into a grungy chair across from his brother, who eyed him warily.

"Here we are, three Himpel's and a bowl of nuts." The barkeep slid them smoothly onto the table. "Is there anything else I can bring you? Some bar pops, perhaps?"

"No thank you...."

"Hubble. At your service, ma'am."

"No thank you, Hubble. You've done quite enough. Now please, give us the room." She waved him away.

The poor man stood there for a moment, wringing his hands, transfixed by Cerillia's faded but still potent beauty. Not only did she have that effect on mortal men; it worked on a few of the immortals too.

She snapped her fingers, breaking him out of the spell. "You can go now."

"Of course, ma'am." He mopped a sheen of sweat off his brow and, with an apparent effort, turned and retreated through a swinging door at the back of the bar, leaving the three of them alone.

Crispin's mother lifted one of the heavy glass mugs and took a sip of beer. A deep crease furrowed her forehead. "Quite dreadful." She snapped her fingers again and the drink transformed into a fluted crystal chalice filled with something frothy and pink. She took a long sip. "Much better."

Crispin stared at his own mug, waiting for her to transform it as well. When no further magic was forthcoming, he sighed, picked it up, and took a sip. It wasn't really that bad, and it would certainly have its intended effect if consumed in quantity.

Minkis scampered down his arm to the bowl of nuts, almost knocking the mug out of his hand.

"Hey, careful there."

"Hungry." He picked up one of the nuts—round and purple with little yellow points on each end—and began to nibble contentedly.

Crispin set down his mug, having no intention of dulling his wits. "You promised secrets?" He sat back, arms crossed, hoping to hurry this along. He did have a human to save, after all.

"Treat Mum with a little respect, you yellow, lily-livered twerp." Aspin glared at him as if Crispin were responsible for all the trouble in the family.

Well, maybe I am. He snorted. *And maybe they deserved it.*

"Enough."

Aspin had started to speak again, but a sharp look from the Queen of Fae silenced him.

"Your brother deserves some answers. And so do you." She drained the glass and set it down on the sad little table.

Crispin braced himself. Was his father a warthog? Had he been adopted from some gods-forsaken world that no one wanted to talk about? *Oh gods, am I actually... human?*

"Crispin is my one true heir."

Now *that* he hadn't expected.

Aspin was on his feet. "What? Him? When I've been at your side, loyal as a fire dragon, while he—"

"Sit down, Aspin." Her voice cut through the rant and all but took the legs out from under her pompous older son.

Crispin stared at the two of them.

Minkis had stopped nibbling to stare with him, seeming suddenly fascinated by the larger beings around him.

"You... you can't be serious." It was disconcerting to actually agree with his brother, for once. "You've never had one good thing to say about me. And Aspin's older than me."

"Aspin's not like us."

Us. That one word knocked the wind out of him. The Queen of the Fae, Her Great Mabness. "How in Hades' dark halls am I like you?"

"We are both the servants of Order." Her eyes bore into his, as if to see whether he understood the true import of what she was telling him.

And suddenly it became clear. "I'm... I'm like Leo."

She snorted in the most lady-like and yet derisive way possible. "Hardly. Leo is a servant of Chaos."

"But I don't have a real father, do I?"

She shook her head. "No more than I did. Nor a mother, in truth."

Aspin looked from Crispin to his mother, and back again. "I don't understand."

"She didn't birth me. She... created me." Suddenly everything made sense. The arms-length treatment he'd received all through his childhood. His attraction to the Red Door. His exile to the Office of the Lost. His love of all things straight and clean and organized. "I'm... Order personified. Aren't I? And so are you."

A smile spread across her face. "Now you see it."

"And my father..."

"Was from behind The Door."

A horrid thought crossed his mind. "Is Leo my—"

"Oh sordid heavens no. There are as many manifestations of Chaos as there are of Order."

Crispin heaved a sigh of relief. For a moment there, he'd been afraid he'd slept with his own father. Which... just no. "But why? What are we, really?" Being so like his mother was profoundly disturbing. All of his life he'd consoled himself that he was nothing like her.

"You are Acorn Man. Belong with Chaos Man."

Crispin stared at his squirrel companion. Minkis's poor grasp of English grammar belied the truth and deep insight of what he'd just said.

Unconcerned, Minkis went back to rummaging in the nut bowl for hidden treasure.

"He's not wrong." Cerillia's face looked a bit sour at the admission, like she'd just sucked on a lemon. "In the beginning, there were two forces in the void. Chaos and Order. Neither one had the upper hand, and worlds were built and destroyed as they fought for dominance. Unimaginable pain filled the young Connected Worlds, until a group of elder mages came up with a solution. They married Order to Chaos in the form of two beings, each made of one pure essence."

"Why did these... beings... agree to such a union?" He didn't like where this seemed to be heading.

"Because they were too evenly matched, and the world would never see an end to their strife if something wasn't done. And because they realized something important: that Order without

Chaos was deadly boring, and Chaos without Order was unsustainable. They each needed the other."

It made a certain kind of sense. He and Leo balanced each other out nicely. "So where is your... consort? The King of Chaos?" He was rather proud of that one. It rolled neatly off the tongue.

She looked away, regret clouding her features like frost on a delicate leaf.

"The Red Door," he said. "You imprisoned him."

"It was the only way. My father did it before me, and his mother before him. Chaos, if left unchecked, eventually seeks to dominate everything—"

"Just like you have?" He frowned. "That's why I was sent to collect Leopold. He was a loose end, a bit of Chaos free in the world, not under your control."

She took a deep breath. "Not exactly. He was meant for you." She reached out to him, her white hand—cold, so cold—touching his cheek. "You just found him too soon. In a few more years...."

Crispin couldn't believe what he was hearing. "You and Bidulla plan to keep him locked up for *years*?"

He'd never seen his mother look uncertain before. "You weren't ready."

Before he could reply, the door slammed open. One of the mages who had been fighting the erosion of the Prickles Hotel stood there breathless. "Oh... thank... the... seven... gods."

There was something strange about him, but Crispin couldn't quite put his finger on it.

The anguished look on his mother's face vanished. "What is it now?" She was once again the cold, bright, beautiful, terrible creature he'd known throughout his childhood. "Speak!"

He essayed a quick bow, but something outside had scared him more than she could. "Come quick. Something is happening!"

He turned sideways and vanished.

Cerillia Ailedrin Moss'caladin swept out of the empty bar and into the light of the new morning. Crispin followed her, and stopped at the threshold.

The world was flat. Or maybe *flattening* was a more accurate description. Color was seeping out of it like the bloom off a rose. All the random jagged lines were straightening out, crackling like broken glass as the change passed through. The mage turned back, and Crispin could see that he was now two-dimensional, thin as a slip of paper. "What's happening?"

Only the Queen and her two sons seemed unaffected.

"Mother, what's happening?" Aspin was actually shaking. Crispin had never seen his brother afraid.

"It's Chaos. It's leaking out of the world." Crispin grabbed his mother by her leather jacket, spinning her around to face him. "Mother, what did they do to Leo?"

She shook her head, staring at the morphing world. Only the twitching of her cheek betrayed her own fear. "I don't know, Crispin. I truly do not know."

26

LEOPOLD

Bewitched proved less than spellbinding, maybe because Leopold had experienced more than enough magic for the time being. Which was kind of too bad. One of his foster families had possessed a huge library of vintage-TV DVDs, and for the several months that he'd lived there, he'd found surprising comfort in bingeing them all.

Now, though, he switched off the TV just as Endora was in the middle of trying to break up Samantha and Darrin's marriage. That struck a little too close to home.

Leopold climbed into bed and tried to fall back asleep, but it was a no-go. He kept thinking about Crispin and wondering how he was doing.

"Maybe I *did* accidentally enchant him into falling for me," Leopold said to the empty room. "And if so, maybe now that we're separated, he's over me." That would be good, right? For Crispin, at any rate.

But Leopold was definitely not over Crispin. He couldn't rationally explain how or why he'd fallen in love so fast. On the face of it, Crispin was his polar opposite: neat and organized and flawless while Leopold was, well, Chaos. Opposites did attract, however. And since when was love ever rational?

He sat up quickly, struck by a thought. Love was messy and unpredictable and sometimes dangerous. It was, he concluded, another one of those things—like magic and art—that could only exist with some Chaos in the world. That idea made him proud, if wistful. Gods, he missed Crispin!

Time was hard to measure in this place, but at least several hours must have passed after that, with Leopold pacing the room and trying to flex his powers. As far as he could tell, nothing happened. Maybe the protective spell on this place was like defensive shields in a sci-fi movie, and if he pelted it hard enough and long enough it would be damaged and eventually disintegrate. That was a plan, anyway. *Sort of.*

His legs grew tired eventually, so he plopped down onto the couch. How would Crispin approach this problem if he were in Leopold's place? Obviously, if it weren't for Leopold, Crispin would never find himself in a situation like this. He would instead happily spend his life perfecting his perfecality score, hanging out with Minkis, and having occasional trysts with hunky men.

That reminded Leopold of Qylzryd, and a new wave of anger washed over him. That rat! That stinking puddle of slug scum! He had betrayed Crispin and kidnapped Leopold for no good reason other than money. At least Juzir had been motivated by concern for the fate of the world—and a destroyed bathroom, for which Leopold still felt a nagging sense of guilt.

Qylzryd was just a mercenary. Crispin deserved much better than that.

"Like me," Leopold said sadly. Because if he were reunited with Crispin—and if Crispin still wanted him—Leopold would treat him right. He'd never sell him out for any reason. He'd listen to Crispin go on about obscure facts that nobody else in the universe cared about, and he would be happy to hear him. Leopold would remind him every day that despite Aspin's bullshit, and despite his mother's somewhat cavalier treatment of him, Crispin was amazing. And loved.

"I am not a *thing* to be archived!" Leopold roared, leaping to his feet. He picked up the chair and rammed it against the wall several times, but neither the wall nor the chair showed any signs of damage, and eventually he dropped the chair and sank to the floor in defeat. He'd spent his entire life feeling like a screwup, but even causing disasters was better than causing... nothing.

He'd never felt so useless.

"Focus, Leo." Saying it out loud helped a little. "Think like a desk fae." *Or like the Skipper.* "Bamboo and coconut shells. What are your assets?"

He took a visual inventory and came up fairly short. He still didn't have any clothing aside from his underwear. There were no windows, no doors. No way to communicate with the outside world. No—

Wait. Maybe he couldn't communicate with the world, but it had communicated with *him* via the television. What if he could do more than get cryptic advice from incompetent ship captains? Though to be fair, it really hadn't been the Skipper's fault. That storm had come up really fast....

Leopold switched on the set again. Static hissed for a few moments before the picture clarified. *Ah.* Another midcentury cishet male's misogynistic fantasy about controlling a powerful woman. Only this woman—who also possessed magic—was more scantily clad than Samantha.

Wearing her culturally appropriated pink costume, Jeannie sat cross-legged on her purple couch, reading a magazine. She didn't say anything, or even look up, so Leopold cleared his throat.

"Um, hello?" He would have felt stupid starting a conversation with the TV, except he'd been talking quite a lot to Thea lately and she was a broken cell phone.

Seemingly unsurprised, Jeanie glanced up. "Oh, hello, master."

Oh gods. "I'm not your master. I'm not anyone's master. Well, that's not entirely right. Uh, if the other person is fully consenting."

She laughed. "Of course I am fully consenting, silly. I am pretty powerful, right? I cannot do much here inside my bottle"—she waved her arms to indicate the curved, jewel-studded walls—"just as you cannot do much inside of yours. But when I am outside my bottle, I can do all sorts of things. If someone tried to be my master and I did not wish it, well, he would regret it very much. But sometimes I wish it very much." She winked.

Lovely. There went another childhood memory, thoroughly ruined.

Leopold sighed. "Well, I don't want to be your master. I just hoped maybe you could help me."

Jeannie put down her magazine and laced her fingers in her lap. "Very well. I can try."

That was something at least. "It's just, they've trapped me here and I can't get out. And I'm in love with an elf—well, a fae...." He still wasn't clear on the difference. He'd have to ask Crispy about that when he saw him again. *If I ever see him again.* "But I'm worried about him. He's got troubles of his own, which I sort of created. Family drama. I want to be reunited with him. Or at least know that he's okay. I hate being stuck here."

"I can understand that. I was trapped in my bottle for two thousand years."

Leopold groaned. He was already going nuts, and he'd been here less than two days. And even if he could survive for two millennia, what about Crispin? Leopold had no idea of the lifespan for fae.

"Leo," said Jeannie softly, "I cannot get you out of your room."

"I didn't figure you could. But I appreciate you listening to me complain." He went to the couch and lay down, staring at the unremarkable ceiling. If all he could do was wallow in self-pity, well then, dammit, he was going to do a good job of wallowing.

"Although I cannot help you, that does not mean it is impossible."

He didn't bother turning his head to look at the screen. "Maybe not, but I'm not going to figure it out. I'm not a figuring-it-out kind of guy."

"Then perhaps you should find someone who is."

"Yeah," he replied hopelessly. That would be Crispin.

It was possible that Crispin did still love him, and if so, it was also possible—likely, actually—that right this very minute he was working away at the problem. And if true, it was even possible that he would be successful. But man, that was a few too many *possibles* for Leopold's taste. Right now, he could really go for a *definite* or even a *probable*.

"Thanks, Jeannie," he said, because she'd been really nice. The TV went back to static, which was actually pretty soothing, so he left it on. It reminded him a little of pure Chaos.

He missed that part of himself. He'd spent his whole life believing—reasonably enough—that he was human, and it had been shocking to discover that he wasn't. But it had also been… affirming, in a way. An acknowledgment that the unsettledness he'd always felt in his core wasn't craziness or a bad attitude but, instead, a source of power. And now it was gone.

And it wasn't as if he entirely minded being human-ish. He liked his body well enough and the things he could do with it, like eating and enjoying a nice spring day and, of course, sex. He wasn't nearly as handsome as Crispin, but Leopold's eyes were a nice color. And being around other people, that wasn't so bad, even if he inevitably messed something up and did something, well, chaotic that upset them. He was, in fact, grateful that Crispin's mother had made him human-shaped and had sent him to Earth.

Yet now, in this place, he wasn't even really human. He'd been reduced to an object. Part of a collection, with no more abilities than a butterfly pinned to cardboard.

Yep, here he was, back to wallowing again. He could do *that* for two thousand years if he had to. It wasn't as if he had any better way to spend his time.

He groaned and covered his eyes with an arm.

He remained like that for a time, but it turned out that wallowing was actually pretty boring. He also lacked the accessories for proper wallowing, such as bottles of alcohol or tubs of ice cream or those plastic yellow squeezy sleeves of chocolate chip cookie dough. He'd never really noticed before how tedious his own company could be.

A new idea trickled slowly into his brain. Jeannie had suggested that he find someone clever to help. Maybe someone else on TV would fit the bill. Someone who solved mysteries.

He thought back to the foster parents' DVDs, trying to remember whether there had been any detective shows among the mix. Did *Adam-12* count?

It was worth a try.

Leopold heaved himself off the couch and turned the channel knob on the TV. At first there was more static, but just as he was about to give up, a cartoon speech bubble appeared. *POW!* It was replaced a second or two later by another: *BAM!* and then *SOCK!* Familiar music began to play.

"Oh," sighed Leopold.

And there they were in their leotards, capes, and masks, grinning at him. Leopold waved and collapsed back onto the couch. "Hi, guys."

It wasn't *Adam-12*, obviously, and these guys weren't detectives. Although one of the actors was named Adam, if he remembered right, so maybe that counted for something.

They did solve crimes, though. Sort of. And jeez, watching this series had led to his gay awakening, when his not-quite-adolescent self had become increasingly aware of how interested he was in Robin and his almost skin-tight clothes.

"I'm not trying to fight a humanoid feline or an Egyptian mummy. You can go away now," Leopold informed the TV.

"Holy doormat, who knew you'd give up so easily?" Robin looked slightly disgusted.

"I'm giving up 'cause I can't do anything. I've got nothing. Look at me! I'm even more scantily dressed than you."

"Clothing does not make the man," said the other guy on the screen, and it looked as if he might be about to launch into a lecture.

Leopold stopped him with a raised hand. "I'm not your *young ward*, okay, so spare me. I'm nobody's anything. And my underwear isn't really the point." He was reminded that the whole *adopt the handsome young guy who likes to wear really tight tights* thing had always seemed a bit suspicious. "My powers are gone. I've got zip."

"Oh?" Robin crossed his arms. "If that's the case, how come you're talking to us?"

That question hadn't occurred to Leopold. If it had, he would have assumed it was just part of the general magicness of OotL. Except... it didn't make sense that Bidulla—or whoever was in charge of such things—would send him TV characters who were potentially helpful. Or that she would choose shows that had comforted him in his childhood.

"Okay, fine. Maybe I can somehow manifest you guys. But that's not helpful. I need to escape this place, but I can't get anything out, not even a message to Crispin."

The older man raised one beautifully tweezed eyebrow. "Maybe the answer isn't getting things out. Maybe it's drawing things in."

They both watched him expectantly, clearly waiting for him to get it.

He didn't, though, and a moment later they hopped into a black car and raced away, leaving him with nothing but a bright yellow screen with a speech bubble that said *KLONK!*

He didn't want to draw things in. What was he supposed to do? Zap Crispin here so he was imprisoned too? As much as Leopold missed him, he would never stoop so low, even if he could. Crispin deserved his freedom.

This is stupid. He clicked off the TV, stomped over to the bed, and fell dramatically onto it. The problem was that he had zero ideas. Which wasn't a surprise, since Crispin had said that creativity came from Chaos, and right now Leopold was fresh out of Chaos. Which sucked. Chaos *did* help make the worlds beautiful. Without it, life would be as pointless and featureless as this room, without even a poster on the walls.

Wait.

Wait wait wait.

Draw things in.

Due to the magic spell or whatever hex the OotL people had put on this room, Leopold couldn't send Chaos outward. But what if he could pull Chaos *inward*?

There was a lot of Chaos in the worlds; any idiot could see that. Incarcerated or not, Leopold was a part of that Chaos. He was Chaos. And the Chaos was him. So all he had to do....

He reached deep inside himself, metaphorically speaking, and discovered a single thread. He gave it an experimental tug, and it moved.

When he pulled harder, it moved some more.

He imagined a fishing reel somewhere in his center. The handle might be a little hard to turn, as if there were a giant fish on the other end, but with patience he could manage.

If this worked, the worlds would become increasingly dull, bereft of music and dance and storytelling and painting and... all of the things that made life worthwhile. Including love.

People would notice pretty fast, and they wouldn't be pleased.

The Office of the Lost would have to do *something*. Like maybe come open the door to find out what he was up to.

Was he willing to hold Chaos hostage in return for his release? Sure. They were already holding him, and he was Chaos personified.

"After all, turnabout is fair play." Grinning, Leopold set about it in earnest, reeling in Chaos.

27
CRISPIN

eo.

He was doing this. It had to be him. *But how?*

A sudden surge of hope swept through Crispin.

The building across the street snapped and straightened, trans-forming itself into an assortment of unbending lines on a plane as flat as Qylzryd's stomach.

Crispin shook his head to clear out *that* particular image. He was very angry with Qyl at the moment, and the memory of the man's magnetic charms was not going to distract him.

Down the street, a series of sizzles and pops accompanied a row of trees as they shivered and flattened. They dropped a season's worth of paper-thin leaves in an instant, which tumbled to the ground in a rustling clutter.

Minkis chittered anxiously on his shoulder. "Not good, Acorn Man."

He nodded. "Maybe not. But I'd bet Leo's behind this."

"What's the little bushy-tailed rat on about now?" Aspin glared at him.

Crispin's eyes widened. "It's happening to you too." His once muscular and very handsome brother was flattening out, becoming a mere wisp of his former self as his cheeks and nose drew back and his hair lost its luster, making him look like something in a funhouse mirror.

"But not to us. Curious." His mother looked *exactly* the same—though was it just his imagination or was her silver gown a little more tattered and worn than before?

The two of them were increasingly out of place in this strange new world.

Her eyes narrowed. "Why is your... pet not affected?"

Crispin glanced at his best friend, who was still chittering away on his shoulder. "I don't know. Maybe because he's so close to me?" He scratched the squirrel under the chin, and Minkis let out a pleased little squirrel growl. "It doesn't matter. Right now we have to get to the Office to save Leo, and put an end to this."

"You think he's responsible?" One eyebrow arched, as if the Fairy Queen conceded the possibility that Leo was more powerful than she'd believed. Or perhaps it just signaled that she thought Crispin was crazy.

"Yes, I think Leopold is doing this. Somehow." His mother's use of the personal pronoun was a marked upgrade from what she'd called Leo before. Progress, of a kind.

"What about me?" Aspin's voice was a shadow of its former self. He was flailing about and ultimately lost his balance and slipped to the ground, floating downward for a few feet before settling onto the equally flat pavement. "Help me! Don't leave me here!" Even his voice sounded dull and toneless.

Crispin sighed. "You'll be fine if we can get all of this fixed." He knelt and began to roll up his brother into a tight scroll.

"What are you doing?" Aspin demanded. "Mother, you can't let mpprhhllggg." The rest was lost as Crispin tied the roll closed with a neat bit of ribbon from out of his backpack. He tucked Aspin safely away inside.

His mother hid a smile. "So what do we do now?"

He stared at her. "You're asking me?" She'd never asked for his advice, not once in his entire life. The world really had turned itself inside out.

The Mother of Fae gestured at the still-flattening city of Odds. "This is your mess as much as it is mine. Perhaps it *is* time for the two of you, after all."

He blinked. Things were shifting, and not just outside of him, in the world. He wasn't sure he was ready for the weight of responsibility that a relationship required. And not just any relationship. With his soulmate. How could this be happening? He was just a quiet desk fae.

You are Order, personified. What the little voice inside of him proclaimed still seemed strange to him, but maybe not so surprising. All of his life he'd been good at organization, and at OotL he'd had the best perfecality score for years. He took a deep breath and squared his shoulders. *I can do this. Besides, Leo needs me.*

"We need to go to the Office. Between the two of us, we can get this sorted out."

His mother nodded. "I'd take us there, but I find myself... diminished." She snapped her fingers, but nothing happened.

Maybe it was the lack of Chaos in the air? He almost felt sorry for her. Almost. "Not a problem. I can get us there." He pulled out his travel device. "Thea, take us back to the Office of the Lost." He waited for a portal to open up.

Her lights flashed, then went out. "I'm sorry, Crispin. There seems to be some sort of block." It was good to have her back to her normal, competent, non-singing self.

"Flying faeries of Flathium Four!" *Bidulla.* She'd managed to revoke his access somehow. She must have known he'd be coming.

"There has to be another way." His mother seemed... shorter now, more... mortal? She also looked tired.

Another way. Who else had access, that he could get to quickly? *Juzir.* Someone Bidulla trusted, who had just been to OotL. "Juzir can get us in."

An arched eyebrow greeted his suggestion, a gesture that at one time would have sent him scrambling back to his room in fear. "Didn't he betray you?"

Crispin snorted. "Yes. Him and Qyl. It may take some work to get him to agree. Fortunately I know just the creature for the job." He'd never thought he would willingly return to the giants' world—what with them having a sweet tooth for fae and all—but a friend was a friend. Crispin straightened up, pulled his shirt taut, and addressed his friend-cum-travel device. "Thea, take us to Vlotho."

The air shimmered, and a small travel portal appeared in the air before them. It looked a little weird around the edges—black and white where it usually sparkled with color—but the purple forests of Vlotho beckoned them from the other side.

"After you." He held out his arm, and his mother, after looking at the portal as if it might bite her, stepped carefully over the threshold of the shimmering image. Crispin followed, feeling a strange surge of energy as he passed through the flat surface.

It snapped shut behind him, and three things happened at once.

He noticed Minkis was gone.

His backpack exploded, depositing a full-size, very angry, and entirely three-dimensional Aspin on the ground next to him, a red ribbon tied around his temples like a headband. "Crispin, I should—"

A booming voice shook the purple trees, sending a flock of nesting white somethings skyward in a mad flapping frenzy.

"WHO DARES INVADE MY... oh, is that you, Crispin?" The owner of the voice squatted, squinting at them through a giant eye.

Crispin waved. "Hello, Fromlith. So good to see you again. Hope you don't mind that I brought some company."

A grin, as hideous as it was welcoming, showed a row of teeth, each one nearly half Crispin's size. Next to him, Aspin had become as still as a statue.

It was good to know the effects of the Great Flattening could be reversed. The draining of Chaos from the Connected Worlds must not have reached Vlotho yet.

"You are always welcome, Master Moss'caladin. And who are your friends?" His breath could have knocked out a were-ox, and not just due to the gale force of it.

"These are my brother, Aspin..."

Aspin managed a bow and almost fell over.

"...and my mother, the illustrious Cerillia Ailedrin Moss'caladin, Queen of the Fae."

Fromlith blushed. "I am honored to welcome Her Majesty to my humble abode." One giant palm indicated his cottage, which was almost large enough to hold all of the Prickles Hotel and still have room for a giant teapot. He stood and assayed what he must have thought was a gentlemanly bow, scaring the flock of maybe-birds once again. "To what do I owe this honor?"

Crispin stood on his tiptoes in a failed attempt to match Fromlith's stature. "We need your help to... *enlist* the services of a certain archosaur wizard who owes me a favor."

Fromlith sat onto a giant stone chair that the bulk of his body had previously hidden from view and he scratched his chin, a sound akin to a woodsman sawing down a tree. "Me mother's a-visiting soon for her summer stay, and I was planning to finish off the addition before she arrived." He indicated a large pile of stone that had apparently crushed two or three of the pretty purple trees when it had been laid down. "Perhaps a week from Frorsday?"

Crispin exchanged a look with his mother. He had no idea when Frorsday was, but a week or more away was too long.

The Queen of Fae cleared her throat. "Mister...." She glanced at Crispin, one eyebrow raised.

"Flokrion." He whispered it, but Fromlith probably heard anyhow. Giants had excellent hearing, what with the ears that were as big as a fae. Or a human.

"Mister Flokrion, I'm afraid our request is quite urgent. Something is sucking all the Chaos out of the Connected Worlds, and if we don't put a stop to it, your beautiful house may soon collapse, like a house of cards."

That got Fromlith's attention. He sat up and then looked worriedly over his shoulder at his home. "You don't say."

Crispin tried again. "Look, Leo's in danger. You remember Leo, right?"

Fromlith leaned forward so that one of his huge eyes was just above Crispin. "Leo's in danger?"

Crispin nodded. "Someone has taken him, and we have to get him back. Will you help us?" He took a deep breath. "I'm sure my mother can send someone, once this is all over, to help you build your addition."

Cerillia hissed, but at a stern glare from Crispin, she silenced and finally nodded. "I would be honored to help you enlarge your... house. It's truly like nothing I have ever seen before."

Giants weren't great with nuance, and Fromlith rose to full height, beaming with pride at the perceived compliment. "So kind of you to say, miss. It's built of nothing but the finest stone from Mount Aspire—"

"It's truly lovely." Crispin cut him off. "But we must hurry." A stand of trees in the distance was markedly losing its brilliant color.

"Of course. Do I need anything?"

Crispin shook his head. "Just your giant self." He pulled Thea out, relieved.

"You know, we giants are resistant*ish* to magic."

Crispin laughed in spite of the gravity of their situation. "I'm quite aware. That's why you're perfect for this position."

Fromlith blushed, momentarily turning as purple as the forest.

"Thea, can you take us to Earth 2?"

"Of course, boss. But how is *he* going to fit through?"

Fromlith chuckled. "Don't worry about me. You three... or four...?"

Thea flashed. "Four. Thank you for recognizing me." It was said with a bit of an edge, as if *someone* had been remiss in that department.

"You four go through, then I'll follow."

Crispin frowned. Thea was right... the portal was barely large enough for fae-sized entities. "You sure?"

Fromlith gestured them toward the portal, and the wind of his hand's passage nearly knocked Crispin off his feet. "Go on, little ones."

Crispin sighed. If Fromlith said he could do it, well, maybe giantish magic included the ability to... smallen?... when necessary. "Come on then." The portal showed the same tidy park he and Leo had arrived at, what seemed like a lifetime before.

But where was Minkis?

"Mink?"

The squirrel was suddenly there, on his shoulder. Or had he been there all along?

"Hello, Minkis. Good to see you again." Fromlith sounded genuinely happy to see the little squirrel.

"How do you two know..." Crispin sighed. "Oh, never mind." One more mystery for later.

He was so tired. He just had to hold himself together long enough to save Leo, and then he could rest.

"Can't we just go home?" Aspin sounded whinier—and younger—than usual.

"Just be glad you're three-dimensional again." Crispin wished his brother was anywhere else but here. It would make things easier.

Cerillia suppressed a smile.

Crispin set the example, stepping confidently through the portal into a warm, rainy summer afternoon on Earth 2. The rain smelled like spring.

His mother and Aspin followed. "Thank you, Thea. I'm sorry if I overlook you, sometimes."

"You're welcome, Crispy."

Oh no, we're not going to let that get started. "Crispin, please."

"As you wish. Cris*pin*."

They all expectantly turned back to the still-open portal.

A massive thumb slipped through, grasping the edge of the shimmering portal. It began to tug, dragging the edge of it upwards with a hideous howling screech. The door between worlds grew in fits and starts, fighting the giant's grip but losing in ever weakening stages until its top edge finally jumped all at once a good thirty feet into the air with a loud crackling *snap*.

Fromlith stepped through, his giant feet shaking the park, and then let go of the poor, abused portal, which popped out of existence like a soap bubble.

Crispin stared at the space where it had been. *That was interesting.*

Giants were surprising creatures, far beyond the lunkish (and somewhat flesh-eating) traits usually assigned to them in the stories. *Thank the Red Dukes that Frommy's a vegetarian.*

Then he looked around.

Their arrival on Earth 2 had drawn a crowd of archosaurs and their humanish pets.

Leo, we're coming! They'd better snap to it and find his former wizard friend, and then move on to the Office before the Chaos Wave caught up to them.

Fromlith dusted himself off, causing cries of consternation from the crowd. "Where to, my little friends?"

28

LEOPOLD

Fishing for Chaos was exhausting.

It wasn't a terrible or painful task. In fact, every little bit of Chaos that Leopold reeled in felt satisfying, like adding a rare figurine to a collection or fitting a Lego piece properly into place. And it wasn't as if he had anything better to do with his time. It was either Chaos-fishing, napping, watching ancient TV, or feeling sorry for himself. Honestly, he could do two or three of those things at once, which was better multitasking than he usually managed.

But catching all those parts of himself and drawing them inward was mentally taxing. If he didn't concentrate, those parts slipped away from him, and then he had to redo his work. He wasn't especially good at concentrating; he'd never done much of it in the past.

So eventually he needed to take a break. He locked his imaginary Chaos fishing reel in place so the line wouldn't play out, and he collapsed onto the couch with a heavy sigh. He desperately wished there was something else to distract him in this prison. Chores to do. Food to eat. Books to read. Someone to talk to.

He'd led a fairly solitary life, not because he chose to but because his knack for causing disaster drove people away. Maybe nobody knew he was made of Chaos—that wasn't the sort of thing most folks would assume—but they could sense *something* off about him. Something hazardous.

His loneliness had been painful when he was a kid and never got picked for teams or invited to birthday parties. Things got worse after his parents died and he bounced from foster home to foster home, dragging his meager belongings in a plastic garbage bag that inevitably tore at the most inconvenient times. By the time he reached adulthood, he told himself he was used to solitude. *Lone wolf*, he assured himself. *Individualist. Hardcore introvert.* He'd never been fully convinced, though. And his recent time with Crispin had blown all of that out of the water.

Gods, it had felt so good to spend time with someone. Even if a good chunk of it had involved escaping disaster or death.

Oops. There he was, self-pitying again when he was supposed to be on break. "You're not on the clock, Leo," he said. "Chill."

Easier said than done. Maybe he should get back to fishing. He had no idea how big his task would be. How much Chaos was there in the Connected Worlds?

Suddenly, an old memory resurfaced. It had been sunk deep in his unconscious since he was a kid, but now here it was, bobbing along on the surface.

When Leopold was nine—a few months before his parents' fatal camel accident—they took him to a little cabin somewhere in the woods. Due to limited finances and his dad's work schedule, they rarely went on vacation, so this had been a real treat. Even though bears broke into their car, Leopold slipped and sprained an ankle, and all three of them ended up with poison oak rashes. In between the calamities, they'd had fun.

One day they'd fished in a river, although nobody caught anything except bushes on the opposite bank. Dad got a fishing hook stuck in his thumb. Leopold's rod broke. When they took a break for lunch, a downpour began, instantly soaking them and ruining their sandwiches. But they'd laughed almost the whole time, even when

Mom tumbled into the ice-cold —but thankfully not very deep—water. Leopold's parents had behaved as if it was amusing that everything went wrong; Dad said something about Murphy's Law, whoever that was. They'd ruffled Leo's hair and told him he was a great kid and they were glad he was there. He'd believed them.

Now, on the couch somewhere in the bowels of the Office of the Lost, Leopold let out a shaky sigh. His parents had loved him, no matter how much of a mess he was.

After a few minutes, he got up, switched on the TV, and shuffled back to the couch. He was looking for entertainment rather than advice, but if Robin or Jeannie wanted to pop back in, he wouldn't object.

Instead he got a cartoon.

At first he was disappointed that it wasn't *SpongeBob*, which had been a childhood favorite. In fact, he still watched it now and then. This TV, however, only seemed to receive much older shows. Then he realized it was *Rocky and Bullwinkle*, and that was okay too. His foster parents had owned parts of that series on DVD.

In this episode, Bullwinkle the moose could predict the weather via a bunion on one hoof. Bad guys broke into the home he shared with Rocky the squirrel, bound and gagged Rocky, and started to kidnap Bullwinkle. All of which hit a little too close to home for Leopold, considering his recent misadventures. Intending to change the channel, he got up from the couch, but then the image on the screen shifted a little. Instead of a cartoon, Rocky was now a live-action squirrel.

A live-action squirrel who looked really familiar.

"Minkis?"

The squirrel shook himself free of the ropes, tossed aside the gag, and scampered forward. "Chaos Man!" he squeaked.

Yeah, okay. Well, the squirrel wasn't *wrong*. "How did you get inside—" Leopold stopped abruptly because those sorts of explanations weren't important right now. "Are you all right? Is Crispy all right?"

"Acorn Man's sad and angry and good."

"Sad and angry?"

Minkis used a hind leg to scratch behind one ear. "He's looking for Chaos Man."

A *puff* of hope filled him. Followed by an equally strong *huff* of fear. "Is he angry at me?"

This time, Minkis gave him an incredulous look, as if Leopold were the stupidest person he'd ever met. "Anger at lizard man and big man that tastes...." Minkis made a gagging sound. "He loves Chaos Man."

"Oh." Relief felt as sweet as a delta breeze on a hot summer night. But then Leopold remembered his previous concerns. "I love him too. But I'm afraid I might have accidentally magicked him into loving me back."

"Love *always* magic, silly man."

"Okay, fine. But it's not right to bespell someone into—"

Minkis called him something in Squirrel that sounded distinctly unflattering. Leopold would have objected, but he was already conversing with a squirrel on television. Actually arguing with him seemed like a step too far into insanity.

"Acorn Man is for Chaos Man. Chaos man is for Acorn Man. Kismet."

Minkis sounded so sure of himself. He could be just making this stuff up, but Leopold decided to believe him.

"Okay," he said with a sigh. "Got it. We were *meant to be*. But now I'm locked up here, and he's out there. Can he come into the TV too?" Surely if Leopold could speak directly with Crispin, they could figure this whole thing out.

But Minkis dashed his hopes. "Only Minkis." Then he winked, which was interesting to see, made a noise like a cat trying to hawk up a hairball, and opened his mouth. A thick little gray cloud wafted out. It floated toward the screen. Then *through* the screen. And then it floated right through Leopold's chest, where it joined the Chaos he'd reeled in.

"You *ate* some Chaos?" Leopold asked.

"Tastes good." Minkis cocked his head, looking around the room, a speculative gleam in his eyes. "Does Chaos Man have acorns?"

"No, sorry. They haven't supplied me very well here." He gestured to indicate the mostly bare room and his mostly bare body.

"No acorns is sad."

Leopold chuckled in spite of himself. "No Crispin is even sadder."

Minkis made a sympathetic chittering noise. "Keep the tail bushy, Chaos Man." He winked again and scampered offscreen. The TV clicked off.

Slightly heartened, Leopold returned to Chaos-fishing.

29
CRISPIN

Crispin took in his surroundings. They were in the same park where he and Leo had arrived—had it been only a couple days before? Time seemed stretched beyond all meaning.

In some ways, it seemed like he had known Leo forever. Perhaps he had, if what his mother had said about the relationship between Chaos and Order was right. But in other ways, Crispin felt as if he hardly knew anything about him.

Juzir's apartment was across town, and Crispin was tired of wasting time. "Fromlith, if you don't mind?"

The giant nodded, lowering a massive palm to the ground.

Crispin stepped up nimbly.

"Giant man." Minkis chittered. "Friend?"

"Yes. A good one." Crispin still wasn't used to Minkis actually talking. How did he know Giant man... Fromlith? And where had he disappeared to when they'd first arrived on Vlotho? *A problem for later.* If he were keeping a ledger, it would be stuffed full of problems for later.

Fromlith lifted them smoothly into the air and then offered his other hand to Cerillia and Aspin. The latter climbed eagerly onto the flattened palm, but Cerillia regarded it with a level of disgust she normally reserved for Crispin and his "lifestyle." She didn't approve of tree living.

"Can't we walk? Although a nice litter wouldn't be unwelcome...." She looked around hopefully, as if a team of handsome, muscular, well-oiled men might materialize, ready to carry her through the city in the manner to which she was accustomed.

There was only a large—and growing—crowd of archosaurs, snapping photos and pointing at the giant in their midst.

Crispin was breaking six laws and about forty-three regulations by bringing Fromlith here and "cross-contaminating" the worlds without prior permission, but he didn't care. If he didn't act—and soon—there would be no worlds to protect. "Hop on, mother. It's surprisingly comfortable."

Fromlith curved his hand, and Crispin settled in. Minkis made a show of scrambling around the edge of the great palm, looking out over the forest below.

"That tickles." Fromlith's hand twitched, and Crispin grabbed hold of his pinkie finger to avoid being dumped over the edge.

Still excited, Minkis chattered, "High, so high! Higher than home tree!"

Fromlith's chuckle dislodged a flock of golden birds from a nearby tree, and they rose with squawks of protest.

"Minkis! Back to my shoulder!"

The squirrel hung his head, but complied. "Chaos Man misses you."

Crispin blinked. He hadn't realized that Minkis had thoughts on the matter. "Maybe so. We'll find him. I promise."

His mother finally gave in and climbed up onto the giant's other hand, her mouth distorted in a moue of distaste.

"Where to?" Fromlith brought Crispin up to get a better look at him.

"See that tall white building with the golden spire? He lives there, on the tenth floor." He wondered if Juzir would hear them coming. Did they have quakes here? "Oh, and Fromlith?"

The giant paused mid-step. "Yes?"

"Try not to crush any of the natives."

"You got it, friend." Fromlith squinted at the ground far below. "Excuse me, coming through." He eased his sandaled foot down, giving the archosaurs time to move out of the way.

"This is going to take longer than walking," Cerillia complained.

"But look at this view!" Aspin was perched at the edge of Fromlith's hand, entranced.

Crispin felt sorry for his brother, for once. The handsome fae had rarely been away from their mother's side, and almost never off the Estate. Now he was like an aardvark in an anthill, drinking it all in with an infectious enthusiasm. Crispin could almost forget they were on a dire mission.

They reached the edge of the park, and something caught his attention out of the corner of his eye. He turned to see what it was, and his mouth dropped open.

A patrol of leathery... things—like bats but larger, with great paper-thin wings and long beak-like snouts—were approaching from the far side of the park.

Minkis strained to see them. "Birds. Big big birds!"

"Careful, Mink. Don't want you falling." They *were* kind of like birds, and as they got closer, their riders became visible: archosaurs in trim blue uniforms with gold embellishments. "The police."

Leo would have said something charming and human and possibly outdated, like "Damn, the fuzz are here." Crispin felt a little pang.

Fromlith continued his journey unabated, heading up a broad city boulevard, finding places to put his huge feet between cars and on empty patches of sidewalk, and the screams that accompanied his trek seemed to be more cries of fear than those of the mortally wounded, much to Crispin's relief. Breaking rules was one thing. Breaking people was quite another.

To his credit, Fromlith seemed to be causing minimal property damage as well, though at least one fire hydrant would need replacing and the center median's attractive assortment of jungle-inspired foliage would never be the same.

"Giant being, please cease and desist this unapproved rampage." The lead flyer held some kind of megaphone.

They thought this was a rampage? It was more of a walk in the park—literally. "Sorry, can't do that. Just going to see a friend. We'll be out of your hair shortly!" Crispin's voice couldn't match the megaphone, but the man seemed to have heard him. He was handsome for an archosaur, with a square jaw and a crest of bright blue plumage that complemented his uniform nicely.

"Negative. Please rein in your giant and return to the park." The flyer swooped close by, circling Fromlith and bringing him to an abrupt halt. The other flyers joined him, making circles around Crispin and his companions. Residents of the nearby apartment building, including their human-looking pets, gathered at the windows to stare.

Fromlith, his brow knitted in concern, lifted Crispin closer to his large face. "What do we do?" he asked, quietly for a giant. "Should I knock them out of the sky?"

Crispin sighed. He didn't want to do any more damage or cause any more harm to life than was strictly necessary. "No, we'll figure out how to deal with this."

"I repeat, please return to the park, the lot of you, so we can sort this matter out." The captain of the police seemed to be growing steadily more annoyed.

Crispin understood. How would he feel if his beloved forest was invaded by a giant, hell-bent on beating a path to one of its biggest trees? Still, he was at a loss about how to deal with it without causing more harm.

"Make cold." Minkis chittered in his ear.

"You're cold?" It was currently warm on Earth 2, like it normally was; most of this world boasted a tropical temperature.

"No. Make. Cold."

"Ahhh." Crispin's eyebrow shot up. Juzir and his people were cold blooded. "Mother, could you... arrange for a little local snowstorm?"

"A what?"

"They don't like cold." He pointed at the flyers circling them.

"Ah. Yes. Of course." Her voice almost sounded approving. She lifted her hands grandly, miming a sprinkling of snow—not strictly necessary, but Cerillia was nothing if not dramatic.

At first he was afraid it wouldn't work—she'd seemed to have lost her powers back in Odds—but then the temperature began to rapidly drop. The air filled with snowflakes, sparkling under the tropical sun, and the flyers began to lose altitude, their wings beating in ever-slowing speeds.

Must be more Chaos magic here for her to draw on. Indeed, none of the city seemed to have flattened, just yet.

"Please... desist. Cold...." The leader's flyer slipped out of the air, falling like a very cumbersome snowflake to land on a five-story building behind them. The steed promptly curled up into a circle, its rider asleep on its back. Soon all of the police force was grounded, and the civilians in the area had slumped to the ground too.

"Nice work!" Crispin let his voice practically shine with approval and was surprised to see the slightest blush bloom on his mother's cheeks. "Fromlith, take us onward."

"As you wish, friend." The giant resumed his careful plodding through the city streets. They made good time, arriving at the shiny white building in minutes.

"What now? A pretty building, but not made to giants' standards." He tapped on a window and the glass creaked, groaned, and then cracked.

"Please, Fromlith, try not to break it. We need one of the residents alive and in good shape."

"Any one of them?" Fromlith brought a giant eye close to one of the windows, looking inside. "We have many to choose from. This one looks particularly delicious...."

"You're a vegetarian, remember?" His giant friend eating a local was the last thing Crispin needed on his conscience.

"Maybe so. But it doesn't hurt to look."

"Anyhow...." Crispin did his best to sound authoritative. "We're looking for a particular one. Juzir. I mentioned him before, I think."

Residents of this building, too, were coming to their windows to see what was causing the disturbance outside.

Crispin spotted his once-friend at last. "Up there." He pointed at a balcony on the tenth floor. "Juzir! It's me!" He waved at his former friend, as if it were the most natural thing in the world to arrive for a casual lunch in the palm of a giant.

Juzir opened his glass door onto the narrow terrace, his archosaur brow furrowed in a clear sign of annoyance but tempered with fear. "What are you doing here in such... company?"

Crispin swallowed his anger at seeing the person who had betrayed him. "We need your help."

Juzir waved his tiny arms in negation. "Sorry, I don't have time. I'm busy overseeing my bathroom remodel, fixing the damage that your *collection* caused—"

"His name is Leo. And if I'm not mistaken, you're paying for it with money you got for kidnapping him. So you don't have the moral high ground here."

Juzir sighed. "Go home. You have no idea what you are up against." He spun his hands over one another and cast a sparkling glow-ball at Crispin, who flinched and then watched it dissipate before reaching him. "What in the Dicharthian hells?"

"Giants are resistant to magic, remember? *Now*, Frommy."

The giant reached forward and scooped up Juzir in the same palm that held Crispin, lifting them into the air.

Crispin took a couple of deep breaths to clear away the dizziness from the sudden ascent.

Juzir looked over the edge of Fromlith's palm, panicking. "Put me down. You have no right—"

"You lost your rights when you invaded my son's house and stole his future husband." Cerillia sounded as indignant as Crispin had ever heard her.

"His... future... what?"

Crispin grinned. "My future husband." He liked the sound of that. "Order and Chaos. Opposites attract, you know."

Juzir stared at him. "You're... Order personified?" Then he nodded, grinding his impressive teeth. "That makes a strange sense. That's why he's here." He pointed, unexpectedly, at Minkis. "I'm sorry I didn't recognize you before."

"Um, yes. He's my...." He was going to say *pet*, but that wasn't quite right. "Friend."

"Friend of Acorn Man." Minkis nudged Crispin's cheek with his own furry one.

"Sure. *Friend.*" He looked over at the Queen of Fae. "So he's the one?"

She nodded. "I sent him away for his own good, and to learn about the joined worlds. One day, he will take my place."

All the grayish-brown drained out of Juzir's handsomely scaled face. "Your Majesty." He bowed to Crispin as well as he was able on the uneven surface of Fromlith's palm. "How may I be of service?"

"Oh, get up, Juzzy. I'm still just good old Crispin." Was this what it was going to be like? People constantly bowing to him and deferring to his every whim?

He hoped his mother had a long way to go before she felt the need to turn the Estate over to him.

"I'm sorry, Crispin. I didn't know...."

"Water under the bridge." Although to be honest, his old friend was on shaky ground; it would take more than one act to redeem himself. "Can you get us into the Office?"

"Of course." He stared at Minkis. "But there's one thing you should know first...."

30
LEOPOLD

Time was weird in this place. Not only were there no clocks —or windows to mark day and night—but Leopold also didn't have any of the usual bodily urges that helped him gauge the hours. The only way he could measure time was with TV shows, but the characters kept stopping to chat with him, so that wasn't terribly helpful either.

When he took a break from fishing, he had nice chats with Hoss Cartwright, Gomer Pyle, and Maxwell Smart, and that was pleasant enough. None of them had any tips on how he might escape his current prison—or at least contact Crispin—but he did learn quite a lot about horses and the Marines.

For a few minutes he'd actually hoped that Maxwell Smart might be helpful, but it turned out that even though he knew a lot about KAOS, an evil organization, he didn't know much at all about Chaos, the stuff Leopold was made of and now hoarding.

Leopold did feel stronger as he collected more Chaos. More... himself. But he didn't seem able to do anything with that strength, which was supremely frustrating. He couldn't even change the color of the stupid walls. *Man, I hate white walls.*

It was Sheriff Andy Taylor who finally gave Leopold an idea. It started out as an amiable conversation about small towns, and then Leopold remembered what had annoyed him when he'd watched reruns of the show years later. "There's no such place as Mayberry and there never was. You created this false paradise that makes a lot of people all fuzzy-eyed nostalgic. But where were the African Americans and the segregation? Where were the cops who enforced white supremacy and persecuted people of color? Where were—"

"Now, just hang on there," the sheriff drawled. "It's only a television show. A li'l bit of escapism to make folks happy. You can't begrudge someone a li'l happiness, can you?"

Leopold crossed his arms. "I can if it creates false narratives and unreasonable expectations."

The sheriff kept on smiling. "You know, the children who watched me and Jeannie and Samantha? Just a few years later they were burnin' bras and draft cards and riotin' at Stonewall. So maybe we weren't so bad after all."

Leopold was pretty sure that the social activism of the sixties and seventies wasn't fueled by inane fifties sitcoms, and he was working up a good argument in his favor when Sheriff Andy waved a hand. "Y'know, sometimes there's not much we can do at the moment to change the world around us. When that happens, well, we gotta change ourselves instead. Kinda reshape ourselves and learn new things so we *can* change the world." He turned to look at something offscreen, then faced Leopold again. "Well, sir, I have to go. Looks like Opie and Barney have got themselves in trouble again. You take care, now."

Leopold was left glaring at a blank screen.

"Reshape ourselves," he grumbled. "I was recently a deer creature—among other things—and I started out as Chaos clouds, so I guess I've done plenty of reshaping. Yet here I am." He stomped his foot for emphasis.

No. Wait. He stomped his *hoof*, because for a split second, that's what he had. And when he concentrated hard, he had a hoof again. Two of them, in fact.

He flexed the Chaos inside him like a muscle, and he had birds' feet with sharp talons, similar to a giant eagle. Then he had enormous furry feet like a Sasquatch. Webs like a duck. Tentacles, although that was frankly pretty disturbing so he went back to nice human feet again—except he gave them magenta-and-cobalt stripes, just because he could.

Was the containment spell failing? He eagerly jumped up onto his colorful feet and tried to make a door appear in the wall.

Nothing happened. No door. No window. Not even a peephole. He wasn't affecting the room at all.

But he *was* changing himself, just like Sheriff Andy had said. Apparently the spell stopped him from using Chaos on the world around him but didn't stop him from utilizing it on his own person. *Okay. So how can this help me escape?*

He experimented with changing his size, but even though he made himself as big as Fromlith, he just ended up squished uncomfortably in the now too-small room. He couldn't punch a hole in the walls or stomp through the floor. Then he made himself tiny, but the room truly had no exits, not even one big enough for an ant.

It also didn't help when he shifted his color, his species, or his general shape. Being a dodecahedron was briefly amusing—but not helpful.

Leopold stomped again, this time out of frustration. What had the sheriff said? *Reshape ourselves and learn new things.* How the heck was he supposed to learn anything when he was stuck in this room? He couldn't even google stuff!

"How can we learn without the internet?" he asked out loud. Because people *had* done so, once upon a time. He'd seen memes about it. They'd learned through literature and teachers, but he had access to neither. They'd also learned through experience, through trying things and using their senses.

Senses? Huh. What if he could use his to figure out where he was in OotL and whether there was anyone nearby who could help? He couldn't see through the walls. Yet the room couldn't be completely sealed or he would have run out of oxygen by now. And if air could flow in and out from outside, maybe so could sounds.

Leopold concentrated. He wasn't sure what animal had the best hearing abilities, but he knew bats were pretty good at it, so he started with that. He made his ears grow bigger and added muscles so they could twist around. It felt weird—sort of stretchy and tickly—but not painful or unpleasant. Then he did his best to make his hearing incredibly acute. He closed his eyes and focused.

And... yes! From far away came snatches of conversation. One of the desk fae was discussing lunch options with another, while a trio of them were bragging to each other about their latest exploits. Apparently one had recently collected the Flame of Egeaqesh, whatever that was, and was very happy with herself over it.

Leopold heard pens scratching on paper. He heard faint barks, growls, squawks, and honks, presumably from other creatures that had been locked up in this place. He heard a toilet flush, followed by a running sink. He heard someone drop a coin that bounced and rolled across the floor. He heard footsteps.

None of this was getting him anywhere, though. He swore a few times. "This is stupid. Why am I listening to advice from a fictional 1960s police officer? I give up. I—"

Wait.

Was that screaming? And shouting? And what were those rhythmic pounding noises?

The pounding noise grew faster and he realized it was footsteps. *Heavy* footsteps. A tendril of hope sprouted inside him. He heard several voices all talking at once:

"—must protest, Mother. You're playing favorites and choosing him when you should really—"

"—supervise the workers. Who knows what they're doing to the bathroom when I'm not—"

"—retirement might be a nice option for me as long as I know my Estate will be properly—"

"—not built for people of my stature and I really should—"

"—*squeak chitter chitter*—"

"—figure out which of these thrice-cursed doors is the right one to—"

Crispin. That last one was *Crispin*!

Leopold leaped with joy and followed it with a little dance, waving his hands in the air. "He came for me! Crispy came to rescue me!"

His elation grew to panic, however, when he realized that Crispin and whoever was with him were being chased, and that there were a *lot* of rooms in this place, and that Crispin had no idea which one was Leopold's.

Leopold needed a way to steer him. If sound could enter the room, it made sense that it could leave as well. If it was loud enough.

He focused now on his vocal chords. *I need to be like a whale.* Their voices could be heard for hundreds of miles. Or, if you believe the *Star Trek* movie franchise, their voices could be heard by aliens— who sent a probe that was destroying Earth. Leopold didn't want to turn into a whale because the room was too small and too dry, but maybe he could vocally project like one.

"Crispy!" he shouted. Which was a mistake because he still had super-hearing and that yell *hurt*. He added a new feature to his ears: an automatic volume decrease when he was the one yelling. Then he tried again. "Crispy! I'm here!"

And from far away: "It's him! It's Leo! Fromlith, did you hear that? It's my Leo!" And then, after a brief pause: "Which room is yours?"

Possibly there was a number or some other identification on the door, but Leopold couldn't see it. He shouted back. "Don't know! Follow my voice!"

"Okay!"

Leopold was so overcome with excitement that his heart

galloped and he could barely breathe. Despite that, he sprinted around the room, yelling Crispin's name the whole time and then, for good measure, belting out the theme song from *Gilligan's Island*.

The running footsteps—which must have been Fromlith's—came nearer. "Keep singing!" Crispin said. "You're getting louder!"

Leopold gave him an entire medley of theme songs: *Brady Bunch. Fresh Prince of Bel-Air. Laverne & Shirley. Friends.* He was about to resort to *The Dukes of Hazzard*, which was slightly horrifying, but was saved when something crashed through the wall.

Some*ones* crashed through the wall.

Leopold scrambled back to avoid being squashed but leapt forward again when he saw Crispin leap off Fromlith's hand.

"Crispy!"

"Leo!" Crispin stared at him for a long moment, and Leo started to grow concerned. "My, what big ears you have."

"What? Oh, these! Sorry." He swiftly restored his ears and vocal chords to their normal shapes and capabilities. "Better?"

Crispin grinned. "You look good to me no matter what."

And like in some corny old movie, they flew into each other's arms and kissed, and the music swelled dramatically, and— That wasn't music. It was sirens.

Leopold grabbed Crispin's arms. "We need to get out of here before they arrive and find a way to stuff *all of us* in prison. Hurry!"

With a solemn expression, Crispin shook his head. "We can't run, Leo. They'll track us down and collect us. That's what we—I mean *they* do for a living, remember?"

Leopold didn't fancy the idea of spending his life as a fugitive, and he certainly wouldn't wish that on Crispin. "I can take us to... that Chaos place. I bet they can't get in there. I'll make it look just like your treehouse, I promise. We can even—"

"Leo." Crispin's voice was soft. "We need to confront this. We need to figure out why they've been so insistent on collecting you. And that means... we need to go see the Oracle."

That made sense, even if it didn't make Leopold happy. He just wanted to be free of this place.

He wondered what the Oracle would be like. Some grand fire-breathing dragon? A bunch of old Greek women playing harps and looming... or whatever they did with looms. Or maybe something more like the Wizard of Oz when Toto pulled back the curtain. That would be awesome.

He shot a sour look in the direction of the figures still perched on Fromlith—and man, did Aspin ever look pissed off; that part was good, at least—and grunted. "This stupid Oracle bosses people around and ruins lives. Who is it, anyway?"

Crispin got an odd look on his face and sighed. "I think you'd better ask Minkis."

31
CRISPIN

The life Crispin wanted was at his fingertips—he could feel it. His life mate, his mother's approval, and a future he'd never dreamed of.

Including King of the Fae, not that he was sure he wanted that. He loved working, but being responsible for the Estate and all of that magic sounded like heaping handfuls of responsibility. Still, something about it appealed to him. He'd be the literal Keeper of Order.

Fromlith had left a path of destruction as he'd widened—and heightened—the corridor to make room for his own passage. A piece of the broken doorway wall crashed to the ground, reminding Crispin of how out of his control the current situation was. *Some Order-Keeper I am.*

"You okay, Crispy?" Leo's concern brought him back to the present.

In response, Crispin hugged him tightly. As long as he had Leo on his side, he could accomplish anything. "Yes, I'm much better now."

"What were you saying about Minkis?" Leopold looked around. 'I don't see him. Wasn't he with you?"

"He's... gone ahead. It's... complicated." Juzir had told Crispin something that had shaken him to the core. He turned to his giant-friend. "Fromlith, can you and Juzir keep Bidulla and her minions occupied?" She'd thrown everything she had at them, from a trio of Mazurian mercenaries to the entire office staff of OotL. Crispin wasn't exactly sure where all the minions were right now.

Because Juzir's magic was limited here by the Office's dampening properties, he couldn't port them around the place willy-nilly, but he *could* make life difficult for Crispin's former supervisor.

"You got it, future King."

"I can help." Aspin pulled his sword. "I know I've been an ass to you, little brother. But what you did today...." He blushed. He actually blushed. "Love you, little bro. I'm proud of you."

Crispin blinked. He was fairly certain all thirty-seven known hells had just frozen over, even the one made mostly out of soured mead. "Um... thanks, Aspin."

His brother crushed him in his over-muscled arms, pulling him so tight that the air squeezed out of Crispin's lungs in an undignified gasp.

"I... um... love you too?" he squeaked. He didn't mean for it to come out as a question, but there it was. "You... need... to let... me go." That last part was nothing but a raspy whisper.

Aspin didn't seem to notice the question mark. He dropped his arms, and suddenly Crispin could breathe again. "So what now?"

Everyone turned to face him, including Minkis, who had apparently just returned. "What now, Acorn Man?"

Crispin felt a little queasy. He wasn't used to being the one that people turned to for answers. Especially not all the people, all at once.

Leo leaned in and whispered, "You can do this."

Crispin squeezed his hand gratefully. "We go to see the Oracle."

If Juzir was right—and it would explain *so many things*—the Oracle would know who was behind this, and why Crispin had been sent to collect Leo.

The corridor shook. "That's our cue." Juzir winked at him. "Go!

We'll keep Bidulla and her cronies occupied. You're going to owe me more than a bathroom remodel after this."

Fromlith winked at them with an enormous eye through the broken wall. "Go get them, Your Future Highness." He lumbered off in the direction they'd all come from, and Juzir scurried after him, casting fiery spheres as he went.

"Come on, then." Crispin climbed over the wreckage, taking Leo's hand and helping him through the door.

Thea whistled a happy tune in his pocket.

"Hey, I know that one. It's from the *Wizard of Oz*." Leo frowned. "Well, we just *saw* a wizard, so I'm not sure it's the most accurate...."

Crispin laughed. He'd missed Leo's mental wanderings. "Close enough, I suppose. The Oracle is... magic. Of a sort. He/she/they always know what needs to be collected, and where." Ahead of them, the white corridor was still fae-sized, not having been pounded out of shape by a passing giant. "Come on."

They started down the hall, checking the doors as they passed, each neatly lettered with a unique numerical code. Other than that, there was nothing to set them apart.

They followed the hall past a couple hundred more doors, and then the corridor split into three directions.

Crispin had never seen a floor plan of OotL. He imagined it would be surpassingly strange-looking, the way the corridors combined, split up, and recombined.

Not only that, but the layout seemed to change from time to time. Usually he just *knew* where things were, or they came to him as he had need of them. But maybe Bidulla had blocked that, too?

He scratched his head, staring hopelessly at the three tunnels.

"Um, Crispy?" Leo's warm hand touched his shoulder. "Are we lost?"

"Not... exactly." He could still sort of feel the Oracle, as if its eye was on him. But he couldn't sense *where* it was. "Maybe if we...."

The hallway shifted, momentarily flashing in a blur of bewildering colors. When things settled, Bidulla was standing in front of him with sour-looking mercenaries at her back.

His enormously tusked boss seemed as surprised to see him as he was her.

Crispin fell back and heard the whisper of Aspin's sword being drawn.

The mercenaries settled easily into a fighting stance, drawing what seemed like a thousand daggers that sparkled under the harsh fluorescent lights.

Crispin had mere seconds before this devolved into a bloody melee.

"Stop!" He put all the strength of his position as the future king of the fae into his voice, and the hallway shook.

Everyone froze.

Bidulla blinked and then looked him up and down, as if really seeing him for the first time. "You've changed."

Coming from her, that was high praise. "Yes, I have. I'm not the meek little desk fae you sent out to collect Leo."

One of her huge furry eyebrows raised at the nickname. She glared at Leopold as if he were a cockroach stuck to her shoe. "This *thing* is a danger to the Connected Worlds. Surely you've seen the damage it has done to hundreds of thousands of citizens. It must be *contained*."

Crispin didn't like the way she said that last word. "Leo is not a thing. You can't just bottle him up and leave him alone for the rest of eternity." His anger was threatening to boil over. He took a deep breath to calm himself and felt Leo's warm hand slip into his. "Besides, look how well that worked the last time. Where was he when he did all this *alleged* damage?" It was real damage—he'd seen it himself—but he wasn't going to give her the satisfaction.

"What did I do?" Leo bit his lip.

"Nothing that can't be fixed." He squeezed Leo's hand.

Bidulla charged on, as ogres tended to do. "We'll do better. Lock him up in a place so deep and empty that he'll never be able to break out."

"Like behind the Red Door?" He glanced at his mother.

Cerillia had the grace to blush. "There is no *safe* place. Trying to bottle him up... to bottle Chaos up... it's always going to find a way out."

Bidulla blinked again, as if seeing Cerillia for the first time.

And perhaps she had. Ogres were also notoriously short-sighted. "My Queen." She went down on one knee. "Surely you must see how dangerous this... *thing* is."

Cerillia drew herself up, and for a moment she was her old self— powerful, mysterious, and scary as the Oark of the Black Forest. "This *thing is* my future son-in-law." She put a hand on Leo's shoulder. "I made a huge mistake when I exiled his father through the Red Door. Chaos only works if there's Order, and Order can only exist when there's Chaos to be organized."

The ogre sputtered. "But Your Majesty—"

Cerillia took a regal step forward and placed one hand on Bidulla's oversized, hairy chin. "Look at him." She forced Bidulla's gaze down onto Leo's face.

They locked gazes, and Bidulla's eyes went wide. "It's... he's... so beautiful. Why did I never see that?" Her eyes rolled up and she slumped, hitting the ground and causing the floor under Crispin's feet to shake.

Leo leapt forward. "Is she okay?" He knelt next to the ogre. "She's still breathing."

"Just overcome. She'll be all right." Cerillia grinned. Her glamour had departed once more, but she still had that air of royalty.

The mercenaries sheathed their knives and stepped back.

Crispin stared at his mother. "What did she see?"

"From Chaos comes beauty. She saw into his soul." There was a deep longing and sadness behind her words that tugged at Crispin's heart.

The mercenaries were staring at one another, unsure what to do now that their employer had decided to take a little floor nap.

Cerillia snapped her fingers. "Come with us. I'll pay you double what the Office offered."

The leader—a woman dressed in black with a red sash, her black hair shaved close to her skull—cleared her throat. "Your Highness." She essayed a deep bow and the others followed her lead.

Crispin stifled a laugh. Power and money could buy almost anything. "Where is the Oracle?" He looked ahead down the hall and then back the way they had come. "It could take all day searching this place to find it."

Leo frowned. "Needle in a haystack."

Such cute colloquialisms. A thought came to him. "Leo, take my hand."

Leo practically leapt up from where he'd been kneeling next to their fallen nemesis and he reached out.

Their touch was electric, sending a surge of love and potential through Crispin. He felt a foot taller and twice as strong as Aspin. "First, you need to let out all that extra Chaos you've been holding in. Send it back where it came from. Can you do that?"

Leo frowned. "I don't know. There's no television—"

"Just let go, Chaos Man." Minkis hopped onto Leo's shoulder and chittered something into his ear.

Leo's eyebrow shot up. "Just like that?"

Minkis bobbed his head. "Easy peasy."

Leo closed his eyes, and the air around him swirled as if he were surrounded by a heat wave.

Crispin knew his part. He reached out, drew in the growing flood of Chaos, setting it in order, and channeled it back to where it had come from.

He could feel it, rolling through him like a flood and then back out into the Connected Worlds. Buildings and streets, trees and people, birds and sky filling with color, plumping out with restored vigor and life, with curvy lines and conflicting impulses.

The entire building shook with the power as it poured from Leo into Crispin and then found its home once again.

It lasted for an eternity, or maybe five minutes, but the thrill of working with Leo like that....

Crispin opened his eyes. A beatific smile lit up Leo's face, and Crispin saw, for just an instant, what Bidulla must have seen in him.

Chaos wasn't the enemy. It was impulse and change and complicated, conflicted beauty. Free will and love and brilliant colors. And it was war and hatred and jealousy and strife, and all the million other things that made life... well, *life.*

All during his own life, Crispin had struggled to stamp out chaos, to put things in perfect order in his home, his job, and his heart. But Order without Chaos was flat and dead and boring.

And Chaos without Order was insanity.

All of these thoughts passed through him in an instant, and then it was done.

"Did I do it? Is it fixed?" Leo, waiting for his answer, looked as eager as a puppy.

Crispin smiled. "Yes. Yes, you did."

"What just happened?" Aspin looked from Leo to Crispin and then to his mother.

"Your brother and his future husband just figured out who they are. Together." Cerillia's smile was tinged with sadness.

Perhaps she regrets exiling her own other half.

Crispin nodded. "Leo set things right."

"I'd kiss you again," Leopold said, "but don't we have an Oracle to find?"

"We can spare a couple seconds." Crispin threw his arms around his Chaos Man, and this time their kiss was different. Their essences mixed, and the tingling spread from Crispin's lips and warmed his whole body. *If that's what a mere kiss is like....*

They broke apart.

"Dude." Leo's voice made the word a sacrament.

"Dude." Crispin grinned again, and Leo returned it.

Minkis leaped back onto his shoulder.

"So how do we find this Oracle?" Leo's eyebrow rose in that adorable way of his.

"We bring it to us." Crispin took Leo's hand again and felt the welcoming surge of Chaos.

The Office halls shifted around them, blowing apart like a slow-motion explosion. For a moment it was all exposed, every nook and cranny, every sealed room holding its secrets. Then it came back together, reassembling itself.

The door to the Oracle was suddenly right in front of them.

"Whoa." Leo's mouth hung open.

"Whoa, indeed. Not even the wards of OotL can stand up to the two of us when we work together."

"Right? That's so much better than an elevator." Leo's eyes twinkled.

The door before them split in two, the crack opening around one side of the giant, winking eye.

Crispin's pulse raced. He'd never been to see the Oracle before. Only Bidulla and a few of the higher-ups had O-Level access.

They stepped into the medium-sized chamber, maybe five meters square. The transparent walls showed a forest scene with little half-seen somethings scampering among the branches.

In the middle of the back wall, a huge eye blinked at them, almost a twin to the one in the entry door, but much larger.

"Who calls upon the great and mighty Oracle?" The deep voice shook the room, coming from everywhere and nowhere, all at once.

Crispin frowned. This wasn't what Juzir had told him to expect.

"It's the Wizard of Oz." Leo was grinning like a madman.

"What?" Crispin had never heard of a place called Oz, and certainly not of a wizard who hailed from there.

Leo jabbed a finger at the lump in Crispin's vest pocket. "Thea. Thea was right. This is the Wizard of Oz." He stalked forward and punched the eye right in, well, the eye.

"Leo, don't—"

But it was too late.

The eye crumpled like a piece of tissue paper, folding back on itself to reveal a series of compartments. And in each one—

"Squirrels?" Leo stumbled back a step. "Why is it filled with squirrels?"

Minkis chittered, and the forty-odd squirrels that had been hidden behind the eye chittered back.

"That's what I was trying to tell you." Crispin still couldn't quite believe it himself. "The Oracle is *squirrels*."

32
LEOPOLD

When Leopold was a little boy, he and his parents had lived in a house near the outskirts of Stockton. The house had felt too small for Leopold even then—his frequent fits of youthful energy banging him into walls and furniture—and it seemed as though parts of the house were always needing repairs.

But he had his own bedroom, and just outside was an ancient oak tree with wide, gnarled branches. When he woke up in the morning, the first thing he always did was look through the window toward the tree. Frequently he'd find a squirrel or two staring back.

The squirrels had been cute enough, but he'd found the experience somewhat unsettling. It was as if they were spying on him. He'd even complained about the creatures to his parents once but hadn't found much sympathy there. "They're just curious," his dad had said. "Maybe they think you're a little nuts." Then he'd chuckled at his own joke. Which was, Leopold had thought at the time, actually pretty funny.

Then Dad had done something to distract Leopold from the topic, and Leopold had never mentioned the squirrels to his parents again. He'd never quite trusted them, however, with their bright eyes and twitchy tails. When he'd met Minkis, Leopold had made an exception to his general policy of squirrel avoidance because Minkis clearly meant a lot to Crispin and, well, Crispin meant a lot to Leopold.

Now, though, it wasn't just Minkis he was facing but rather four dozen of the fluffy gray rodents, all of them chittering at once. If there hadn't been a whole crowd of people there to see him, Leopold might have run away.

Instead he took a deep breath and turned to stare at Crispin. "The Oracle is squirrels?"

Crispin didn't seem any more thrilled—or any less shocked—than Leopold. "Apparently."

"But... how? Why?"

Minkis hopped from Crispin's shoulder onto Leopold's and waved his little front paws in the air. "Acorns! We gather acorns. Sometimes we plant them. Sometimes trees grow." All of his furry compatriots squeaked their agreement.

"I don't get it." Was he just being his usual dense self, or was this another level of crazy in a week that had already brought him a lifetime's share?

Crispin gave Leopold's arm a little squeeze, and that sparkly magic thing crackled briefly around them. "They're metaphorical acorns, Leo."

Leopold shook his head. "What's a metaphorical acorn?"

"I think what Minkis means is that he and his, uh, colleagues, collect bits of information? And when they act on that information—by giving appropriate oracular predictions—there are often positive results."

"Oh." While all of the squirrels chattered something that sounded like agreement, and while Minkis gave Crispin a tiny high five, Leopold thought about this. "I suppose it sort of makes sense. Squirrels scamper everywhere, so I guess they'd have access to all kinds of data." Maybe that's what his childhood squirrels had been doing.

But that still left questions. He turned his head in an attempt to make eye contact with Minkis, which wasn't easy considering Minkis's proximity to his face. "Why do you do it?"

"Keeps us busy, Chaos Man. It's fun."

Well, that was reasonable enough. He'd done plenty of things for lesser motives than that. "How do you guys know what data is important? And how do you decide what predictions to give?"

Minkis made a tiny little squirrel sigh, as if Leopold were way too slow on the uptake. "If you plant enough acorns, at least *some* are bound to grow."

Which meant, Leopold assumed, that lots and lots of the items currently in OotL's collection hadn't needed collecting at all, and now they were just sitting pointlessly somewhere in the vast building, sort of like years-old Beanie Babies in a closet.

Which probably didn't matter if the items were inanimate objects and was maybe not so bad for the last members of those species that would otherwise have gone extinct. But what about him? Had there been a good reason for the squirrels to send the desk fae with the highest perfecality score after a guy who'd screwed up everything for his entire life?

"What's the matter?" Crispin asked softly.

"The squirrels make mistakes. What if I'm one of them?" His whole life felt like a mistake. Why should this be any different? But the thought of losing Crispin threatened to shatter his heart.

Crispin's eyes widened. "You're no mistake!" He grabbed Leopold's hand, hard, grinning at the magic that flowed between them, through them, out of them. "Feel that? That's us, Leo. And it's amazing! That's a pretty huge metaphorical oak tree, don't you think?"

Their combined powers did feel wonderful, and Leopold loved seeing Crispin so happy. This wasn't the fussy, uptight creature who'd come to collect him in Sacramento. This was the man that Leopold loved.

Except that was a problem too, wasn't it?

Leopold gently extricated his hand, but only so he could turn and place both of his palms on Crispin's shoulders. Minkis, of course, remained on Leopold's shoulder, watching with bright eyes.

"Crispy, you need to think about this carefully. You got a job with OotL 'cause your mom arranged it. You got sent after me because squirrels said you should be. Maybe you fell for me because my chaosness—chaosity?—be-spelled you into it. Aren't you pissed off about everyone else screwing with your fate?" He took a deep breath. This was the hardest part to say. "You're the most incredible person I've ever met. I think you deserve to be in control of what happens to you."

For a moment, everyone was still and silent. Even the squirrels. Crispin's eyes were as big and shiny as an anime character's. "Do you mean it?"

"I'd rather spend the rest of my life *curated*—locked up in a room and talking to old TV characters—than force something on you." Wow. That was completely honest. Leopold had never sacrificed anything for anyone, and it felt easier than he'd expected. Because, well, he loved Crispin. And if he had to make this declaration in front of a fairy queen, an ogre, a stuck-up older brother, and an assembly of squirrels, all while wearing nothing but his underwear, so be it.

Crispin let out a noisy breath. "I wish Mother hadn't been so sneaky—stop glaring at me like that, Mother—and Bidulla had been more forthcoming. I wish we hadn't almost been eaten so many times. I wish Minkis had been more honest with me." Crispin gave Minkis a severe look and the squirrel managed, briefly, to look abashed. "And by the way, it turns out that I'm an agent of Order, and we're apparently fated to be together."

Leopold blinked. "You're *what* now?"

"Order, Leo. Just like you're Chaos. Yin and yang. We belong together because neither of our natures is any good all by itself, but combined we can do anything."

"Oh." Leopold blinked a few times. That made sense.

"But you know what? It doesn't matter. I don't care how we got here or even why—I'm just really, really glad that we got here. Together. Because there's no place that I'd rather be than with you."

It was kind of hard to hug and kiss someone with a squirrel on your shoulder and a whole audience watching, but they managed it, and it was even better than before. Usually Leopold felt swirly and wild in... well, in his soul, or whatever equivalent he possessed. When he kissed Crispin, though, his inner tornado settled into something calmer and more soothing, like a warm breeze on a tropical beach. At the same time, he could feel Crispin's inner self, usually as carefully stacked as a wall of interlocked Legos, jiggle and warp a little into pleasing curves and interesting swirls. Judging from his tight embrace, Crispin enjoyed this as much as Leopold.

Then someone cleared her throat and Leopold remembered where they were. He drew slightly apart from Crispin and turned to eye Minkis again. "Okay, fine. If Crispy's okay with this... situation then so am I. But at least give us an explanation. Why was it so important that I get collected?"

Minkis and the other squirrels made exasperated noises, but before they could answer, Cerillia stepped forward. She didn't look as shiny and glamorous as the last time he'd seen her, but honestly, he liked this version better. She seemed more real. And she wasn't staring imperiously at him, which was a nice change.

"Leo," she began. He was going to interrupt and explain that no, his name was Leo*pold,* but maybe that ship had sailed. There were worse fates than being stuck with a nickname given to you by a beloved. Besides, if *Crispy* could handle it....

Leopold managed a small smile. "Yes?"

"My son is capable of great things—"

"Of course I am!" interrupted Aspin. "Last week I slew an entire flock of cockatrices, and—"

Cerillia stopped him with a raised hand. "My *other* son is capable of great things. Just as you are, in fact, Leo. Alone, however, each of you would likely cause more damage than good. But *together!*" She pressed her palms against one another, her eyes glittered, and she was more beautiful than ever. "Together you can create so much joy, and prevent so much sorrow."

Crispin puffed out his chest a little and Leopold felt an unusual surge of pride. And something more: possibility. Which was, in his estimation, infinitely more precious than perfecality.

But Leopold had more to say. "You could have just introduced us, though. Would've been a lot easier."

She looked a little stern. "Proper introductions were on the agenda, in fact. But the Oracle suggested that we send Crispy to collect you, so we did."

"Crispin," muttered the former desk fae in question, but without much real heat. He did, however, furrow his brow at Minkis. "Why couldn't everyone have been straight with us from the start?"

"The best trees aren't straight, Acorn Man. They twist and turn."

Cerillia laid a hand on Crispin's arm and gave him a gentle smile. "To be honest, I had reservations about the wisdom of you partnering with Leo. Chaos is dangerous and unpredictable. And I had doubts about what he was like as a person. I wouldn't want my son married to a schmuck."

"Leo is *not* a schmuck!" Although Crispin was impressed that she knew the word. He wrapped a protective arm around Leopold.

"I know that now. I didn't then."

Her explanation didn't make perfect sense. But Leopold was hardly the type to demand consistency and solid logic, and if he remembered his mythology properly, the fae weren't exactly famous for careful, cool-headed decisions.

However confusing Cerillia's motives had been, however irritating the Oracle, however bullheaded Bidulla, and however obnoxious Aspin, here they all were. Here *Crispin* was, holding him tightly and looking a lot more sure of himself than the guy who'd knocked on Leopold's door one rainy Sacramento day.

"I think," Leopold said to Crispin, "it's okay. If we hadn't gone through all those adventures together, I'm not sure we would have fallen for each other. I would have blown you off as a bore with a stick up his, uh, butt. And you would have been horrified by the walking disaster zone that I am."

Crispin gave a slow nod. "But this way we showed our true selves, bit by bit. And Leo, I love your true self. Even the messy parts. Maybe especially the messy parts."

"And I love you."

The squirrels cheered. Cerillia beamed. Aspin rolled his eyes. Bidulla saluted.

Juzir popped his head into the doorway, loud booms announcing that Fromlith wasn't far behind. "Hey, what did I miss? Where's Bidulla? And... hey? Why are there so many squirrels?"

Crispin and Leopold laughed together. "I'll explain later, Juzzy."

Thea started played Etta James.

Leo and Crispy stared at one another, and Leo saw the true beauty of Order in Crispy's eyes. They kissed again—the very best kiss so far, with even better yet to come.

EPILOGUE

Crispin checked himself in the mirror. Everything was in place, his brand-new bowtie crisp and green as the forest canopy, his gray tweed vest neatly pressed. He was letting his hair grow a bit longer—his one concession to Leo's admonition that he "loosen up a bit." In fact, he had loosened up much more than a bit over the last few weeks, and if he was honest with himself, that wasn't a bad thing.

A sly whistle emanated from the bed.

He turned to find Leo—still deliciously shirtless—staring at him.

"Looking sharp. You sure you don't have time for...." He patted the mattress next to him.

Crispin considered it. After all, he was the boss now, what with Bidulla being sent on administrative leave due to "a series of poor judgement calls that damaged the reputation of the Office." That had almost destroyed the Connected Worlds, more like, but whatever.

His mother didn't need him yet, though she was making noises about eventually stepping down. The longer, the better, as far as he was concerned.

He looked around the space they shared. Together they had

magicked it bigger, as it had been too small for two men, let alone two men and Minkis, who also seemed to have gotten a promotion and was home less and less. He was still talking—had he always been able to? Crispin's best friend was a little cagey on that matter— but Crispin let the new Ambassador to the Oracle have his secrets. The idea to make the treehouse bigger on the inside but not on the outside had come from Leo, from some TV show about a blue tele- phone booth, apparently. Crispin had promised to watch it with him, but the last couple weeks had been a whirlwind.

The place was a compromise between Chaos and Order, stuffed full of Crispin and Leo's stuff that was—at least technically—put away, even if toes of socks and sleeves of shirts did hang out of mostly closed drawers and the refrigerator was almost bursting with half-empty containers. What once would have driven Crispin to distraction now reminded him that Leo lived here. Truly *lived* here.

Leo slid up behind him and kissed his neck. "At least let me make a little contribution." He wrinkled his nose—something he called The Samantha—and Crispin's bowtie shifted down on the left, just a little. "There. Perfect."

"*Im*perfect." But Crispin resisted the urge to straighten it. "So what are you going to do while I'm gone?"

"Juzir said he'd give me a tour—a real one this time—of the Connected Worlds. At least, all the good ones." Leo grinned. "Dude seems to think he owes me something."

Crispin smiled in return. "And you're... milking it?" He was still getting used to Earth idioms.

Leo flashed his pearly whites, which were just a little crooked. Charmingly so. "All the way to the bank."

Crispin frowned. What did cows lactating have to do with an institution where humans kept their money? It didn't matter. It was all part of Leo's messy charm.

Maybe he would have time for one more quick—

A sharp banging at the door brought him back to the present. Or rather, to the past, when Juzir and Qyl had shown up to take Leo away from him.

They shared a look—Leo was clearly thinking the same thing.

Wordlessly, he gathered up his clothes and disappeared into the bathroom, snicking the lock closed.

We have a bathroom lock now? Crispin brushed away the thought. "Coming!"

He hoped Leo wasn't in trouble again. They'd fixed everything; there were no more flat citizens lying about aimlessly. Well, except on Tarkon, where most of the wildlife and half of the people were naturally pretty flat. And they'd had a big party to smooth over the waters with all their new friends, including the Mucklins, even though Molly the moth-woman had planned to feed them to her children. That was all in the past.

He swung open the door, half expecting an angry mob.

Instead, it was Aspin, staring at him forlornly. "Hey, Elly...."

The old, much hated nickname brought a rebuke to Crispin's lips, but it died when he realized how dejected Aspin looked. "All clear!" he called over his shoulder, and to Aspin, "Come in. What's wrong? Did something happen?"

Aspin nodded, looking as if he'd eaten Minkis.

"Who is it?" Leo appeared, dressed formally for company—which for him meant flip-flops, jeans, and a loose white T-shirt that he'd made a half-hearted attempt to tuck into his pants. His hair, which usually stuck straight up, was slightly more tamed. "Oh, hey Aspin!"

Leo never held a grudge, one of the many things Crispin loved about him.

Aspin stepped inside and threw his arms around Crispin. "She's gone, Elly. She's gone."

"Who?" But then it dawned on him: Aspin had only one *her*.

He confirmed it. "Mother."

Crispin stiffened. "Mother is dead?" *I'm not ready to take over yet.*

Aspin ended the embrace, returning to form. "No, you idiot. I said she was *gone*. Three days ago, and no one knows where or if she will come back. You have to help me find her."

"Gone." Crispin sank down onto their newest furniture addition, the old couch from Leo's Earth apartment. It was lumpy but yet the most comfortable thing that had ever graced the treehouse.

Leo stared at him, blinking, then sank down onto the cushion next to him. "So that means...."

Aspin sank down onto one knee. "Hail to Crispin Eladrin Moss'-caladin, King of the High Holy Fae."

Oh crap.

Book Two, Searching for the Lost, is coming out in late Summer, 2026.
Mark your calendars!

ABOUT THE AUTHORS

J. Scott Coatsworth

Scott lives with his husband of 33 years in a Sacramento, California suburb, in a little yellow house with a brick fireplace and a couple pink flamingoes.

As a writer, he has always lived between *here and now* and *what could be*. Indoctrinated into fantasy-sci fi by his mother at the tender age of nine, he devoured her library. But as he grew up and read the golden age classics and modern works, he began to wonder where the people like him were.

After he came out at twenty three, he decided it was time to create stories he couldn't find in the bookstores. If there weren't many gay characters in his favorite genres, he would reimagine them himself, populating them with men who loved men and other queer characters. He would remake them to his own ends. And if he was lucky enough, someone else would want to read them.

His friends say his brain works a little differently - he sees relationships between things that others miss, and gets more done in a day than most folks manage in a week. Although he was born an introvert, he learned to reach outside himself and connect with others like him.

He writes stories that subvert expectations, and transforms sci fi, fantasy, and contemporary worlds into something new and unexpected. He runs Queer Sci Fi, QueeRomance Ink, and Liminal Fiction with Mark, sites that bring people like us together to promote and celebrate fiction that reflects us.

He was recognized as one of the top new gay authors in the 2017 Rainbow Awards, and his debut novel "Skythane" received two awards. In 2019, he won Rainbow Awards for three other books, and became full member of the Science Fiction and Fantasy Writers of America in 2020, where he was the chair of the Indie Authors Committee for two years.

He has written and published more than forty stories, including thirteen novels.

Kim Fielding

Kim Fielding is very pleased every time someone calls her eclectic. She writes fantasy, mm romance, science fiction, horror, and whatever else her muse demands.

Winner of the 2021 BookLife Prize for Fiction, a Lambda Award finalist and Foreword INDIE finalist, she has migrated back and forth across the western two-thirds of the United States and now lives in Oregon, where she will never have enough bookshelf space.

She's a university professor who dreams of being able to travel and write full time. She also dreams of having two daughters who fully appreciate her, a husband who isn't obsessed with football, and a house that cleans itself. Some dreams are more easily obtained than others.